MARVEL

A NOVEL OF THE MARVEL UNIVERSE

CAPTAIN MARVEL

SHADOW CODE

NOVELS OF THE MARVEL UNIVERSE BY TITAN BOOKS

Ant-Man: Natural Enemy by Jason Starr

Avengers: Everybody Wants to Rule the World by Dan Abnett

Avengers: Infinity by James A. Moore

Black Panther: Panther's Rage by Sheree Renée Thomas

Black Panther: Tales of Wakanda by Jesse J. Holland

Black Panther: Who is the Black Panther? by Jesse J. Holland

Captain America: Dark Designs by Stefan Petrucha

Captain Marvel: Liberation Run by Tess Sharpe

Civil War by Stuart Moore

Deadpool: Paws by Stefan Petrucha

Morbius: The Living Vampire – Blood Ties by Brendan Deneen

Spider-Man: Forever Young by Stefan Petrucha

Spider-Man: Kraven's Last Hunt by Neil Kleid

Spider-Man: The Darkest Hours Omnibus by Jim Butcher, Keith R.A. DeCandido, and Christopher L. Bennett

Spider-Man: The Venom Factor Omnibus by Diane Duane

Thanos: Death Sentence by Stuart Moore

Venom: Lethal Protector by James R. Tuck

Wolverine: Weapon X Omnibus by Marc Cerasini, David Alan Mack and Hugh Matthews

X-Men: Days of Future Past by Alex Irvine

X-Men: The Dark Phoenix Saga by Stuart Moore

X-Men: The Mutant Empire Omnibus by Christopher Golden

X-Men & The Avengers: The Gamma Quest Omnibus by Greg Cox

ALSO FROM TITAN AND TITAN BOOKS

Marvel Contest of Champions: The Art of the Battlerealm by Paul Davies

Marvel's Guardians of the Galaxy: No Guts, No Glory by M.K. England

Marvel's Midnight Suns: Infernal Rising by S.D. Perry

Marvel's Spider-Man: The Art of the Game by Paul Davies

Obsessed with Marvel by Peter Sanderson and Marc Sumerak

Spider-Man: Into the Spider-Verse – The Art of the Movie by Ramin Zahed

Spider-Man: Hostile Takeover by David Liss

Spider-Man: Miles Morales – Wings of Fury by Brittney Morris

The Art of Iron Man (10th Anniversary Edition) by John Rhett Thomas

The Marvel Vault by Matthew K. Manning, Peter Sanderson, and Roy Thomas

Ant-Man and the Wasp: The Official Movie Special

Avengers: Endgame – The Official Movie Special

Avengers: Infinity War – The Official Movie Special

Black Panther: The Official Movie Companion

Black Panther: The Official Movie Special

Captain Marvel: The Official Movie Special

Marvel Studios: The First 10 Years

Marvel's Avengers – Script to Page

Marvel's Black Panther – Script to Page

Marvel's Black Widow: The Official Movie Special

Marvel's Spider-Man – Script to Page

Spider-Man: Far From Home: The Official Movie Special

Spider-Man: Into the Spider-Verse: Movie Special

Thor: Ragnarok The Official Movie Special

A NOVEL OF THE MARVEL UNIVERSE

CAPTAIN MARVEL

SHADOW CODE

AN ORIGINAL NOVEL BY

GILLY SEGAL

TITAN BOOKS

MARVEL

CAPTAIN MARVEL: SHADOW CODE
Print edition ISBN: 9781803361802
E-book edition ISBN: 9781803361819

Published by Titan Books
A division of Titan Publishing Group Ltd
144 Southwark Street, London SE1 0UP
www.titanbooks.com

First hardback edition: May 2023
10 9 8 7 6 5 4 3 2 1

FOR MARVEL PUBLISHING
Jeff Youngquist, VP Production and Special Projects
Sarah Singer, Editor, Special Projects
Jeremy West, Manager, Licensed Publishing
Sven Larsen, VP, Licensed Publishing
David Gabriel, SVP of Sales & Marketing, Publishing
C.B. Cebulski, Editor in Chief

Special thanks to Sarah Brunstad.

A CIP catalogue record for this title is available from the British Library.

Printed and bound by CPI Group (UK) Ltd, Croydon, CR0 4YY.

For my crew who, like Carol's, always answers the call.

G.S.

1

WHEN SHE was training to become a pilot, Carol Danvers would have said nothing compared to the feel of commanding a fighter jet as it hurtled across a cobalt sky. Back then, she had no idea of all the ways her life would change. She never imagined she'd know the exhilaration of rocketing through an endless darkness punctuated by the glimmer of stars that were now within reach. Carol was no poet, but the possibilities of an infinite universe at her fingertips made her wax lyrical. With the push of a button, she could send this spacecraft to chase the farthest pinpricks of light. In fact, she had reached many of those distant planets, had landed there and explored. That pleased the deepest part of her soul that was never satisfied being anchored by gravity.

The alien part of her soul?

Carol wondered if all Kree wanted to fly farther than the instruments could measure. Maybe she inherited the need to take flight from her mother, along with her blond hair and the angle of her jaw.

The bedrock upon which Carol had built her life shifted when she learned her true heritage not long ago. She was half-alien, born to a Kree mother and a human father. The Psyche-Magnitron had not bestowed her powers, as she always thought; it had awakened them. Not only did she have an alien mother who'd been a powerful and important member of Kree society, she had a fully alien half-sister. The revelations made her see her family, her experiences as Captain Marvel, even herself, differently, like she was at the eye doctor, being asked which lens made things clearer and which made them more blurry. Metaphorically, of course. Carol's more than 20/20 vision was definitely inherited from her mom, Mari-Ell, Captain First of the Supreme Protectorate, Champion of the Kree Empire, Daughter of Hala by Bloodright and Starlight.

What a mouthful.

Most days, Carol could tell you what she knew to be true about herself. But she couldn't say how she felt about any of it. Growing up, telling Carol *no* had had the effect of activating hyper-mode. She'd work harder than anyone else, longer than anyone else, work herself into the ground, even when the world told her she'd never be able to do it. Especially then. She'd attained every goal she set for herself, realized every dream. Everything she'd fought to accomplish—pilot, astronaut, super hero, Avenger, Alpha Flight leader—she'd attributed those achievements to her grit, her determination. And maybe her stubbornness.

Now she had to reckon with the fact that there had been other factors at play. She'd tried to dissect which of her traits came from being human and which were Kree. It made her head spin. No matter how long she pondered, she could never answer the question that plagued her. Did being an alien make those accomplishments more worthy—or less?

She'd spent so long coming to grips with *having* alien powers that working through what it meant to actually *be* an alien felt like diving into a vortex.

Been there, she thought. *Hard pass on doing it again.*

The crackle of the ship's comms drew Carol out of her thoughts. Fortunately, flight demanded her full attention. She'd have to navel gaze some other time—like never—or else risk piloting her borrowed spacecraft into a star. The *Peregrine* was a first-of-its-kind decasonic microcraft, designed to fly small crews to remote planets at outrageous speeds. In theory, anyway. The designers were still figuring out how far it could reliably go without losing thrust and overheating. Hence, working with Carol for flight tests, since no other qualified pilot could bail out in deep space and find her own way home. She'd only been at the command of the *Peregrine* a few times, but it was fun. The cabin was sleek and streamlined, a tad claustrophobic, if she was honest, but the ship's movement was not unlike how it felt propelling her body through space—lithe, maneuverable, and fast. She wasn't about to let a bunch of *feelings* prevent her from enjoying this ride.

"Earth to Danvers," a familiar voice called through the comms. "Literally and figuratively. Danvers, do you read?"

Tony Stark would find a way to pester her, even here. She considered ignoring the call, but since that tactic never made him go away, she flicked the lever. "I read you, Tony. What do you want?"

"Is that any way to greet your long lost best friend?"

"I saw you last week." Carol already regretted opening the comms channel. "And don't let Jess hear you call yourself that."

"You think I can't take Spider-Woman in a fight?" Tony's mock-wounded tone sounded almost convincing.

"I think we're not going to invoke trouble with hypotheticals."

"Did you know that at some fan cons, they have 'versus' sessions where they debate the merits of super hero skills to decide who'd win a one-on-one? I have it on good authority that Iron Man is always a moneyline bet. "

Carol rolled her eyes. No doubt "good authority" really meant firsthand knowledge. "Tony, do we have to have the talk about cos-playing as yourself again?"

"There's no evidence of that that anyone can find," he said. "Anyway, Danvers, I need a favor. Where are you?"

"Off planet." Carol checked her gauges. She was just a couple of hours from being on-planet again—on Throneworld II.

"I know that. Couldn't geolocate you through your phone. That only happens when you're in outer space."

"What did we say about tracking our friends' devices without permission?"

"Only do it for ethical reasons, like determining whether you need to rescind the APB you put out on a missing friend?"

"Tony, no. You didn't." The resulting silence stretched uncomfortably through the time and space between Carol's speeding craft and Tony back on Earth. She groaned. "Who'd you call?"

"Jess. And maybe Monica."

Monica Rambeau, A.K.A. Spectrum, wouldn't get as high-stress as Jess, but she'd check in at least twice.

"Also, possibly Jenn."

Aw man. Jennifer Takeda, A.K.A. Hazmat, would definitely fret. Carol's notifications were going to be a mess when she got back to Earth.

"I'm not AWOL. I'm going to visit Lauri-Ell."

Months had passed since Carol last saw her half-sister, Kree Accuser Lauri-Ell, who was currently on Throneworld II. The pieces of Carol's shattered past were inescapable, it seemed. The *Peregrine* test flight had offered her a chance to kill two Chitauri with one punch. Figure out if the ship could reliably reach as far as they hoped, plus stop by to see Lauri with a built-in exit strategy. She'd have to get the craft back to Earth promptly—no time to linger and talk about dysfunctional family matters.

"Ah," he said, pausing respectfully for a beat. He might not know everything going on in Carol's mixed up mind, but he knew enough. "Perhaps it's not the best timing, but I do need a favor. And it's a little bit time sensitive."

She sighed. Tony had the tact of a wrecking ball, but when he called, something was usually up. "What's going on?"

"Bad reception..." Tony breathed heavily into his mic, faking a crackling sound. "You must... space tunnel."

"Tony, you designed this comms system. Are you telling me a Stark invention can't handle a little interstellar space debris?"

"Stark technology is *completely* trustworthy." His voice leveled, all faux-brokenness vanishing. "The same can't be said for everything else. I need you, Carol. Right away."

The comms line went dead, leaving her no chance to ask for further details.

She was overdue for this visit to Throneworld II. Jess had been telling her for months that she needed to go see Lauri-Ell, spend time among the Kree. Figure out the parts of herself that were currently more mysterious than the black hole she'd done some fancy flying to avoid about an hour ago. Jess would be a pain about it until Carol finally listened. She really shouldn't turn back.

But Tony's words and tone reverberated in her mind. Okay, so he had a bad habit of needing her right when she finally took a few days for herself. He also had an annoying tendency to be strategically ambiguous when sharing intel. Still, she trusted him. And he never missed an opportunity to engage in a battle of wits with her. Today, he'd not only passed up sniping back when she teased him about Stark tech, but he'd gotten defensive. That was peculiar. Concerning, even.

Maybe she'd head back, see what more Tony had to say. This was early stage test flight. Nothing urgent. Plenty of time to assess the *Peregrine*'s long distance flight capabilities. The engineers could tweak its comms systems in the meanwhile. She definitely had feedback on how easy it was to hail this craft. It needed a feature that let the pilot set their call status to "away" or "unavailable" or "leave me alone, Tony Stark" or something else universally relevant like that.

Carol splayed her fingers over the instrument panel, adjusting her altitude and easing back on the yoke to chart a course for Earth. Throneworld II wasn't going anywhere, nor were all her questions about herself.

2

"JASON, MY phone's been off for all of two hours. How bad could it possibly be?"

Laurence Faber strode through his penthouse, phone pressed to his ear. The place was empty. His wife had combined a business trip to London with a visit to their daughter at LSE and wouldn't be back for several days. The extensive staff that kept the Faber family and business organized, clean, clothed, fed and transported had all gone home for the night. Faber balked at the idea of live-in staff; he valued his privacy too much. Thus, he returned home more often than not to a quiet, empty house. He passed the great room, where the Tiffany side lamps were dimly lit, welcoming him home, loosening his bow tie on the way to his study.

Jason, his executive assistant, was high strung. Made him fantastic at managing the details of Faber's work, but prone to dramatic reactions. One of these days, the annoyance of the fuss would outweigh the efficiency Jason offered. Not tonight, though. His zealous assistant had hunted down someone on the waitstaff at the charity gala Faber had been attending and paid them to yank Faber aside to check his messages. Fourteen texts from Jason insisted, more and more vehemently as they accumulated, that Faber leave the event at once and get home.

"Mr. Faber, it's bad. DigiTech is the lead story. Not just on Bloomberg—the general news channels are covering it, too."

The study was Faber's refuge, the only room in the house over which he'd had complete design control—if by complete, one meant the power to make suggestions that his wife and her designer would then approve. The dark paneling, high ceilings, double-decker bookshelves and mile-wide polished oak desk resembled the university library fantasies of his youth, back when he thought he'd be an economics professor. Instead, junior year of college, he'd lent a few thousand dollars from his savings to a friend who wanted to start up a delivery service that brought students homecooked meals to their dorms during exams. That friend became his wife, and her business mushroomed into one of the largest food delivery services in the world and made Faber his first fortune. His wife still ran that company, while he went on to a long and illustrious career as an angel investor.

Tossing his jacket on the leather couch, Faber helped himself to a glass of whiskey from the decanter at the wet bar. The remote that brought out a TV, cleverly concealed behind a mirror over the fireplace, sat beside the tray of cut glass tumblers. Faber twirled it in his fingers, debating whether he had the energy for the latest DigiTech roller coaster.

He'd bought shares in the company a year or so ago at the urging of his sometime investing partner, Marian Sutherland. DigiTech Systems, Inc. had been a sleepy old computer hardware company, nothing like the wave-of-the-future AI people were so excited about. Most investors Faber knew were prone to join the cult of every new Silicon Valley hotshot who emerged wearing a turtleneck and a perpetual scowl, promising to revolutionize tech. Faber snorted. Everybody said *their* thing was *the* thing. He sat out those flash-in-the-pan opportunities and never regretted it.

He had that in common with Marian. They met early in their careers and discovered a complementary style characterized by thoughtfulness and intuition over glitz. She was as careful an investor as he'd ever met, doing twice the diligence he did. She brought DigiTech to his attention when the company's newly hired president announced she was looking for an involved board. That piqued Faber's interest. The sunset of his investing career was approaching and he knew it. His daughter was training to be the next head of Faber Investments, and she'd want to do things her own way when she took over. He respected that. Out with the old. He'd do the same, in her shoes. The current crop of young whizz kid founders didn't want anything more than his money. All his years of buying and selling companies, building empires, disrupting industries, reorganizing the way business is done—that knowledge and experience went to waste when all he did was cut a check. He wanted to have a hand in a company's success before he hung up the checkbook for good. He wanted a legacy.

Investing in DigiTech had, frankly, been more lucrative than betting on a Vegas long shot that paid out. He'd been minting money since they diversified into software, a vote that had been one of the first Faber supported when he joined the board. The success made it difficult to understand the recent rash of stock sell-offs. Laurence wasn't losing sleep over it, though. People made foolish investment choices all the time. No doubt the news was covering those with their usual doom-and-gloom predictions about collapses. The media never got the investing mindset right.

Still. Might as well take a peek at what they were saying, if for no other reason than to let some of the helium out of Jason's voice. He flicked a button on the remote and found a twenty-four-hour news network. Instead of the usual image of a talking head above a crawl, there was footage of Marian Sutherland being led from the very same charity fundraiser he'd left not thirty minutes ago. In handcuffs.

Laurence Faber choked on his whiskey, spitting half the mouthful across the marble countertop. The tinny sound of Jason's voice piped up from the phone that sat abandoned on the tray beside the decanter. "As I said, sir."

Faber stabbed at the phone screen, disconnecting the call and silencing his assistant's told-you-so superiority. So the kid had been right. That mattered little in the face of the arrest of his fellow DigiTech board member. He pumped up the volume in time to catch the newscaster intoning breaking news in a fake-grave timbre.

"—Sutherland, a prominent investor known for her land development portfolio, recently forayed into the digital space when she purchased substantial shares in DigiTech Systems. She's in federal custody tonight and sources tell us she'll be charged with securities fraud, in connection—"

Fraud? Marian? She was as T's-crossed-and-i's-dotted as they come.

Faber paced toward the French doors that led from his study to a private balcony overlooking the city. Normally he loved the feeling of towering over the world, lights spreading below in all directions. He imagined it felt a little bit like flying through space. Tonight, the view gave him vertigo. Maybe a blast of the January wind would ease this dizzy spell. He opened the door but the barely concealed glee in the newscaster's tone caught his attention again.

"—a felony which carries a penalty of twenty years in prison and a hefty fine—"

Felony. Jesus. He definitely needed air.

Faber turned back to the balcony and gasped. Not two feet from him stood a figure shrouded in darkness. *What the*—? The glass slipped from his hand and shattered on the hardwood, splashing liquid across his loafers. No one had been standing there a moment ago, he was sure. Was he hallucinating?

Faber backed up a step. The figure glided forward with a swish that brought Faber's eyes to the ground. The light was dim, but he could see fabric swirling around—a *cloak*? And was there a kind of glow emanating from the figure?

"Knock, knock, Mr. Faber."

If this was a hallucination, it was an especially vivid one. The voice was low and pleasant but unfamiliar. "Who—who are you? How did you get here?"

"Aren't you going to invite me in?"

He sure as hell was not. Faber fumbled in his pockets for the phone that wasn't there. The device sat on the wet bar behind him, where he'd left it after hanging up on Jason. Dammit, if only he'd left the line open, he could shout for his assistant to call 911. He glanced over and saw the screen light up with an incoming call, no doubt from the young man himself. He had to get to that device and tell Jason that… an ethereal cloaked figure had turned up on his balcony?

He'd sound like he had been overcome by a flight of fancy. He had a hard time believing it himself, despite the evidence his eyes supplied.

Besides, he wouldn't really call this thing ethereal. That shine wasn't a pleasant firefly kind of glow. It was sinister. He couldn't make out anything important about this creature—it held itself like a person. But it glimmered. And his penthouse occupied the thirtieth floor of this building. There was no way a human could just appear on his terrace in the span of a few seconds. He felt suddenly short of breath and clutched his chest, thinking bizarrely that he'd rather the intruder get him than a heart attack.

Wait, no. No way was he going down to a caped balcony prowler. Faber scrambled back, his shoes sliding in the liquid he'd spilled.

The figure flashed out of sight, leaving behind a faint blur. Faber grabbed for his phone—which was already in the hands of his visitor, who now stood beside the bar. *How?* Faber could not formulate a coherent question for himself, let alone speak it aloud. He'd scarcely seen the person—or whatever it was—move. It disappeared and reappeared in a way that should not be possible.

"I don't think we'll be needing this, will we?" The figure dropped the phone on the ground, pulverizing it beneath a boot heel.

Faber had not turned on any lights when he entered the room, and he cursed himself for it now. The flickering TV was useless in his efforts to make out a face. That voice, emanating from deep within the hood of the cloak, had a songlike cadence, smooth and rich and even. Like a yoga instructor. It would have been calming, had it not been coming from a glowing figure that had flown onto this thirtieth-story terrace in the middle of the night.

16

"We wouldn't want Jason's paranoia to disrupt our little chat."

They knew his assistant? Who the hell was this?

"I don't have cash here if that's what you're looking for," he said, fighting for a level tone of voice. He handled multi-billion-dollar negotiations for a living. Surely, that's all this was. A transaction. They wanted something from him and he wanted his life. He just needed to understand this, er—person's goal, and he could do a deal for his survival.

"Not as such, Mr. Faber."

The figure came no closer; it was more than an arm's length away, but Faber felt it looming over him, smothering him. More than a human arm's reach, anyway. But the speed with which it moved…

"Then what?"

"Tomorrow morning, you'll receive an offer to buy your DigiTech stock. You'll accept the offer."

That caught him off guard. He narrowed his eyes, trying—pointlessly—to make out something beneath that hood. DigiTech was trading high at the moment, probably near peak. It was no coup to get in on it now, unless—"You want me to give a below-the-market order?"

"The offer will be market value."

"How much stock?"

"All of it."

Faber fought against the instinct to just say yes, to agree to anything as long as this creature left him alone. He stiffened his knees to keep them from knocking. This made no sense. Selling and buying high? There was no money to be made. He was missing something. The creature hadn't done anything particularly threatening, other than magically appear on his balcony and order him to sell stock he wanted to keep. And yet, he was plagued by the sense that this was a robbery of some kind. "It's a bad deal. If you—or uh, your investor is looking for a good deal, I could provide some advice. A—a tip. I have access to all kinds of valuable information."

"You assume we don't have access to the same information?" A slight ripple of the cloak gave the only indication of the figure's movement, but it had unmistakably drawn closer to Faber. "Perigee Partners doesn't need your tips."

Faber swiped a hand across the back of his mouth, leaning back to preserve his space, his safety. His head told him the effort was illusory, but it made him breathe easier. A little. Perigee Partners, Ltd. was a holding company, the ownership well-shrouded behind layers of legal protections. Faber had done some research when they first began acquiring DigiTech stock, and there'd been no red flags. As he thought through it now, he realized they were the buyer in many—most?—of the recent stock sales. They had amassed quite a lot of shares. Faber cast about in his memories, trying to recall how many exactly. With his portion added to what they'd already acquired, he thought Perigee might gain a controlling interest in DigiTech. Again, the sense that there was more at play here than he understood pricked at his conscience. Faber didn't like surprises. "What if there was another stock? Any other stock. I'd cut you a good deal."

The figure stayed silent, motionless and glowing, and then a gloved hand waved toward the television. An image of Faber and Marian filled the screen—a photo taken earlier that very night as the two posed together with the emcee of the event, some star too young for Faber to have recognized.

"Such troubling news about your dear friend. Allegations like these, they can't help but spread. Like a virus."

Was the creature creeping closer again? It was too damn dark in here. Most of the light seemed to come from the glow filtering from beneath that nonsensical cloak. "Marian and I haven't done a deal together in years. I don't have anything to worry about."

"Don't you?"

His pulse began to throb again and he felt a sensation like the one he experienced two years ago, right before the "episode" he refused to call a heart attack. He needed air. He needed space. Over the years, Faber had dabbled in a few gray areas when it came to securities law. Who didn't? Investors collectively lobbied to keep the statutes vague so they'd be able to argue the line wasn't where any prosecutor wanted to draw it. But that was all. He was nearly certain. He paid an army of lawyers to ensure he remained firmly within sight of the right side of the law.

"You own a big share in a surgical laser tool manufacturer. Cutting edge, minimally invasive, all the buzzwords that attract doctors and patients, right? How strange that soon after launch, they signed an exclusive deal with a company that makes the precision prisms needed for those laser tools. That resulted in a substantial price increase and boxed out competition. You were an early investor in the prism manufacturer, weren't you? Few people know of that."

No. No one knew about that. Rumors, maybe. Nothing concrete.

"Wouldn't it be interesting to learn there were records of your involvement in those deals? Records showing you traded stocks based on your access to confidential information about that deal?"

"Those records don't exist." The tech guys said there was no trace. Scrubbed. Wiped. Double deleted. They assured him.

"In your files, perhaps." The figure was moving, closing in. Faber's pulse raced even faster. "Larry—I can call you Larry, right? Like friends. It would be better for you if we were friends."

"There's no proof."

The figure hummed, low and satisfied. "Everyone keeps files, Larry. You can't control what's out of your reach, can you?"

Had he ever corresponded with Marian about the laser/prism companies? She had been part of that deal. Had the Feds got ahold of her files? Who was this creature working for?

"Call your broker, Larry. Give the order to sell. Unless you think, as Marian Sutherland did, that you can play games with me. And if twenty years in a federal penitentiary aren't enough to persuade you to be reasonable, we have other ways." The figure's hands shot forward, balls of light blooming on the upturned palms.

Faber gasped, pressing a hand to his chest. The light from the pulsating energy balls reflected in his wide, terrified eyes.

"Tomorrow morning, Larry. I wouldn't want to have to visit again."

3

AFTER PILOTING the *Peregrine* to its top secret hangar, expertly maneuvering the ship down through the rooftop bay doors, Carol turned the craft over to the anxious aerospace engineers tasked with developing and testing it. They immediately swarmed the ship, examining every steel plate, every bolt, every wire, every blinking light on the instrument panel. The clink of their gear and buzz of their excited conversations echoed through the cavernous belly of the hangar, which had been outfitted with the most advanced tech military money could buy, but was empty of vehicles other than the single prototype ship Carol had just returned. She watched the flurry of activity with bemusement.

"How'd she run?" The ranking engineer on the team beelined toward her as soon as she popped the ship's door open.

Carol grinned as she dropped to the floor beside Senior Master Sergeant Alexander. He stood a head shorter than her, his coveralls rolled neatly at the sleeves and ankles, the pockets bulging with tools and devices. She'd run into the Georgia Tech-trained aerospace engineer a number of times over the years, as she consulted on military research and development; he had a knack for being involved with the most cutting-edge projects.

"You thought I'd take your baby out for her first test drive and wrap her around a tree, didn't you?"

"Or planet," Alexander laughed, running a hand over his regulation buzz cut, the line above his ears so perfectly straight he probably had a level in his grooming kit. The hair at his temples had silvered since Carol last saw him, though the gleam in his eyes made him look like a kid on his first mission. "No overheating issues?"

"Well, I didn't make the full trip. But for as long as I had her in the air, no. And I pushed her hard." Alexander pumped his fist in the air, and Carol quirked one eyebrow. "You're unusually excited about a ship *not* overheating, Master Sergeant. What didn't you tell me before I took her up?"

"We're trying out a new thermoacoustic cooling system. Combines sound waves and inert gas to create a refrigerant effect. Super powerful. Lightweight. Energy efficient. No moving parts." He launched into an animated mini-lecture on how the cooling system worked, which Carol did her best to follow. "It actually recovers energy waste, converts thermal management from a burden to an asset."

She smiled. This was her favorite version of Alexander, the one hyped about physics and unable to resist sharing his delight. Nothing like hearing from an inventor thrilled about his latest invention. "Sounds like a dream."

"It could be. We've been experimenting to make sure the combo doesn't cause drag on the thrust."

"I think you're nearly there," she said, giving him a complimentary nod before heading to the locker room.

Carol strode across the hangar, returning salutes from the various scattered airmen who interrupted their work to acknowledge her. She no longer technically held her Air Force rank, but when she had, she'd far outranked all the personnel in the hangar, including the Senior Master Sergeant. Most of the soldiers she worked with now still honored that, and the part of

Carol that held tight to the memories of working herself raw to earn that bird on her flight cap appreciated the gesture. But she didn't dawdle. They had work to do, as did she, the vibration of the phone in the pocket of her flight suit reminded her. Inside the locker room, she glanced at the device screen, counting no less than five texts from Tony. The first had come minutes after she entered the atmosphere. She wrinkled her nose, making a mental note to uninstall whatever tracking app he put on there. Honestly, Carol hadn't expected him to wait that long to nag her. He probably expected her to come directly to the meeting location without taking the time to change. But she didn't want to get a reputation with the supply officer for having sticky fingers. She'd already "borrowed" an unfair share of flight suits over the years.

Carol opened Tony's most recent message and found he'd dropped a location pin. No further information. With no hint at the expected dress code for this mission, Carol swapped her flight suit for her preferred civvies—her "Carol Danvers" uniform. She'd stowed a set of jeans and a black sweater in the locker on base while she worked with the *Peregrine* team. As a nod to the chilly New York morning, she tugged on a leather jacket and pulled a black toque over her hair. Tucking tendrils in around the edges, she reconsidered the length for the millionth time. The short 'do had been much easier for upkeep, but Carol liked the long wheat-colored waves currently spilling from beneath her hat. Kept her neck warm this time of year.

Absently, she slammed her locker shut, studying that location in a map app. It would be a long walk from the base. Carol wouldn't have minded a chance to stretch her legs after the flight, but that would also give her time to mull over why she'd been so quick to brush off the meeting with Lauri-Ell. Flying, as always, would be much faster and provide her less time to stew. It was about efficiency, really, like Alexander and his thermoacoustic cooling system.

Maybe that was a little self-serving, but hey, no reason you couldn't do well for yourself and do good for the world. Carol slipped out of the gargantuan hangar into the bustle of the Air

Force base. She glanced around, admiring the hum and hustle. Carol rarely longed for her military days, though sometimes she did miss the dynamism of a place like this, of a massive crew focused on achieving a common mission together. Maybe she did need Tony's quest, if for no other reason than to shake off the nostalgia tugging her back in time toward a past she could never relive. Shaking her head, she gathered her energy, dug the balls of her feet into the ground, and lifted off.

○————————○

SHE WAS still blocks out from her destination when she caught sight of the crowd. From her vantage point, the sidewalks brimmed with ants she knew to be people. Tens of thousands of them, all thronging toward the convention center. That must be where she was headed.

Tony, she groaned inwardly, *please tell me your emergency did not have to do with attending a fan con!*

Carol dropped down and joined the horde on the street— none of whom wore costumes of any kind. They did, however, sport badges on lanyards and totes emblazoned with a black, silver, and purple logo. The crowd ebbed and flowed, some heading in the direction of the convention center, others peeling off and entering the buildings around them—mostly hotels—all of which were marked with banners bearing that same logo. The banners displayed letters each a full story in length—GTSS. What in the Multiverse was that?

Two blocks later, she bumped into the answer. A massive glass arch, at least ten stories high, stretched across the street, the apex rising even higher with a glowing black, silver, and purple logo declaring this to be the entrance to the Global Technovation Supernova Show. As Carol watched, glass elevator platforms hoisted convention attendees up the arch. The structure itself proved to be a touch screen. Wherever someone threw out a hand, displays burst to life, leaping off the screen, coating people in augmented-reality experiences. Here, a 3D map rendered itself in the air; there, a flying car burst out of the arch, its sides emblazoned with a booth number on the convention floor; and there, a VR display coated a viewer in a billowy virtual ballgown that looked real enough to touch.

A tech con? Carol shook her head, wending her way through the crush toward the convention center entrance, where Tony's latest text told her he was waiting. He was abstruse on the best of days, but this might be a new record. Around her, sign-throwers and product-hawkers created chaos, yelling, dancing, inviting people to scan codes with their phones to claim giveaway items. Convention employees wearing jackets with light-up displays on the back attempted crowd control. Carol saw now that the logo comprised what looked like a star falling into a black hole.

She wondered if there was a deeper meaning behind naming a convention about futuristic tech after a stellar explosion that resulted in the progenitor dying. Something about disruption of the old ways? Carol liked Tony's tech buds best in limited doses, but she'd heard plenty of platitudes like *innovate or die* even in the insignificant time she'd spent with them. A smirk rose to her mouth. She'd bet a ride in the *Peregrine* they hadn't consulted an astronomer before they named this con.

The entrance teemed with security and attendees negotiating the complex dance of mass ingress and egress. Carol noted a still spot among the crowd. Tony Stark, in his own civilian gear—expensive jeans, a designer jacket, and sneakers that cost more than Carol's rent—stood off to the side, leaning against a barricade, eyes glued to his phone. He wore no hat, probably so his spiky dark hair wouldn't get unintentionally instead of intentionally mussed.

"Surprised you're not in the Iron Man suit, Stark," she grumbled as she reached him.

"One time, Danvers," he said, holding out a GTSS badge to her. This one, unlike most she saw around her, was silver and inscribed with the letters VIP and matched the badge hanging from the lanyard around Tony's own neck. "I did that *one time*."

"One time too many. What I am doing here?"

"Besides making fun of me? Come on, we're going to see a panel."

Incredulous, Carol followed Tony as he powered through the convention center lobby to the exhibition hall. Left on her own, she might have liked to poke around the demonstrations a little. She wouldn't mind seeing what the car bursting out of the arch had been all about. It was high time someone besides Tony Stark had access to a flying car, in her opinion. But Tony had not a minute to spare for the exhibitions, marching past the most lurid of future-tech spectacles. He must really want to see this panel, she mused, because this stuff was normally Tony's catnip. With Carol on his heels, he turned into a massive auditorium that was full to overflowing. From the size and the crowd, she guessed this panel must be one of the main attractions of the convention. A cordoned-off area toward the front of the room declared itself reserved for VIPs, but despite their badges, Tony steered them away. Instead, they climbed over knees and stumbled on tote bags to find two seats tucked in the shadow of the sound engineer's panel.

The chatting of eager convention-goers making plans to meet up for later panels collided with the sound of audio recordings promoting sponsor products being played at full volume from the speakers that dotted the perimeter of the room. Together, they brought the noise level to a painful decibel.

"Let me guess, Banner, Lang, and Cho were all busy?" Carol said, naming everyone she could think of that would be a more natural companion to attend NERDCON with Tony.

He shushed her vigorously, drawing the attention of a few people seated around them. Carol slunk into her seat, pulling her toque lower and scowling. Tony might not mind being swarmed at places like this, but he knew she hated that kind of attention. She wasn't anonymous these days, even as Carol Danvers, but she preferred not to have more eyeballs and camera phones focused on her than absolutely necessary. She missed the days when her Captain Marvel suit was enough to protect her secret identity.

She'd stumbled across one too many overblown opinion pieces about her half-alien status rendering her a questionable ally when she was just trying to read the news. Hala knew what they'd make of her attending an event like this.

Luckily, the dimming of the house lights and the sudden flare of blue-white spotlights shining on the stage claimed the crowd's attention before anyone beyond the closest few rows distinguished that Iron Man and Captain Marvel were sitting among them.

Two figures emerged from backstage. Carol recognized neither, but a disembodied announcer introduced one as the interviewer—a tech reporter named Miller—and the other as the apparent star of the show, Griselda Seales. Carol leaned forward, involuntarily drawn toward the woman. Though she was of average height and dressed in the same jeans and blazer combo as Miller, she commanded the stage. Her dark hair draped to her chin on one side, hanging smoothly over one eye and coming to a razor-sharp edge, while the other side had been shaved close to her scalp. It was impossible not to focus on her. The crowd roared at the mere mention of her name. Carol didn't pay much attention to tech culture, but she was guessing this woman was the kind of star that transcended Silicon Valley and became a pop culture sensation.

Seales, graceful even in tall pumps with a pointed toe and a telltale red sole, trailed Miller to a pair of stools positioned center stage. Carol caught sight of an odd kind of glint around Seales's feet as she moved. She rubbed her eyes with the heel of her hand, wondering if maybe it had been a trick of the light. But no, there it was again.

"Did she *flicker*?" she whispered out of the corner of her mouth to Tony.

He chuckled. "Good observation, Danvers. She's a hologram."

"What?!"

"Shhhh," he hissed again, more harsh than teasing this time. Carol glanced over and found his face puckered like he'd just sucked on a lemon.

Interesting. Tony hated this woman.

On stage, a massive IMAX-sized screen flashed up yet another logo Carol didn't recognize. Luckily, this one didn't require decoding. In staid blue block letters, the words *DigiTech Systems* rotated and twirled and even leaped off the screen to circle over Miller and Seales's heads. Despite the backlighting, Seales remained as visible she had been a second before. Didn't holograms disappear or fade to blinking pixels in that much light?

"She looks solid," Carol said. "Without that little flicker when she was walking, you could never tell she was a projection. Incredible."

"Nice bit of tech, but pretentious as hell, if you ask me."

She side-eyed him again and he looked even more petulant. Tony didn't wear his feelings on his face often, but he couldn't hide them now. "How so?"

"She only makes appearances in holo form. Showy nonsense."

Says the man who wears a sparkly red and gold suit, she thought. Carol didn't mind snarking back and forth with Tony, but theirs was a mutually admiring antagonism. He seemed genuinely ruffled by Seales. She stifled both her smile and the rejoinder on the tip of her tongue and turned her attention back to Miller, who'd wrapped up a fawning intro of Seales and moved on to talking about the company.

"Just over one year ago, DigiTech went from an unexciting, unadventurous hardware manufacturer to the hottest tech property in the world with the release of its revolutionary operating system, BOS-MA."

The audience screamed its approval.

"Oh, you've heard of it?" Miller teased. "Nah, who am I kidding? GTSS attracts the savviest tech crowd in the world, so you are all probably BOS-MA alpha users, aren't you? I mean, if your stack isn't running on BOS-MA, is it even running? Amirite?" Cheering, laughter. Carol wrinkled her nose. This was a language she didn't speak, though everyone else in the room was fluent. "And now little ol' BOS-MA is here." Images began materializing on the screen behind him. First, a picture of the Federal Reserve Bank. Then some private banks. Then the Wall Street sign. "And here." A power station. A dam. Logos for all the major voice and internet communications providers. "And here." Images of every type of phone and tablet.

"Basically, everywhere! If you've upgraded any time in the last year, you're running on BOS-MA. And the woman responsible for it all, Wall Street's darling, technology's savior, the wunderkind, is sitting right here beside me, on these dime store stools! Seriously, guys, we couldn't get a couch? A love seat? An armchair? Something?" Miller mock-wobbled on his chair, flinging his feet out and rocking on the flimsy plastic stool. Seales sat—"sat"?—serenely on her own seat and smiled at the antics. The expression lay flatly on the holographic face, showing too-bright teeth but failing to carve laugh lines at the corners of her mouth. Now that she was looking for them, Carol picked out more signs that there was no flesh on those bones. It was more than a little disconcerting.

Tony's phone pinged, then lit up, and this time he was the shushee, drawing the crowd's ire. A few made infuriated shut-it-down gestures.

"Come on," he said, without bothering to whisper. "I've seen enough of the clown show."

"Tony, what? Why—" He'd dragged her all the way down here, gotten VIP passes and dead center seats with a view, to watch two minutes of introductions? Carol didn't even know what that BOS-MA thing was yet. But Stark was already on his way out the door. She scrambled after him, clambering over the irritated attendees in their row, whom they'd *just* crawled around on the way in. Carol whispered apologies over Miller's renewed droning about the operating system's humble origins as a military technology.

In the light of the lobby, Tony's wrinkled brow betrayed his irritation. He strode toward the exit to the building, tearing off his GTSS badge and grousing under his breath. Carol raked her memories for the last time she'd seen him so riled up and came up blank.

It wasn't until they were outside, back in the brisk winter air, that it dawned on her. She grabbed his shoulder and pulled him to a halt, forcing the crowd to eddy around them. "You're jealous!"

"Absolutely not," he said. "Of what?"

"They're lauding her as the greatest tech genius on Earth or whatever. You're used to that being you."

"Every significant piece of tech in the last seventy years has come from Stark Industries. Or, at least, from a Stark. But here comes this nobody working for a hardware manufacturer who resurrects a defunct military tech that becomes the world's leading OS? I mean, *DigiTech Systems*?" He flung his hands out, palms up, to indicate the absurdity of such a thing, and narrowly avoided dealing a resounding thwap to a guy walking past. Carol shot the startled man a brief, apologetic look, as Tony ranted on. "They were assembling motherboard components a minute ago. And not even very good ones."

"Okay, but so what?"

"I think it's odd I'd never even heard of Griselda Seales." Tony shook off Carol's hand and resumed his march through the lobby. He picked up speed toward the exit, wending his way through the crowd, down the convention center steps and into the flow of folks heading away from GTSS.

"Do you know everyone in the tech world, Tony?"

"Most of them, yes," he said, waving a hand dismissively. Of course he did, she thought. "Where did she come from?"

Carol nodded back toward the building, where no doubt Seales was still answering interview questions and being cheered like a rockstar. "Why not go straight to the source? Ask for an audience with the new reigning queen of tech?"

"She's not—no way is she—that's not what she is!" Tony spluttered, stuffing his hands into the pockets of his peacoat. "Anyway, she won't speak with me."

Carol eyed his stiff-shouldered posture and his sullen scowl. "Maybe she's too busy running a company to deal with jealous competitors."

"Busy, I can respect. But Griselda Seales refuses to let even her staff go near me. She fires anyone who mentions my name. You might think this is professional jealousy, but it's not. DigiTech's rise was meteoric and our atmosphere doesn't have capacity to withstand a meteor crash."

"Lot of space analogies there, bud," Carol said. "Come on back to Earth."

Throughout Tony's rant, they hadn't stopped moving, progressing onto a quiet side street populated with storefronts and office entrances and one modest coffee shop.

Tony paused, turning to Carol with a grave expression. "Seales is manning an empire that now forms the basis of our entire interconnected technology network—an empire that's suddenly a fortress of secrecy. They even had military records about the creation of the OS purged. BOS-MA's too important to the world to be treated like a trade secret formula for a sugary soda."

He'd slipped back into speaking that dialect of computerese she wasn't fluent in, but the bigger point wasn't lost on her. Carol sighed. "So, what, you want me to go talk to her? Impress upon her the importance of transparency my way?" She was goading him. Carol's way involved brass tacks and the Kree-equivalent of brass knuckles. But she never deployed it against civilians, and he knew it.

"I've got something better." Tony prodded her shoulder, spinning her toward the coffee shop's big picture window.

"Caffeine?" she deadpanned. "You're hyped up enough without another cup, I think."

Tony pointed through the window to a woman sitting alone in a corner booth. Past the condensation and the decorative winter snow scene painted on the glass, Carol made out a puff of curly brown hair under a bright yellow beanie, and a matching puffer coat the woman hadn't unzipped or removed, despite being indoors. A black turtleneck poked from the collar. "Mara Melamed, daughter of Dr. Iris Melamed, granddaughter of Professor Shelley Melamed."

He said this grandly, with the air of an announcer introducing a famous guest on a talk show. A bit like Miller had with Seales. Carol did not, however, react with the exuberance of the GTSS crowd. She merely looked at him. Tony groaned and rubbed his hand across his face.

"Shelley Melamed is the father of modern computer science. He founded the program at Empire State University, ran the most forward-thinking lab the industry had for decades. Shaped two generations of thinkers. His daughter Iris followed in his footsteps and then went into the private sector at—wouldn't you know it— none other than DigiTech Systems."

Carol nodded toward the woman sitting in the coffee shop. "That her?"

"That's his granddaughter, Mara. Grad student at the U. Met her guest-lecturing a couple semesters ago. She has a mind for patterns like I've never seen. I tried to hire her before the semester was out, but she has romantic ideas about finishing her degree."

Of course he sounded derisive about that. Carol found herself admiring the stranger's steel spine. She had no doubt Tony had wooed and tempted with the kind of money most cash-strapped grad students would kill for. "And we're here to talk to her and not her mother, who works for the actual company you're worried about, because…?"

"Her mother went missing mysteriously about a year ago." Carol's eyebrows rose. "I see you're as intrigued by the timing as Mara is."

"Maybe. The granddaughter suspects foul play?" She didn't wait for Tony's answer. "You agree with her."

"I think it's worth exploring. I'd planned to do so quietly, but Mara went public with some accusations against DigiTech. Let's just say patience isn't her strong suit."

Well, Carol could sympathize with that. A half-smirk lifted the side of her mouth—until Tony, finally, got to his point.

"I need you to look after Mara while I look into all this."

"Look after her?" Carol protested. "I'm not a babysitter or a bodyguard."

"She'd say she's too clever for the former, and she'd agree she doesn't need the latter. She's wrong on both counts. She needs both and more. She needs a mentor."

Tony wheeled toward the coffee shop door, but she grabbed his arm. "I'm not that either, Tony. I don't have interns."

"She's in danger, Carol. She's made an enemy of a very powerful corporation mired in suspicious circumstances that has a lot to lose."

"Look, I get it. But I'm not the one for this. I don't need another lost cause to look after."

"Maybe not. But you need a purpose that reminds you of who you are."

She attempted her best, intimidating Captain Marvel glare, but Tony's expression was more earnest than he usually let the world see. Stark was a master of layered motives, but she couldn't detect any subterfuge in his tone or his eyes. He was worried about this young woman. He suspected DigiTech was up to no good. Carol could understand that.

Now, as for what he thought *she* needed? Though she wanted to argue, she wasn't guaranteed a win on that count. Tony, of all people, knew what it was like to wake up with powers you never asked for. But no one understood what it was like to wake up not even human anymore. Partially not human? She didn't need a reminder of who she was; she needed an understanding of *what* she was. She had no idea how to square her two selves. It was a trick question on a math test. No matter how many times she did the sums, they never added up to the right answer.

"Come on," Tony said, shifting his weight forward, drawing her back to the present, pulling her out of the storm clouds that enveloped her as only Tony could. "Hear her out. Do it as a favor for me."

Her gaze drifted back to the young woman seated beyond the glass, zipped up tight in her puffy yellow coat. Carol studied her hunched shoulders, the way her gaze darted restlessly from the door to the patrons seated nearby and back to the door, and felt a pang of familiarity laced with nostalgia. Like she'd just caught a glimpse of her younger self in a mirror.

If Tony was right—and she trusted him to be right about this, even if she didn't trust him to know what therapy she needed— Mara Melamed needed protection. That was something Carol knew how to do. That was something Carol was good at and didn't require she decide whether her Kree half or her human half deserved the credit.

She turned to the door and preceded Tony into the coffee shop.

4

UP CLOSE, the smooth plains of Mara Melamed's face revealed her to be younger than Carol first thought. Mid-twenties, at most. She wore a pair of acetate-framed glasses that faded from clear at the inside corners to smoky gray at the outside. Beneath them, her eyes were so rimmed with exhaustion circles one could be forgiven for thinking she'd gotten the worst of a hockey brawl. She was just a kid, a clearly troubled one. Carol's heart squeezed, and she fought off the kind of shiver she usually only experienced in the cockpit when the pressure dropped.

Tony slid into the booth and waved Carol onto the bench beside him. "Mara Melamed, meet Carol—"

"I know who you are," the young woman said. Her voice was little more than a whisper. She clutched the collar of her turtleneck, brushing her knuckles across her chin. She took a second, blinking at Carol from behind those heavy frames. "I mean, nice to meet you. I don't mean to be rude. I just—I didn't know Professor Stark was going to bring friends."

Carol rolled her eyes at the way Tony's chest puffed. *Professor.* You couldn't bestow the honorific on someone who thought they were a more deserving recipient.

"An ally. We need them, Mara," he said. "You need them."

Carol cut her eyes at Tony, but he maintained a stone face.

The young woman raised her cup to her lips, realized it was empty, and let her hand fall back to the table. "I can't argue with that. I'm definitely short on anything resembling an ally right now."

"Ah," Tony frowned. "Still no luck finding a thesis adviser?"

"Another one declined this week. At this rate, my thesis is in the running for a unique award: most rejections from professors before even being written."

"I know it feels like it, but you're not beaten yet." Tony's eyes seemed to catch on the dark smudges beneath Mara's eyes, the droop of her shoulders. He rapped his knuckles on the table and stood. "Thesis rejections go down smoother with a fresh cup of coffee. And a donut. On me."

While he made his way to the counter, Carol studied Mara. Or more accurately, the top of her head, since she was staring down at the table as if the secrets to the universe were written there. Or maybe just the secrets to finding a thesis advisor. The coffee shop hummed with the warmth of the building's heat and the noise of the people clustered at tables around them, but Mara sat bundled in her winter weather gear as if she were hiking a tundra. She was a lonely, quiet little island in a sea of activity.

"Is it a controversial topic?" Carol asked. Mara startled, eyebrows pulled down in confusion. "Your thesis."

"More like a controversial author. I wish Professor Stark could be my advisor. He totally gets my exploration of applying pattern theory to predict anomalous events. And he doesn't think I've 'lost perspective to a degree that concerns the faculty as to ability to complete a cogent thesis.'"

"Ouch. Sounds like a direct quote."

"It was. You'll be surprised to hear this, but math professors can be a bunch of archaic tools," Mara said, dripping sarcasm. Carol grinned. "They pretend otherwise, but I know they're afraid to work with me because I refuse to accept the party line about the *gods* over at DigiTech and I won't shut up about it."

Mara had gone from whispering like a cornered mouse to roaring like a wounded animal. Carol leaned her elbows on the table, intrigued to hear more. "But Tony can't become your advisor?"

"He's an adjunct, so he's not technically eligible."

"And yet you call him professor."

"Well," the girl smiled for the first time. It was a mere twisting of lips, a hint of humor, but for the length of a moment, the two-ton weight on her shoulders seemed to lift. "It makes him feel important."

Carol couldn't help but laugh. Kid was astute. "And what is the party line?"

"DigiTech says they fired my mom—their chief software engineer—because she became erratic and unreliable after my grandfather's death. They claim she had a breakdown after getting fired, and now she's off the grid, hiding out because she can't bear the shame she brought to the great Melamed family name." The young woman rattled through all this without taking a single breath, and her tone made clear she was telling a story she didn't believe.

"Your grandfather passed away recently, too?"

"Of a heart attack." Mara nodded, a small pool of tears building in her eyes. She neither attempted to hide them nor brush them away. Though they'd just met, Carol's heart ached for her. There was something uncannily brave about how she spoke her mind without doubting herself and wore her pain publicly. Carol sympathized with the former and admired the latter, which wasn't something she did well at all. "So they say."

"You don't believe it?"

"Absolutely not. And *yes*, I know how it looks," she said, tartly. "He was in his nineties. His last few months, all the revelations, were tough on him. But he always said what happens in the binary is only a little real and he focused on the really real. I mean, four months before he died, he ran a 5K. He was still coding and conducting research. He kept his lab on campus, as professor emeritus, and he went every week before the allegations. Does that sound like a guy that just drops dead of a heart problem?"

O-kay. A lot to unpack there. Including the way she'd begun by acknowledging and then dismissing the weaknesses in her theory. Mara was defensive, and there were crater-sized holes in her assumptions, regardless of her attempts to pass them off. But her passion was compelling. Carol decided to ask the most open-ended question she could think of. "What do you believe happened?"

Mara's eyes still swam with tears, but her gaze was sharp as she sized up the super hero on the opposite side of the table. Perhaps, despite Tony vouching, she wasn't quite sure she could trust Carol. After an uncomfortably long pause, when she spoke, Carol didn't think she landed on a decision, so much as a compulsion to speak her truth yanked the words out of her.

"My grandfather was murdered."

"Why?"

This tripped Mara up momentarily. She stumbled as she started to speak, as if she wasn't used to being offered a platform to make her case. Maybe she just wasn't used to being offered the benefit of the doubt. "I… It's hard to explain. There's a series of events that don't connect logically on the surface but do form a pattern."

"Your thesis topic."

"You notice details," Mara said, sounding the tiniest bit impressed. She leaned back and crossed her arms over her chest. "My otherwise healthy grandfather dies unexpectedly. My mother disappears. Her former employer starts making boatloads—no, shiploads. No! Aircraft-carrier-loads of money. Off software my grandfather invented. There's more, too. Infusions of cash to DigiTech that can't be properly traced. Mysterious bugs affecting BOS-MA competitors right around the time BOS-MA went on sale. If there's one thing I know, it's patterns, and there is a pattern here."

But not a recognizable one. Mara's fervor aside, there weren't many details to support her accusations. The story was thin, nothing that couldn't be dismissed as a series of coincidences. Carol glanced at Tony, who was waiting less than patiently at the counter. Somehow he'd ended up behind an intern wearing a GTSS badge and reading from a long list of orders stored in his phone. The barista looked weary. Tony looked apoplectic. He motioned toward her, silently asking if he should abandon the mission, but Carol waved him off.

"You contacted the police, I assume."

"When my mom first went missing." Mara's hand went back to her collar, knuckles rubbing against her chin hard enough to redden the skin. "The cops didn't bother to look into it. They said grief makes people see connections where there are none. I thought about hiring a private investigator. But my grad student stipend wouldn't come close to paying for that and we don't exactly have family money. I tried talking to some professors at the university, too. My grandfather was such an important member of the community, I thought they'd call for an investigation. Or raise questions about DigiTech. Or something. Instead, they told me to stop making trouble."

"And then, suddenly, you couldn't find a thesis adviser?"

"Even though it's a really good topic." The tears that had pooled in Mara's doe eyes spilled over. "I figured, what did I have to lose? Literally no one was paying attention to the biggest tech story of the century. I had to do something drastic. So I gave an interview to a blog and it kinda went viral. And that's when Empire State University brought out the big guns."

Carol raised one eyebrow.

"They called me in to meet with the chair of the mathematics department, the dean of students, and the dean of career services, who told me how many interns and graduates DigiTech hires. They said they were worried about my stability and my failure to make progress on the thesis. They threw around words like *academic probation* and I got the message. DigiTech matters more to Empire State than I do. I had two choices—shut up or find myself forced to withdraw from the PhD program." Her voice cracked. "I'd be the first Melamed in five generations not to earn my PhD. My grandfather was so proud I was following in his footsteps. He'd have been disappointed if I quit."

Carol could feel how the double-bind tore at Mara. She wanted that degree, but she wanted justice for her grandfather. Not to mention, she believed her theory and she wanted to convince the world she was right. Oddly, Mara mentioned Shelley Melamed quite a bit when she spoke about honoring the family legacy, but not her mother. Her mother was also a computer scientist, part of the heritage of high achievers. Perhaps a bit of bad blood there? Ruefully, she thought of Mari-Ell, her own mom. Carol knew a little something about how complicated mother–daughter relationships could be.

Carol leaned forward, set an elbow on the table and her chin in her hand, mirroring Mara's posture. She studied the young woman across the scarred Formica table, noting her tear-stained cheeks, the mark her anxious knuckles had made on her chin which had yet to fade. Mara was clearly grieving. Maybe her judgment was clouded, as the authority figures in her life believed. But maybe it wasn't. She'd impressed Tony Stark with her brilliant and analytical mind and Carol didn't subscribe to the theory that emotions rendered brains incapable. Mara hadn't shared anything that suggested actual evidence of criminal activity, but Tony was suspicious of DigiTech, and the establishment had tried pretty hard to shut Mara up. In Carol's experience, higher-ups trying to intimidate a young woman into silence wasn't proof of wrongdoing on its own, but it was a strong indicator. Smoke and fire, and all that. More often than not, this kind of institutional effort to gag someone added up to something.

By the time Tony returned to the table with a round of steaming coffees and half a dozen donuts, Carol had Mara's phone number stored in her contacts and an itch to find out more.

5

THE FOLLOWING day, Carol knocked on a familiar apartment door, balancing a coffee carrier and a very fancy donut box filled with gourmet flavors like Nutella cappuccino, and strawberries and cream, and maple bacon glaze. She knew better than to show up at Jess's apartment this early without a peace offering, so she'd circled back to that coffee shop. If anything was likely to soften Spider-Woman's heart, it was extravagant baked goods. After a beat, the door swung open, revealing her best friend, Jessica Drew, wearing a T-shirt with the collar cut out, an extra disheveled messy bun and a scowl that carved canyon-deep grooves in her forehead. Behind her, a little blond toddler head popped up over the back of the sofa. Gerry, Jess's son, stood on the cushions, wobbling precariously.

"Hi Car-o!" the baby trilled.

Carol thrust the goodies into Jessica's hands and swooped in to scoop him up. It was probably less likely Jess would go nuclear if she was holding a baby, right? "Hi, Ger-bear," she said, giving him a squeeze. "You miss Auntie Carol?"

"Carol Danvers, you have thirty seconds to explain to me

why you're not having a joyful alien family reunion in outer space right now!"

Okay, so mission *not* accomplished. Jess could, in fact, go nuclear while Carol was holding Gerry, if the decibel level on which she'd ended that sentence was any indication. "I do have an explanation." Just not one Jess was going to like very much. Carol stalled. "Where's Lindsay?"

Lindsay McCade was Gerry's nanny, as well as being a sought-after Hollywood stunt double. Made sense for Jess to have a trained fighter watching her kid while she was off Spider-Womaning. Carol hadn't spent much time around the feisty redheaded nanny, but what she knew gave her confidence that Gerry was in excellent, protective hands.

"At an audition. Should be back tonight." Jess kicked the door closed and thrust her chin toward Carol. "Come on, then. Let's hear it. This *explanation*."

"Don't you want some of that coffee first? I had them make it with almond milk." Carol reached out and plucked the smallest cup from the carrier. "And a lukewarm hot chocolate for the kid, here."

She strode toward the kitchen, although considering Jess's was a pretty typical NY apartment, she didn't have far to go before she bumped into the island that served as the breakfast bar and the dinner table. Carol plunked Gerry into a booster seat that still bore the remains of his eggs-and-toast breakfast plate. The fact that it was only 6:15 a.m. and these two had already finished breakfast might explain Jess's grumpy demeanor. Or that could just be her frustration with Carol. Who knew? Hoping to give the caffeine a minute to penetrate, she assumed the role of doting auntie, cleaning up Gerry's tray, transferring the hot chocolate into a sippy cup, and breaking up the most highly sprinkle-coated donut into bite-size pieces for him.

She loved Gerry and she didn't get to play aunt nearly as much as she'd like. But sometimes, in these moments, she felt like she was putting on a show, imitating family life she knew from movies and TV while wearing the slightly ill-fitting costume of the "single aunt." Which made sense since Kree families behaved nothing like this. This wasn't in her DNA. Had her mother also felt like she was playacting in those early days, while she learned how to mimic Earth family life? Had she ever felt her heart squeeze both with love and with astonishment when she handed a gap-toothed toddler a sugary donut and he grinned up at her like she'd just made his day? The feeling spreading through Carol's chest was warm and familiar and achy and new all at once. She smoothed a hand over Gerry's silky baby hair and returned his smile, forcing her thoughts back to the present.

Jessica cast aside the donut box without even peering into it. Carol interpreted that as a very serious, very bad sign, though her friend had, at least, removed the lid from the almond milk mocha latte and taken a long, appreciative inhale. "Out with it."

"Tony called—"

"Tony summoned, you mean." Jessica slammed the cup down onto the counter hard enough that coffee sloshed over the side. She grabbed for a paper towel, glaring. "You were busy. You did not have to take that call. You did not have to come running back on his say-so."

"He had a credible reason."

"You are avoiding dealing with your emotions!"

"Who, me? I'd never do that." Carol lifted her hands and tried to imitate Gerry's innocent, sugar-frosted smile. The one that never failed to disarm both her and his mother. Apparently, her efforts were less persuasive than the cherubic toddler's. Jess tossed the dripping paper towel at Carol's face. She batted it away, then swept it into the trash bin placed strategically beside Gerry's booster seat. She repeated the explanation she'd given herself when she turned the *Peregrine* back toward Earth. "Throneworld II isn't going anywhere. I have plenty of time to visit Lauri and… you know. Talk. About stuff."

"We both know how fast things like *time* disappear."

Carol clenched her teeth. "Don't."

"Carol, it's okay to be nervous about learning more about your Kree side. Anyone would struggle with such a big revelation. But you can't avoid it out of existence."

An image of a metal spear being hurled through space overtook Carol, sending her spiraling back through time and space. The *thwack* that weapon made when it hit her mother's chest and sank through the flesh resonated in her ears, just as it had that day. The memory became intrusive, sucking Carol into the despair she'd felt as her shoulders curled over her mother's bloodied form, the weight impossibly slight in her arms as she flew Mari-Ell back to the lighthouse. There'd been no time, not even enough to say goodbye, let alone learn her family truths from her mother's mouth.

Carol shook her head to clear the image, dislodging her bun. In contrast to Jess's messy top knot, she wore hers the way she'd learned to put it up in the military, smoothed back from her face and knotted at the nape of her neck, though apparently she no longer pinned it up tight enough to withstand a difficult day. Sort of like the bindings she'd sewn over her heart couldn't weather the force of Jess's scrutiny. One vague reminder of her mother and all of her abiding regret burst forth.

She couldn't reconcile all the pieces of her heritage. One half of her felt like a stranger at best and an enemy at worst, and the person she truly wanted—no, needed to help her understand how to live with that dichotomy was gone. She couldn't give in to the painful memories. She would not let the darkness that shrouded her past annihilate all of her. If Carol kept trying to wrestle this demon, it would consume her. Better to leave it locked tightly behind a door in her memories.

Jess meant well, urging Carol to go to Throneworld and learn about being Kree. But she was wrong that it was the best thing for Carol. The best way for her to keep the pieces of herself together was to make productive use of her time helping someone else. Like Mara. She could help Mara find her mother before it was too late. Before Mara knew the kind of regret Carol did.

"Jess, don't. Please." The tone of Carol's voice brought Jess's verbal ambush to a halt.

"You know I love you, right?"

The two friends had gotten better about saying that over the last few years, about articulating how much their friendship mattered before time and danger and evil sorcerers stole too many opportunities to say the important words aloud. Carol pasted a smile onto her face, nodding. She knew but... Jess loved Carol Danvers, the Captain Marvel she thought she'd been fighting alongside for years. As did Tony and all the rest of the team. What about Car-El, daughter of Mari-Ell? Even Carol didn't know Car-El, let alone love her. How could Jessica?

"I know."

Jess studied her, astute dark eyes searching Carol's face. After a long minute, she shook her head and sighed. Not much got past Jessica Drew, so Carol knew she hadn't fooled her. But they'd also spent their whole friendship testing how hard they could push one another and Jess seemed to sense that this was the limit for Carol. At least for today.

She dug out the maple bacon donut and shoved the box across the counter toward Carol. "Fine, I can take a hint. For now. Grab that boring cruller I know you bought hoping I wouldn't eat it and tell me what Tony's all fired up about now."

Carol blew a tiny breath from the corner of her mouth. She wasn't naive enough to assume this was a full retreat from the subject. Jess wouldn't back down that easily. But she welcomed even a brief reprieve from focusing on her messed up personal life.

"Glad you asked," she said, setting the perfectly frosted crimped dough circle on a napkin. She smiled to herself because she had, indeed, bought the cruller for herself. It was the plainest option in the box, which assured her neither Jess nor Gerry would be tempted by it. But to Carol, it was a tiny ring of flawlessness balanced between savory carbs and sugary glaze. "Because this isn't just a social visit. I need your help on a case."

Jess gestured to the icing-coated kid happily smashing his donut remains. "Little busy today."

"Luckily, I need Jessica Drew, crack P.I., to do some digging right here from the comfort of her apartment. There's a company with a dodgy history and a couple of mysteriously dead or missing computer science professors."

"Ooookay." Jess's eyebrows drew together and her mouth pursed. "Not at all what I expected you to say."

Got her. She'd known this constellation of facts would pique her friend's interest. Investigations might be how Jess earned her living, but digging up metaphorical dirt was also part of her makeup. Look how naturally nosy—and suspicious—she was, Carol thought, wryly, recalling all the intrusive questions Jess had asked about Carol's Kree heritage.

While Jess cleaned up Gerry and settled him on the rug with an impressive stack of blocks to build into towers that he'd promptly knock down, Carol relayed what she'd learned from Tony and Mara Melamed.

"So. Let me get this straight. A world famous computer scientist slash inventor dies, and not long after that, a private company strikes it super rich releasing a commercial version of the operating system he invented, and not long after *that*, the chief engineer of the company, who also happens to be the daughter of the original inventor, goes mysteriously missing?"

"Pretty much. That register as odd to you?"

"Circumstantially, sure," Jess said. "This is DigiTech, right? The company behind BOS-MA?"

Carol licked some excess icing off her thumb and said around a mouthful of donut, "Yeah. You know it?

"I installed it a few months ago. It's incredibly powerful—works great with the software I use for investigations."

"What do you know about the system? Or DigiTech?"

"Not a lot," Jessica admitted, reaching for her laptop. "But you know I'd never pass up an opportunity to look into shady corporate shenanigans. Let's see what we can uncover."

Carol settled on the couch beside Jess and watched as she brought the screen to life. She began with a quick internet search, which turned up a spate of articles focused on the wild success of the operating system—glowing testimonials about how it took computing power forward by giant leaps, how it conquered the world faster than a virus. Jess scrolled past those, dismissing them as PR puff pieces seeded by DigiTech itself.

"That's Seales, the CEO of DigiTech," Carol said, pointing to a profile titled *TECH'S LATEST MARVEL*.

"Tony's least favorite person, huh?" Jess clicked through to the article, which turned out to be more press release copy with only a few quotes from the woman herself, and a solitary photo. With two fingers, Jess zoomed in and then zoomed in even more. She zoomed back out and wrinkled her nose. "This is an odd picture. She's more pixelated than her surroundings. Either this is not a publication quality photo or it's a digital manipulation."

"It's a hologram," Carol said.

"The… picture?"

"No, the person. She only appears in hologram form, apparently. Tony thinks it's a pretentious gimmick."

"Tony probably wishes he'd thought of it first."

Carol laughed, starting a search on the iPad she'd brought with her. They'd have to divide and conquer. She hadn't expected there to be so much material about this one company. Who read article after article of business jargon recycling the same press release info? None of it had that telltale marker that it was an ad rather than real journalism, but Carol couldn't discern a substantive difference between those fawning sponsored content articles and this stuff. Parsing through for facts felt like climbing from the depths of those foam-filled pits Gerry liked to play in at the bouncy house place. She texted Jess a link to a story about Seales and Mara Melamed's mother, Dr. Iris Melamed, the power duo behind the company's unusual decision to use BOS-MA to build a new platform for commercial and consumer devices. Then, she flicked open an article she found in Empire State's alumni magazine online to read herself. Instead of focusing on the company, this profile detailed Professor Shelley Melamed's career, including the government-funded research he conducted during the Vietnam War era.

"A lot of these roads lead back to the Melameds," Carol said. "The family patriarch, Professor Shelley Melamed, invents this software—"

"Operating system."

She rolled her eyes. "Fine, operating system." She began reading aloud from the alumni profile. "'Melamed formed one of the earliest research partnerships with the Department of Defense, securing funding to build what would ultimately become the premier computing research lab in the country, here at Empire State. At one point, he employed over one hundred undergraduate and graduate students in the computer science, physics and engineering schools.'"

"A coup for the university, I guess," Jess said. "But if he invented the OS for the military, how did DigiTech acquire it and release it for commercial use?"

Carol scanned the rest of the article, but it made no mention of BOS-MA. That was strange. Even if the article was written prior to the commercial success DigiTech found, if BOS-MA was as revolutionary as all those press releases claimed, hadn't the professor realized what a staggering invention it was when he developed it? And why hadn't the military adopted widespread use of such a powerful operating system before a civilian company re-released it years later?

A brief reference to Mara in the last paragraph caught her eye, and she doubled back to re-read the section about his family: a wife that tragically passed away just a few years after the birth of their only child, Iris, who spend most of her childhood at a girls' boarding school in upstate New York, where she won numerous awards and captained the robotics team, followed by her time at Empire State, where she earned a doctorate in computer science with high honors. According to the gushing article, during grad school, Iris cemented the Melamed family reputation for single-minded genius when she led Empire State to not one but two Gold Medals in the prestigious Stark Awards for contributions to the advancement of computing technology. Her team won the first medal shortly after the death of her teammate and romantic partner, a fellow grad student who died young and suddenly from an undiagnosed heart condition, and the second, just six months after Iris gave birth to their daughter. The final line of the section noted that Iris's daughter, Mara, had been accepted to Empire State's graduate program, but mentioned only that she'd graduated from a local public school.

Hmmmm, Carol thought. The disparity between Mara's education and accomplishments and Iris's was pretty blunt. She wondered if that was the cause of the tension she'd picked up from the young woman when she spoke about her mother. Something was definitely going on there. Tony had, no doubt, done his research on Mara; he wouldn't have offered her a job if he didn't find her trustworthy. But Carol had some questions of her own. She typed Mara's name into the search engine. The first hit was that interview she'd given to the tech blog. Carol skimmed it, finding a more detailed version of the theory Mara had spun at the coffee shop. At the end, an author's note stated: *The authors acknowledge the controversy surrounding Professor Shelley Melamed's early work. For further information regarding his involvement in the scandal, click <u>here</u>.*

Mara had alluded to a public event that agitated her grandfather in his later years. What had she said? Something about the binary not being real? But she'd insisted that backstory wasn't relevant. Carol's eyes caught on those words in the author's note: *controversy, scandal.* Every reference to the Melameds hinted at a tantalizingly complex and ambiguous history that was beginning to feel inevitable rather than irrelevant. Carol was growing convinced that the Melamed family was inextricably woven into this. Whatever *this* was. When she searched further, a torrent of articles with click-bait-ish titles flooded her screen.

DISHONOR ROCKS STORIED TECH FAMILY

CORRUPTION EXPOSED! GOVERNMENT RESEARCHER INVOLVED IN SECRET WEAPONS TESTING

GENIUS OR VILLAIN? FATHER OF MODERN COMPUTING REVEALED TO BE MASTERMIND BEHIND SHAMEFUL ILLEGAL GOVT WEAPONS PROGRAM

They were the kind of pieces she'd normally dismiss as conspiracy delusion, but some reputable outlets reported on it, too. Carol clicked on one of the less sensational headlines and found an article that was pretty shocking, despite the muted language.

Fresh revelations stunned the technology world as the leak of top secret documents proves Professor Shelley Melamed led a government program that illegally tested weapons on civilians during the Vietnam War. The renowned inventor was well known for speeches in which he claimed that technology could make the world a better place. It now appears, from a video filmed during the testing, that Melamed and the officers participating in the testing were aware it would be considered a violation of international law. That video, along with images from the illegal tests, have been shared to nearly every device around the world and viewed billions of times since their release last year. In the wake of the scandal, the Department of Defense declined to comment beyond indicating they are pursuing an internal investigation into the allegations, but Congress has called for hearings into the now-defunct program. Empire State University revoked Melamed's professor emeritus status, and several prominent committees are considering rescinding his awards. The university closed down his campus lab, which had once been the most sophisticated joint military–civilian research facility in the world. Dr. Rebecca Jerome, his one-time research partner and original co-founder of the lab, released the following public statement: "Code is supposed to make people's lives better. Shelley lost sight of his ethical responsibilities as a member of the research community and allowed his pursuit of invention to lead him down an unconscionable path. I can no longer be associated with his gross distortion of our original purpose: to improve humanity's existence through principled technological advancement." She further demanded her name be removed from all literature, patents, awards, and websites referring to Melamed.

The remainder of the articles varied between measured investigations of the leaked video and images to gleeful tabloid takedowns, but they all concurred on the conclusion: Shelley Melamed's lauded place in computer history deserved a big, big asterisk.

Carol set the iPad aside and ran a hand over her face, scrubbing her strained eyes. The mental clouds that had obscured visibility during her conversation with Mara at the coffee shop finally cleared. As someone who'd lived through revelations that shifted how she viewed her family, Carol understood Mara's distress. It couldn't be easy to idolize a man who turned out to be unscrupulous at best and an antihero at worst.

At least, in her case, her mom had just turned out to be an alien.

"Got it!" Jess exclaimed. Carol glanced up in surprise. Her friend stood by the stove, stirring something in a pot, Gerry on one hip, her iPhone tucked between her ear and her shoulder. Carol hadn't even noticed her get up from the couch. "Thanks, pal!"

Gerry plucked the phone from his mother and proceeded to chuck it toward the island. *Good aim*, Carol thought, watching the phone crash onto the granite and slide off the side, *if too much power*.

"That was a P.I. friend with connections to the military," Jess said, settling her son into his high chair. Was it lunchtime already? Carol glanced at the clock and saw hours had passed. "Finally got the answer to how DigiTech got ahold of the code and it's a more banal explanation than you'd expect. BOS-MA was released as part of a declassification effort, along with thousands of other documents, about two and a half years ago. Anyone could have picked it up and used it to develop their own proprietary operating system. It went mostly ignored. Convenient for DigiTech that Melamed's daughter was one of their engineers. She might have been the only person in the world who knew to look for the hidden gem buried in some old military files."

"Chief engineer, right?"

"No, that came later." Jess delivered a bowl of mac n' cheese to her son. "After Seales was hired."

"Were the video and images released with those documents?" Carol, not one to turn down a childhood favorite, grabbed a bowl and helped herself to half the noodles remaining in the pot.

"What video and images?"

Between bites, Carol summarized the scandal that led to Iris Melamed's breakdown and Mara's fall from grace at the university.

Jessica twirled her fork in a circle in the air, silently calculating. "That happened within the last year? The timeline doesn't quite add up. I guess it's possible, given the size of the declassification dump, that it would take a journalist a few years to wade through hundreds of thousands of files and discover the Melamed materials. But it sounds like the videos incriminate military officers, too. Why would they declassify something like that?"

"Good point." Carol dug her spoon into her bowl, surprised when it scraped across the empty ceramic bottom. Gone already? One of these days she'd learn to give herself time to chew. She sighed, dropped the bowl in the sink, and wandered out of the kitchen area. She came to a halt before the window, watching the afternoon traffic roll past on the street below. The orderly rows of cars heading from origin to destination, on a comfortable, familiar path, made sense to Carol. She tweaked the fabric of the curtain aside and then let it fall back, bathing the room first in light and then in shadow. Twisty investigations were more Jess's specialty than Carol's. She preferred a straight line trajectory from bad guys to face punch. Despite a long morning of research, they hadn't pieced together enough of the puzzle to see a picture forming.

"Something's not sitting right with you?"

Carol turned and found Jess standing behind her, a fresh cup of coffee in hand. She held the mug out to Carol, but not even the enticing scent of the caffeine pulled her from her funk. "According to, well, everyone, Iris's breakdown was caused by her father's passing."

"And?"

"If the articles are accurate, she was basically raised by strangers—nannies and then boarding schools. She never mentions her father in interviews. There's nothing to suggest they were close. People grieve in different ways, of course. Maybe their unreconciled issues made his death overwhelming to her. I get that. But why disappear? Even if she wanted to avoid public attention for a while, she's letting her daughter think she's missing—or dead. That seems extreme."

"As someone who's had to keep away from her kid for his safety," Jess said, through pursed lips, "I have a hard time judging."

Carol nudged her friend gently with one shoulder. "You never simply vanished, though. You always made sure his caregivers knew you had to be away for a while, even if you couldn't say where."

"Gerry's young. Who knows if it'll be different when he's old enough to ask for an explanation. Parents make mistakes in how they tell their kids difficult private stuff all the time, don't you think?" Jess did not look at Carol as she finished her speech, but her tone was pointed.

"Jess," Carol warned. It wasn't completely fair of her to get prickly, she acknowledged that. She'd cracked open this door—infinitesimally—by bringing up Iris Melamed's parenting decisions. But that didn't mean she was inviting deep discussion of her situation, analogous or not. This was *mission intel*. "Don't make this about me. Or you. We're focused on the Melameds. At the very least, you have to agree the timing is suspicious. A month after this scandal goes public, the second most prominent and important woman in DigiTech gets ousted from her position."

"Ah, you've drunk the same Kool-Aid as Tony, huh? You don't trust Seales."

"Corporate greed as a motivator? Whoever heard of such a thing."

"I agree the facts don't all add up." Jess retreated to the island, checking on her son. A ray of afternoon light illuminated his curls, briefly giving him a sparkly little halo to top off his melty cheese mustache. "Then again, not every story does. Sometimes the loose ends are just loose ends."

Carol shook her head. "I don't think these are."

Jess wrinkled her nose and then held her phone out, the screen showing a forwarded email message. "Me either, actually. The P.I. friend I called? He got a tip after asking around for me. From a former DigiTech shareholder."

"A whistleblower?" Carol grabbed the phone. The message was vague, just a line or two that whoever was looking into DigiTech might be interested in certain information he possessed about recent stock sales.

"Or a disgruntled rich guy who sold too soon and wants a little market correction via bad press. Worth checking into. I'll set a meeting up, hear what he's got to share."

Carol tapped her fingers against the phone screen, mind skipping rapidly through maneuvers and counter-maneuvers, just like it had when she was in the cockpit of a fighter jet. "I think I'd like to see what DigiTech has to say for itself."

"Straight into the lion's den, eh?"

Carol grinned, gave Gerry a squeeze, and headed for the door. "My favorite place to start."

6

DIGITECH'S HEADQUARTERS inhabited a compound about an hour north of the city. To gain entry, Carol drove through three sets of gates manned by armed guards, facial recognition and bio-identifier technology. The last army base she'd served on hadn't used so many layers of defense. Either this company took its corporate security seriously or it had something to hide.

Beyond the final set of gates, a complex of buildings sprawled across a lawn as green as a fertilizer ad. A few glass-and-steel structures formed a miniature downtown, swapping out the cars and congestion for bike lanes and rows of electric bicycles. Carol parked in a garage tower and set off across the manicured quad, at one the end of which was a towering steel pyramid marked by an LED sign labeled *Visitor's Entrance*. She underwent another identification check in a lobby that sparkled with sunlight beaming through floor-to-ceiling glass windows onto a sea of white marble and polished chrome.

Carol hadn't paid visits to many high-tech headquarters other than Stark Industries, but she'd seen plenty of pictures of Tony glad-handing CEOs. These places always seemed to follow a formula: 50% ultra-modern industrial chic, 50% playground, 100% hive of activity. DigiTech fit the mold, with one glaring exception. As an all-glass elevator swept her up to the top floor, the assistant escorting her pointed out work zones with treadmill desks and brainstorming rooms with foosball tables and reclining pods for naps—all of which stood empty. The only people on campus seemed to be the lobby desk attendant, the assistant, an army of security guards, and Carol.

Shouldn't this place teem with developers and engineers and interns and whoever else made up the human machinery that ran a giant corporation? Sure, DigiTech was probably more automated than most companies, but to the level where almost no personnel was needed?

"Slow day at the office?" she asked, as they stepped off the elevator. The assistant looked confused. Carol elaborated, waving a hand at the empty secretarial bays they passed. "Pretty empty around here."

"Oh, this is a new campus," the assistant said, plastering on a toothy smile. "A lot of staff still work at our manufacturing facilities. We were a hardware company, you know, before we were a software company!"

That wasn't much of an answer. What was the point of the picnic tables and the bean bag chairs and the energy-drink-stocked fridges on every floor? Why have such a big impressive campus if nobody worked here?

The assistant led Carol to a conference room that took up an entire side of the building and retreated after imploring her to make herself at home. She glanced at the minimalist white conference table and teal molded plastic chairs, which were probably trendy but looked neither inviting nor comfortable. Not even the display of still and sparkling water bottles and the extensive snack bar on a counter at the back of the room could render the sterile space homey. Unchecked sunlight blazed through the wall of windows, leaving the room stiflingly hot—like a greenhouse, although Carol hadn't seen so much as an office *ficus* anywhere in the building.

She shed her bomber jacket and paced, waiting for Griselda Seales. As the minutes stretched on, she checked her phone for a message from Jess, who should be finishing her meeting with that DigiTech shareholder, Faber, right about now. They'd scheduled it so that if Jess learned something Carol could use to lean on Seales, she'd have time to report back.

Her phone screen displayed a couple spam messages from companies offering her discounts on products but nothing from Jess. She was a thorough interviewer; maybe Faber had more dirt to dish than they expected. If anyone was going to get every shred of proof of corporate malfeasance onto a recording device, it was Jessica Drew, P.I.

Carol would have to wing this meeting with the tech genius. Couldn't be harder than talking to Tony when he was on a tear about something he'd programmed B.O.S.S. to do, right?

Finally, more than a little late, the door to the conference room swung open and the assistant returned, followed by Seales, whose image dimmed like an overexposed photo as she stepped into the brightly lit room. Interesting that the glow from the screen at that Supernova conference hadn't messed with the hologram, but the overpowering sunlight here did. Sophisticated tech, but not infallible. Tony would be perversely pleased to hear that.

"BOS-MA, shade the room, please." Seales's voice sounded as crisp and clear as if she were right beside Carol. The windows darkened, blotting out the worst of the glare, and the hologram sharpened.

As Seales moved through the room and took her seat, Carol's heightened senses noticed the way her voice moved across the overhead speakers and then to a speaker recessed into the table, cleverly concealed beside an in-surface panel full of coiled wires and power units. Once she knew to look, Carol spied speakers all around the room—an ingenious trick to throw the electronic voice more seamlessly than a ventriloquist. This wasn't the first time the hologram had taken meetings in this room. Perhaps the space had even been designed as a set of sorts, a place where the hologram could put on a near-perfect show.

"Welcome to DigiTech, Ms. Danvers. Or should I call you Captain?"

"Carol's fine," she said, seating herself near Seales.

The hologram? Felt weird to think of her as either a person or tech. Carol resisted the urge to lean forward and study the hologram's mouth movements to see how well it synched up to the sound coming from the speakers, but she couldn't hold back a prying question. "Do you take all meetings in that getup?"

"It's not a costume," Seales smiled, her holographic teeth sparkling. "I find, when I appear as a hologram, people ask questions about the technology that makes this possible and not what designer I'm wearing or how my hair is styled today. I'd rather answer the former than the latter. I have a feeling you can empathize with that, Captain. Am I right?"

Well, that was disarmingly astute. Carol had deflected her share of nonsense questions about hair and clothing and even what she wore under the Captain Marvel suit. Why people felt entitled to demand that information, she'd never understand. Over the years, she'd wondered, periodically, if maybe she would attract less attention if she just went out in the suit all the time, until it became the norm instead of a curiosity. "Fair enough, Ms. Seales."

"Now, what can I do for you? I imagine you didn't stop by just for a tour of our brand new HQ."

"I thought I detected that fresh-paint smell."

Seales folded her arms on the table, saying nothing.

Oh, come on, that was a little funny, Carol thought, quirking an eyebrow. That digitally rendered expression remained pleasantly, stoically expectant without any hint of softening.

"Forgive me for being blunt, Captain. I suspect you're here on an errand for Tony Stark, but I've made clear that I'm not interested in sharing proprietary information with him just because he is who he is."

Guess the bonding portion of the meeting is over.

"I don't know why he thought camouflaging himself by sending an associate would be more effective."

Carol bristled at the implication of that word choice. She was no minion, as Seales well knew, or she wouldn't keep calling her Captain. "I'm not here on his behalf."

"But at his urging?"

"I don't see how that's relevant. Besides, what've you got against him? He's one of the preeminent inventors in the world, not to mention a big investor in emerging technology. I'd think you'd want to impress him with everything you're working on here."

"Who knew Captain Marvel made such a great hype woman!" The hologram laughed, the sound tinkly in a way that grated on Carol's nerves. "Do you accept sponsorship deals? Our ad agency is looking for a celebrity endorser for our next commercial."

She gritted her teeth. "Not a chance."

"He's the competition, Carol." Seales's laughter stopped abruptly. "We have intellectual property to protect. Stark has never hesitated to take what he wants and make it his own, without a mind toward the inventors and employees who suddenly find themselves underlings to the great and powerful Stark. You'll forgive me if I'm wary of his motives in wanting to question DigiTech about our products."

"I suppose that explains all the security around this place?"

"If those are all the questions Tony had for me—" Seales stood, a disconcerting movement considering the chair behind her didn't push back.

Carol steepled her fingers together and resisted the urge to jump up and chase the hologram as it departed the room. First, given the amount of digital monitoring required for the real woman to have a conversation while physically being in another location, Carol suspected the presence of the hologram wouldn't be needed for Seales to hear her. Second, it would make her feel like the paparazzi running after a fleeing star. Third, a Carol chase usually ended up in a face punch and that would be tremendously unsatisfying with nothing but holographic air for her fist to connect with. Or not connect with, as it were.

"But they're not all *my* questions," she said, her tone firm and unruffled. "If you're so concerned about your employees, how is it that your most well-known engineer doesn't work here anymore?"

The hologram paused on its way toward the door and flickered. "Of whom are you speaking?"

"Dr. Iris Melamed? Your chief engineer."

"Ah yes. Very unfortunate that she needed to… step away." Seales affected a dispassionately respectful tone, the kind of faux-concern someone adopted when a bad thing happened to a person they didn't really know.

Odd, considering the papers had spoken about these two women almost exclusively as a duo. In the early articles, they'd done the journalistic equivalent of gushing over the dynamic pair behind BOS-MA's success. Carol's eyes bored into Seales. The advantage of being fake, of course, was a blank robot face was the default setting. The hologram needed to do nothing but maintain its politely disinterested expression, and Carol could glean no intelligence from the smooth digital pixels of her image. The voice gave nothing away either. Clearly, the intimidation factor of the Captain Marvel glare was muted by the distance and the code Seales hid behind.

Time for a more direct verbal assault. "Are you aware her daughter believes she's missing and suspects foul play?"

"Yes, my PR team informed me the young lady gave quite an erratic interview to some social media site. I'm very sorry for Ms. Melamed. I hear she's been distraught since the passing of her grandfather, to whom I believe she was close. Dr. Melamed once mentioned that her father raised his granddaughter. I can understand why recent disclosures about his career would upset someone in her fragile state."

The news pieces Carol read had danced around saying that Mara was raised by her grandfather, not her mother. Much like Seales was dancing around giving a direct response about Mara's mother. "Have you heard from Dr. Melamed lately?"

"In what capacity are you inquiring, Captain? I doubt you're working with local law enforcement, as there's no investigation that I'm aware of. I'm not clear on your role here and why DigiTech should answer your questions."

Another dodge. Seales's spoken word sleight of hand was impressive. And annoying. Carol's steepled hands tensed, nails digging into her fingertips. "Why not? Got something to hide?"

Another laugh. "Oh, Captain. So earnest. So simple."

Carol backtracked. She couldn't compel Seales to provide answers to her questions and antagonizing the woman wasn't going to get her anywhere. Her instincts cried out that something was off, though, and as her patience wore down, she struggled to keep the barbs from her tone. "Ms. Seales, I'm just surprised, considering your earlier professed concern for your employees, that you're not at least a little worried about one of them disappearing."

The hologram hadn't moved since it first paused on the way to the door. Despite the initial lifelike impression it gave, its inhumanity was becoming more pronounced to Carol. A person would have been shifting their weight, pacing, crossing one foot over the other, looking down at the ground or over Carol's shoulder toward the windows or even at a phone. The flickering image of Seales stood, arms at her sides, preternaturally still. It was more than a little disconcerting.

"Ah, but she's no longer one of my employees, is she? I'm sure you know we didn't part ways on the best of terms. Thus, DigiTech would hardly be the place she'd call when she emerged from her isolation."

"I hear you booted her because she got too emotional."

"The details of her termination are confidential, Captain. Nor would I want to speak ill of the unwell. The Melamed family has been through enough. I'm empathetic to their troubles. Such a shame to see a family who'd done so much for the industry be dragged through the mud. But you know what they say. Never meet your heroes."

"You mean Professor Shelley Melamed? Or Dr. Iris Melamed?"

Seales threw her arms out wide, as if she'd suddenly remembered she was supposed to be moving, imitating a living, breathing being. Her smile practically glowed, the extraordinary white that of a photo filter rather than human teeth. "When you learn the truth about someone you believe you know well, that can upend your whole world view, wouldn't you say?"

Carol suppressed a flinch. Her alien background wasn't secret anymore, and it had caused plenty of suspicion to swirl around the Captain Marvel persona. Logically, she knew Seales couldn't mean her. Still, the comment pressed against the sore spots in her emotional armor.

"There are enough rumors circulating about Iris without her former employer contributing any more," Seales went on. "While I'm sorry she wasn't able to continue as our chief engineer and I appreciated her contributions to our success, the incident likely precipitated an inevitable change. She's a brilliant woman, but at that stage of DigiTech's growth, we needed a… stable presence in the role. I'm sure Iris has gone on to something that better suits her talents."

Considering that, as far as anyone knew, Iris hadn't gone on to anything at all, Carol found that statement more than a little presumptuous.

The hologram swung toward the door. Seales's voice faded as it hopped from speaker to speaker, following her to the exit. "I'm afraid I have another meeting I'm already late for. Wish Tony my best, would you, Carol?"

As the hologram left, the window shading dissipated, flooding the room in light. Carol squinted against the sudden brightness.

She swept her jacket off the chair where she'd deposited it and headed to the door, trying to clear her thoughts. She never imagined she'd meet someone as uniquely infuriating and impressive as Tony Stark, but today she might have done just that. Griselda Seales was as pretentious as he had complained, though. As the assistant escorted Carol out, she couldn't rid herself of the feeling that she'd just been swimming laps in a pool—using up a whole lot of energy but covering the same ground.

ON HER way off the compound, she pulled up her messages. Still nothing from Jess. Carol did a quick mental calculation—six hours since last contact. They'd go days without talking when Jess was in the middle of an investigation or Carol was off planet, but not when they were on a mission together. Jess would at least reply to Carol's messages with a hold your horses gif. An eye roll emoji. Something.

Maybe Jess hadn't heard the pinging of five—okay, eight texts. Tony Stark's bombard-until-you-get-what-you-want tactic hadn't worked, and Carol couldn't quell the anxiety tightening her muscles. Carol dialed her best friend's number. Silence. Dead air. No ringing. Not even a digital recording telling Carol the user she had dialed was unavailable and to please try again later. Nothing. A flash of heat swept over her. Hadn't she left a voicemail just a few hours ago? Why wouldn't the line at least connect now?

Carol pulled off the highway in a suburb halfway between the DigiTech compound and the city. Five minutes past the exit, she spied an outdoor shopping center bounded on one side by a parking lot and on the other by a park. The lot didn't offer much privacy, but it gave her a place to step out of the car and suck down a lungful of cold, fresh air. Was this how Jess, Jennifer, and Monica felt when she ghosted them? Like their gut contained a flammable concoction made from two parts worry and one part irritation? She was going to holler at Ms. Jessica Drew when she finally surfaced. You don't go radio-silent without warning your team.

She strode to a bench at the edge of the park and hoisted herself onto the backrest, feet on the seat. She pulled a hat low on her head and threw on some big dark sunglasses Monica left in her car a while back. The last thing Carol needed while she put out a friend-APB was to be swarmed by autograph-and-selfie seekers. Taking a deep breath and pushing her tension into a tiny compartment at the far back of her brain, she pulled out her phone and tried Jess again but it was still a dead line. She checked in with Lindsay, who had been at a playground in the city with Gerry all morning and hadn't heard from Jess.

Not good, not good. Hadn't her friend just said she'd never disappear on her son?

Okay, Carol. Retrace her steps. Jess had been planning to go see Laurence Faber, the DigiTech shareholder, but she had not mentioned where the meeting was supposed to take place. Carol cursed herself for not asking for those details. Where would a guy like Faber take a meeting with a P.I.? Perhaps his office? She could undoubtedly find that address online and pay a visit, but there was no guarantee he'd still be there. She didn't even have confirmation that's where Jess had met the man.

Wait. Tony had hunted Carol down in space with that blasted tracker app of his. Maybe he'd put it on Jess's phone, too.

Carol dialed his number to the background soundtrack of a peewee soccer game that had started up in the park. The kids couldn't have been older than five or six, wearing miniature cleats and using pop-up goals. While she waited for him to answer, she imagined Gerry out there in a few years and tried to decide what kind of soccer parent Jess would turn out to be. There seemed to be two camps at this game. One set of parents had professional-level tail-gating setups with folding sunshades and picnic chairs and coolers and tripods with phones aimed at the field to record video. The rest stood ten feet beyond the makeshift sidelines, wearing sunglasses, clutching large coffees and talking to no one other than themselves.

She grinned. Come to think of it, it wasn't that hard to figure out where her friend would be.

"Carol!" Tony's voice boomed across the airwaves. "Fortuitous timing. I'm on campus with Mara and—"

She cut him off. "I can't find Jess. I need you to do your tracker thing. Use her phone or whatever."

"What's going on?"

A faint whirring caught Carol's attention, reminding her vaguely of the sound of a civilian drone. She squinted toward the field, wondering if one of those parents was intense enough to get aerial footage of a tot soccer game. In the distance, she caught the suggestion of movement, more of a glint against the background of the sky then a defined shape.

"She hasn't checked in after her meeting with Faber and something's not right."

"Faber?"

"She flushed out a DigiTech shareholder who said he had information. She went to meet with him. I haven't heard from her since."

"We're on it." His voice faded, but she caught enough to hear him instructing someone, Mara maybe, to activate his tracking software.

Carol jumped off the bench. The drone hum had grown loud. Between that and the yelling and coaching whistles from the game, noise pollution had pulled her focus in too many directions. Weren't there ordinances against this stuff in public places? She couldn't afford distractions. Maybe she should get back in the car and head to Tony's place.

Tony's voice came back strong. "What is that ghastly noise?"

If he could hear the drones over the line, she wasn't overestimating the decibel level. "Some kind of drone. People take suburban youth soccer more seriously than I thought."

"Soccer? Carol, where are you?"

She spun around, intending to find the drone operator and give him her most intimidating *shut that thing off* stare. What she saw halted her on the spot and set her pulse racing. That wasn't a drone taking footage of the game.

And it wasn't just *one*.

A phalanx of flying objects buzzed through the sky. They were too large to be civilian, but Carol had never seen anything like them in military use either. She tensed, watching the devices soar and dip, then execute a sharp turn toward the game—all together, in formation. More precisely timed than a squadron of fighter jets. A bunch of hobby drone operators could not pull off that maneuver.

She needed to check this out. As she closed in from one direction and the drones from the other, the field of children between them, she finally got a good look. They were forged from dark, shimmery metal and had wing extensions crooked in the middle giving them an arm-like quality. Were those weapons on the end? Definitely looked like a barrel capable of firing a projectile. Not something you'd see on a non-military device.

"They're armed!" she shouted, pressing the phone to her ear. "What the hell is someone doing bringing armed drones to a soccer game?"

"What the hell are *you* doing at a soccer game?"

She ignored Tony's incredulous tone, eyes flitting around the scene, assessing, just as she had in the cockpit in every mission she'd flown. Information processed swiftly through her brain— the distance between the drones and the civilians, the number of devices. Dozens of armed unmanned crafts and hundreds of people, including children. She knew nothing about the drone operators or the purpose of having these crafts here, but her intuition told her they were something to worry about. Crafts like this did not belong in a civilian park. If they were hostile, this could be a mass casualty event.

"Tony, call emergency services and send them to my location. Pull my coordinates from my phone."

"Carol—"

She shoved the phone into her coat pocket, then removed it and tossed it on the bench. She unwound her signature red sash, drawing on her energy to pull from it the high-tech Stark-invented fibers of her Captain Marvel suit, forming them into the shape of her uniform around her body, and then securing the remaining material to her hip. She wore this fabric as comfortably as her skin. The Hala star on her chest and at her hip encapsulated who she was and what she stood for. Protecting the innocent. But Carol was the power, not the suit. This was no costume she hid behind. It was her identity.

She dug the balls of her feet into the grass and lifted off. The crowd had finally taken notice of the drones. A murmur arose from the field, more interested than worried. A few arms pointed up, followed by more than one cell phone, filming. The children stopped playing and raised their eyes skyward. Carol ground her teeth. Why were they all so willing to risk harm in the hopes of getting footage that would be the next big viral sensation? She'd been an internet oddity more than once in her life. It wasn't as fun as they imagined it would be. Or perhaps they naïvely believed no harm could come to them at their afternoon outing.

She rose into the air, splitting her focus between the civilians and the drones. There was still a chance, a small one, that this was some kind of prank, and she didn't want her arrival to cause the scene to devolve into chaos. If she swooped in hot, she might create a panic. That would have the opposite effect from what she intended, which was an orderly, expeditious evacuation before those drones opened fire. Given the sheer numbers of people, she'd need assistance to make that happen, and as quick as she knew Tony would have alerted the authorities, it could be a few minutes before a team got into position.

Did they have that much time?

Carol knew she needed more information. She wasn't a hothead, despite Monica's repeated admonitions that she couldn't go tearing off into danger whenever the back of her neck prickled.

Okay, *sometimes* she was a hothead. But decisions came to her fast. It was her training and her nature. And Carol had learned to trust her gut.

First step: Find the pilots. She propelled herself higher, keeping her distance to avoid becoming a competing airborne curiosity. How far away could the operators be? High-end civilian drone models had a range of four or five miles, she thought. She saw no one in that range around the field who looked like they had a remote control in their hands. *Aw, hell.* Military grade unmanned aerial vehicles were a bigger problem. The best of those had ranges as far as several thousand miles. And absolutely no upstanding reason to be hovering over a suburban soccer field.

Carol leaned forward and her body shot through the air. Maybe if she had a different vantage point? A mighty buzz built up as the crafts aligned into a squadron, pressed tightly together with a spearhead, turning in formation. No way should they be able to get that close together without knocking into each other, taking damage, and falling out of the air. No way should they be able to act flawlessly in concert. Almost like they were one living organism.

The sight of them sent a spike of anxiety through her. The crowd's fear instincts kicked in too, warning them of what Carol had felt from almost the second she saw the drones. They were in danger.

Carol had to do something before pandemonium ensued. She flew over the crowd, calling for calm, scanning the horizon. There was little shelter in sight, but help would arrive soon. As the herd of people began to run toward the parking lot, Carol realized she needed to create a diversion, draw the drones away while people escaped. She swooped upward, streaking past the lead drones. Their attention, thank Hala, trained on her, and as she raced away from the soccer field, the drones on her tail released their first volley. Before she could identify which device had fired the shot—they were too tightly packed together—a projectile whizzed past her and exploded into the turf, sending up a spray of grass and dirt that showered her and the people clustered around. She couldn't ID the ammo—too large for a bullet, too small for a missile, but potentially deadly in this space, against this crowd. With a roar, Carol called up a surge of energy. It pulsed beneath her fingers for a second before she whipped around and blasted the drone at the tip of the spear.

Direct hit! With a satisfied smile, she watched the photons crackle over the glimmery shell of the drone, like it had been electrified. And then, the metal blew apart. Her expression soured, eyes wide, smile forgotten, as the drone shattered, raining burning shards. One sliced past her uncovered face and another blistered her scalp, unable to do much damage to her superhumanly durable skin. Her strength, stamina, and healing abilities would protect her from the worst of this scalding metal rain, but they'd be deadly to the crowd below. Dammit! She was still too close to the civilians.

Carol shot upward through the air, searching for a place to lead the drones that would take them away from the crowd. She spotted a wooded area behind the shopping strip and zipped that way, as her mind raced to process the drone's curious explosion. A photon blast should not have caused that. Carol had never encountered a weapons-capable drone built from such a brittle material that shattered like glass. Either it was a dangerous design flaw or it was a secondary, more deadly weapon buried within the first, intended to inflict maximum damage. Her stomach roiled.

At least she'd scored a direct hit on the spearhead. That ought to have them in disarray. Carol glanced back and—*no. How could that be?* The phalanx structure remained intact. She'd expected them to scatter. Protect themselves individually. The drone operators *must* have eyes on, but even so, it was extraordinary that they'd reconstituted an attack formation so quickly and with such precision. Who was controlling these things?

Carol checked her six and watched as the drones dropped low, rocketing after her. Targeting her. Recognizing her as a threat now that she'd downed one. Yes! In that, at least, they behaved as she'd expected. To stalk her, the phalanx left the crowd alone, creating time for an orderly evacuation. But Hala help her, they acted in shocking synchronization, moving as one cohesive unit. Almost as if they were sentient. The tech was unfamiliar to her, and the operation of it suggested training, coordination, and sophisticated research. *Expensive* research. The kind that only the military and certain defense contractors could afford. But those entities wouldn't be conducting a test of the weapons' capabilities near civilians! Or would they? Her mind flashed briefly to the Melamed scandal, to the dark recent history it revealed. She felt a rush of anger toward the professor and the government officials who'd approved those tests, followed by pity for Mara, who had probably never seen the damage done by weapons like this up close. If she had, she might have more conflicted feelings about her grandfather and his research, be less ready to jump to defend his actions.

Carol wasn't naïve enough to believe that nefarious decision-making by people in power was a bygone relic of the past, which meant she could not rule out anything, just yet. Who in the military would be working on something like this? Besides the military, who had access to this kind of weaponry? Carol could think of a few possible culprits with the savvy to build something this sophisticated and the stomach for civilian casualties. She'd find and interrogate every one of them, if she had to. *After*. First, she had to take out the threat, and she'd have to do it without lighting up the drones with energy blasts. She had no idea how far the blast radius would reach, and while the crowd was now well behind her, she wouldn't take unnecessary chances with them.

She pressed her legs together and hurtled toward the treeline, going from zero to Mach one in seconds, using windshear to drive the drones' projectiles away from herself. Carol took a few hits, grateful for her Kree powers and her suit, which made the explosions she flew into uncomfortable, but not lethal. She itched to blast these hideous things out of the sky, photon energy boiling beneath her skin like lava.

As far as she could tell, the devices fragmented into shards that fell—more a disintegration downward than an explosion outward. Carol's brain sifted through options and she frowned as she realized her next move. Maybe, rather than blowing them up, she needed to take them down… ah hell. She was going to have to pull them out of the sky one by one, wasn't she? Her best— her only—move was to smash them to the ground, trusting the terrain to contain the debris. And that meant she was going to have to catch them. *Great*. This would be slow. And painful. Her least favorite kind of fight.

Carol targeted a drone in the middle of the pack, dodging projectile fire. If the lead drone didn't sit at the spearhead, it had to be protected in the center. With inches to go, she twisted and smashed into the object, shoulder first. Up close, she saw the drones were the length of a person, but not as bulky. Though the material resembled metal, as she'd surmised, it wasn't ordinary steel. Her suit slid across the smooth, shimmery surface of a brittle composite with which she wasn't familiar. Wouldn't the engineers and Tony love to get their hands on this?

But there was no time for analysis and sample collecting. Carol was taking heavy fire and she needed to figure out if her smash-the-suckers-into-the-mud plan was any good. She cinched her arms around the drone body and dove for the ground, targeting a clearing she'd spotted in the wooded area. The device battled her, surging when she held back, turning to one side and then reacting to her counterpressure by pushing to the other, for all the world as if it was trying to escape from her grip. Too fast and too agile. The best unmanned aerial operators Carol knew were hindered by the limitations of a drone's movement capabilities, and by the delay of waiting for satellite imagery to show what was happening in the field, as even the most sophisticated transmissions could suffer seconds-long lag. None of that stymied whoever was operating this drone. For a wild second, Carol felt it could think for itself.

The notion of an AI-capable drone with such human-like processing capabilities chilled her more than the wind.

She picked up speed until she resembled a torpedo blazing through the air, then barreled for the ground. At the last second, she let go, and with a tremendous grunt forced the drone away from her, toward the earth. Without the midair dramatics, the drone slammed into the ground, and as she'd hoped, the fallout went down rather than out.

Carol expelled a relieved breath. She was going to ground every last one of these damn things, and then she was going to find whoever set them loose and punch them into oblivion. The shriek of sirens from the field alerted her that rescuers were arriving on scene. Tony's mayday had worked. If he'd known how bad it was, he probably would have suited up and joined Carol. Perhaps she shouldn't have hung up that call with him so quickly. Or left her burner phone with her coat back at that bench. He'd want a look at these drone things anyway.

But there was no time to second-guess her choices. More than a dozen drones were still aloft, bearing down, opening fire. She launched herself into the air. The drones swung to meet her in unison. She managed to grab one, and the momentum whirled her like a yoyo. She pushed her shoulders forward, groaning as she resisted the spin. Painstakingly. Agonizingly. Clawing at the drone so she wouldn't lose her hold. Carol had learned to use gravity to propel herself and maneuver in midair. She hadn't fought it like this in years. But finally, second by tender second, she sucked herself out of the rotation and secured her hold on the machine, then dove, kicking the wing of another drone as she sped past. The thing rocked, but didn't spin out. Instead, it adjusted trajectory mid-flight and refocused on her, firing projectiles. Carol instinctively spun to put the metal in her arms between her body and the shooting, to use as a shield, then stopped. She didn't know what would cause the metal to rain hellfire. Was it just her energy blasts or would they disintegrate from friendly projectile fire too? Not a risk she could take.

She whirled back, taking the brunt of the projectiles to her body, and kicked again, putting all her power into it. The drone corkscrewed down. Carol flung the one in her arms after the first and they smashed into one another. Shattering, not exploding.

Small favors, Carol thought, snatching a third from the air and adding it to the smoldering pile of molten rubble. After destroying half a dozen that way, she was beginning to feel it. She could see no operator on the field of engagement, and yet these drones acted like a *thinking* organism. The collective really did behave like it had a single, shared brain. She'd broken their formation twice, and each time they'd reconstituted without delay and without needing to regroup. Without waiting even a minute for a commander to relay new orders. To accomplish that, you'd need the best trained group of operators with the quickest reflexes using the fastest communications systems ever invented, relying on drones with the greatest maneuverability and the highest response rate she'd ever seen.

That was too many "–ests" in one sentence to be plausible.

A barrage of projectiles blasted at her and she flew into the storm. By now there were news crews in the sky, foolishly circling close to where she battled the drones. She dodged two copters, while a third took a hit that sent it spiraling down, heavy black smoke spewing from its tail. She might be invincible, but they weren't. She couldn't risk causing another crash, and the drones were clearly trained on her. Carol reversed course, yanked the helo out of its spin, guided it to a gentler, survivable, crash landing, then grounded herself.

In the center of the field, she shoved her hair out of her eyes and stood straight, refusing to show her exhaustion. This had been a dog fight the likes of which she hadn't experienced in years. Even as a fighter pilot, she'd been able to fire ranged weapons to take out foes. This bone-wearying, energy-draining, aerial hand-to-hand combat sapped her.

The remaining drones hovered above her, weapons quiet. They might have limited battery capacity. They might have run out of firepower. Their operators might have done a runner. But you could never presume your enemy was vanquished. The minute you did, they'd surprise you.

Carol gritted her teeth and started to move. She made it ten steps before they responded. As one, they zipped to the ground, slowing only five feet before crash landing, sending spindly metal legs with tracks shooting out from the bottom. Like an aircraft lowering landing gear. The tracks were already rolling forward as another row of drones came down, these lowering not tracks but pincher grips that attached one device to the other. Row after row settled together, wings tucked, weapons out.

Carol found herself facing a wall of shooters. Her pulse spiked. What the hell were these hybrids? They'd shifted from air to ground combat—*because she had*, she realized. They stopped flying in response to her alteration of tactics. And in this formation, with her energy on the wane, they might have enough rapid firepower to slow her down. She considered blowing them all up, but the fallout would be hard to contain. The wall towered as high as three men. Did she go high and take off the top? Or low and try to crumble it from the bottom? No telling how hard it would be to bust those claw grips apart, and that was assuming the wall wouldn't just reform.

Whoever was behind this was so gonna get face-punched. As soon as she figured out who that was. For now, if she wasn't going to be able to simultaneously outfox and out-muscle these things, her choice was easy. Muscle won.

She bent her knees, preparing for a head-on collision, and used the force of her push against the ground to propel herself. She put all her remaining energy into speed, pelting toward the wall without bothering to dodge bullets or take any evasive maneuvers that could slow her. *Faster faster faster.* Her shoulder slammed into the wall at close to her supreme speed, a tiny part of her brain grimly satisfied to recognize she'd hit max faster than the *Peregrine* with less time and space and no need for fancy experimental cooling systems. With a mighty roar, Carol shoved until she felt the bindings between the drones give.

They reacted as quickly as they had all day, attempting to break themselves apart rather than go down together. But nothing was faster than Captain Marvel. She drove the wall over backward and powered them through grass, through earth, down down *down* until she'd made a crater of what had once been a wooded copse beside a soccer field and a strip mall. Carol hauled out of the dive, briefly taking flight to emerge from the pit, praying to the Supreme Intelligence that if there was a drone or two left in the air, it would be easy for a helo pilot to spot and dodge. As she ascended, she fired a barrage of photon blasts, blowing the remaining drones into an unrecognizable heap of sizzling metal.

Carol clenched her fists and hovered to catch her breath. The wreckage around her made suburbia look like a war zone. The park had been torn to shreds. Emergency vehicles filled the parking lot and still more raced to the scene, sirens screaming. So much destruction. But at least the civilians were secure. The emergency responders had managed to guide them to safety while Carol battled the drones on the far end of the field. An exhausted sort of relief weighed her down momentarily, before anger surged.

Who the hell was responsible?

Carol wracked her brain, listing every villain who might pull off a stunt like this. A bold attack on civilians in a populated area, relying on cutting edge technology. She'd flown the most advanced aircraft the human *and* alien worlds had to offer, but the way those drones worked in synch without a visible command center was brand new. Carol dropped down to where a crime scene team had set up. With people finally out of harm's way, they would get to work. She requested their commander send the remains of one of those things to Tony for further investigation.

Stark would have been a potential perp, if he wasn't on the right side of the law. This was the type of tech that he coveted. Did Tony have an evil doppelganger?

Oh. *Oh.*

The Fixer.

7

NORBERT EBERSOL'S base, he liked to say, was everywhere and nowhere. He was mobile; he didn't need a lair to wreak havoc. He needed only himself and a few toys, gadgets like the ones Carol has just watched ravage a suburban park. With the tech on them, the Fixer wouldn't have needed to be in close range, but she had a feeling he was nearer than not. Her lip curled with distaste. Ebersol was the type that wanted to see the whites of their eyes. He was also the type to be drawn to the Supernova computer show.

She zipped to her car, grateful that Tony had retrofitted her vehicle with biometric door handles scanned to her fingerprints so she didn't have to go back and search the field for the now-lost jacket that contained her car keys. She was even more grateful for the backup cell phone she found in the glove box. Phones had a tendency to get pulverized into glass powder and chip bits, so she'd learned to keep a supply of cheap flip phones in her car and her apartment. They were old and basic, with no apps, not even internet, but they served their purpose, and each one already had contacts programmed into speed dial.

"What's your situation?" Tony demanded, picking up before the first ring finished.

"Contained," she said wearily, sinking down in the driver's seat of the car for a moment's rest. The hand-to-hand combat had exhausted her. She was low on energy reserves.

"Good. Listen, Carol. I haven't heard from her yet."

Jess. With her focus on preventing suburban destruction, she'd temporarily put her friend at the back of her mind, but her concern flooded back at Tony's tense words. She rested her forehead on the steering wheel. "Dammit. That's not a good sign."

"I'm with you on that." His normally insouciant tone was low and serious. "I asked Monica to head to Jess's apartment. See what she can find."

Carol exhaled slowly through her nostrils, but her relief at the help was tempered by mounting stress. Where the hell was Jessica?

"You going to meet her there?"

She should. Twilight had fallen while she handled those drones and Jess had now been out of contact for an entire day. But she couldn't. "Not yet. I need to take care of something first."

"That something have anything to do with the unusual robot carcasses some suburban PD just delivered to my doorstep?" he asked. "Or why you're calling me from your backup phone?"

Carol hummed a non-answer because he didn't need her to confirm his suspicions. "Where would hacker types who want to be at the Supernova convention but are too controversial to actually attend the show officially hang out?"

"Dive bar called Binary."

Memories of the time she'd spent in cosmic form, packing the power of a star and rocking a seriously superior head of fiery hair, flooded her. "Really?"

"Not everything's about you, Captain Marvel. Binary has a computer meaning, too."

Yeah, she knew that. "Well, I still think it's ironic," she said, through a clenched jaw, "because I'm about to go light the place up."

"Carol. What's going on?"

"Fill you in later. Keep trying to locate Jess." Carol stepped out of her car, touch-locking the doors behind her. She put the chaotic clean-up scene to her back, her mind and body rapidly refocusing on her next objective. "Meanwhile, see what you can figure out about the robot carcasses. Which were some kind of UAV I've never encountered before. Tony, they were nasty."

"Like there was any way I *wasn't* going to sic B.O.S.S. on those things."

"Do me a favor, get a couple of images of the wreckage over to Senior Master Sergeant Alexander."

"Your Air Force R&D pal? You think he'll be able to identify them before me?" Tony demanded, around an offended huff.

She rolled her eyes. Hadn't he just admonished her for making everything about herself? Tony could learn the same lesson. But she'd have to school him with a witty comeback about that another day. "Actually, I want to double check those things aren't theirs."

Tony's brief silence spoke volumes, but he knew better than to press for details, given the urgency in her tone. "Got it. And hey, Carol, I like that bar too. Don't go all Binary on the whole place, if you can help it."

"Roger that."

CAROL FLEW straight for the convention center. Had it only been two days ago when she'd joined Tony to watch that DigiTech panel? Time ought to move predictably, not at seemingly variable speeds. There had to be some magical explanation for the whole "time flies" thing, right? Someday, she was really going to have to ask Stephen Strange to explain to her the phenomenon that made time feel like it could speed up and slow down at will.

The week-long tech extravaganza had yet to come to a close and conference attendees filled the streets, despite the hour. She realized the panel sessions lasted into the evening, and the outdoor dog-and-pony shows did, too. All the displays that captivated Carol earlier in the week now illuminated not only the streets but the night sky. The light pollution was so powerful she wondered if her former colleagues on Alpha Flight Station were tracking it as some sort of disturbance to be monitored. She might have, had she still been up there.

She zipped through the flashy projections, prowling the area in search of her target. Three blocks from the action, where the crowds finally thinned and the fancy displays receded into the background, she saw a dingy maroon awning and an old-fashioned neon sign that read BINARY'S in an early computer-era font. Carol dropped lightly onto the sidewalk. The windows were covered with posters advertising the Supernova show, preventing her from getting a glimpse of the interior. Based on the apparent age of the shabby, rusted awning, Carol had feeling that when they picked that font for the sign, it had been futuristic rather than retro.

Carol set a hand on the door and slipped inside an '80s bar that was definitely out of date, not styled to be a throwback. Tiny bistro tables crowded the room, and a bar ran the full length of one side. Every step caused her boots to briefly paste themselves to the floor. There wasn't much décor beyond posters of early-era Apple and Microsoft products, but there was a crowd.

She pushed through the crush of smelly, sweaty bodies. The room teemed with people, many of them still wearing Supernova badges. They stacked three deep at the bar, clustered around the little tables, and lined the walls. At the far end, a large group had pushed a few tables together, littering the scarred wood with glasses, beer bottles, and a heap of technology.

And there, leaning so far back in a chair that the front legs popped off the ground, was the man Carol sought. Norbert Ebersol, A.K.A. The Fixer. Not exactly Tony's doppelganger, but he did keep his dark hair shaggy and sport a neatly trimmed circle beard. And he did sometimes run around in a red mechanized power suit. Tonight, he wore a plain black T-shirt as he held court for his gathering of admirers, his high-pitched laugh carrying over the general bar noise and drilling a hole in her ear. As Carol suspected, he didn't sport a conference badge. Of course, Ebersol wouldn't be so basic as to buy a ticket to anything like the Supernova show. He'd skulk around the edges with an affected superiority that couldn't quite mask his secret fascination with the event. Villains like him were disappointingly predictable. Nostrils flaring, she honed in on the table in front of him, scanning the tech.

Yes! She spotted a controller device double the size of a large cell phone. It reminded her of the handsets her brothers once had for their remote control airplanes—the ones they refused to let her have a turn at but that she'd always snuck out for a spin when they disappeared to friends' houses and sports practices. The device in front of Ebersol had buttons, vertical and horizontal joysticks, even possibly a signal transmitter. Exactly the controls you'd need to remote-pilot a drone.

Carol was off the ground before she formed a plan, powering high enough to clear the bar patrons. Barely. She sped toward Ebersol, grabbed him by the shirt front, and hefted him out of his chair. With a toe, she launched the controller into the air and caught it with her free hand.

"You!" The Fixer squawked. "Release me!"

She ignored him, as well as the excited rumblings of the bar-goers and the cell phone cameras they'd whipped out to film all this. She flew straight back out of the room, bursting through the front door hard enough to damage the hinges and circling the corner to the alley. Once she cleared the dumpster, she slammed the Fixer against the wall. His head bounced off the brick.

"Why did you attack that soccer field? What's your game?"

The Fixer's legs flailed. His hands clutched at hers, but she batted them away and slammed him into the wall again, this time making a Fixer-shaped crater in the brick.

"Where did you get the drones?"

"What are you talking about?"

She smashed the device against his chest. "What the hell is this?"

"A gaming controller," he cried, grabbing at her hands again. "Let me down."

"Who are you working for?"

"I work for no one, Captain Marvel," he snarled, attempting to knee her.

She slammed him into the wall once more and he moaned, but no matter how she demanded, no matter the force she applied, Ebersol rebuffed her questions, professing ignorance. She kept up the interrogation until he sagged and stopped struggling. Carol hesitated, gripping his collar tightly. His strength might have flagged, but the vigor of his denials had not.

Ebersol seized on her hesitation. "You're making a mistake, as usual," he said, his voice weak but shrewd. "Flying head first into the nearest answer without any evidence it's the correct one. That hubris'll be the death of you one day."

She stilled, her anger teetering on the edge of too far. What caused her to race off to find a face to punch instead of a connection she could prove? She usually considered her ability to leap into action to be one of her most positive qualities. Were there, possibly, a few occasions, like now, when she had to admit it steered her off course? Carol shrugged, trying to shake off those unnerving and intrusive thoughts. Airborne interrogations were a poor moment for navel-gazing. Come to think of it, she couldn't name a good time for that kind of self-introspection, but it certainly was not now.

Carol peered into Ebersol's eyes, seeing fury but also frustration and confusion. He was scared, but no more than anyone would be hanging twenty feet in the air and being slammed repeatedly into the wall. He was not nervous. Not the way he would be if he was lying. Would he be able to resist bragging, seeking an acknowledgment of some kind, if those drones were his tech? Or, like Tony, would his ego-fueled pride erupt from him and demand recognition of his genius? He accused her of hubris. *Takes one to know one*, she thought. Which meant…

Aw, hell. The Fixer wasn't acting like a villain who'd been caught.

Carol let herself drop ten feet, her hair streaming upward as she fell. Ebersol screamed, and kept screaming as she let go, sending him plummeting to the ground. He crumpled to the dirty pavement.

"You're out of control, Captain Marvel," he groaned. "You're a menace. An alien menace! They should lock you up, not me."

Adrenaline rushed through her, and energy crackled just below the surface of her skin. She itched to let loose a barrage on him, teach him how insults would be answered. She'd always been better at *show* than *tell*. But she gritted her teeth and breathed the tension away. She wouldn't prove him right by letting her pride make the decisions about who and when to punch. Jess, Mara, and DigiTech were the priorities now.

"This isn't over, Fixer," she spat, throwing his device to the ground beside him. It fragmented into sharp-edged plastic pieces. "I'll be watching you."

He snarled, but Carol was already flying away.

8

THE US Army Special Combat Capabilities Directorate at Fort Henry William was the most heavily guarded installation on base. Clearance higher than top secret was required just to know the SCCD was housed here. The Senior Chief Weapons Engineer personally approved each clearance before any personnel was permitted entry, regardless of rank. No visitors proceeded past the main entrance of the R&D building, and a metal door as thick as those on a bank vault, regulated by biometric scanners, protected the inner sanctum.

The SCCD formed as an offshoot of the Combat Capabilities Directorate in the wake of revelations about aliens. Their mission was to conduct weapons development with their eyes on space rather than terrestrial enemies. Few people knew the SCCD had been created, let alone what it did. Its existence was Sensitive Compartmented Information. The motto on the SCCD's wall, for those privileged few granted entry into its halls, was "The Future of Combat Emerges Here."

Colonel David Finke, third highest ranking member in the SCCD officers corps, sat on the top floor of the lab building in his interior office, a spare, small, anonymous box with only one advantage—proximity to the roof exit. With such a high rank, Finke might have been able to grab a window for a little natural light, but he liked to escape to the roof, unnoticed, for a breath of fresh air when the gloom of the lab became too much. Or when he needed to check the personal phone he wasn't supposed to have. Watching his holdings closely required round-the-clock attention and he couldn't let a few security regulations put his portfolio at risk. Tonight, though, he was too absorbed in reviewing test results to sneak away to check the sell order he'd placed earlier in the evening, hoping to dump some crypto before it tanked.

He opened the link on a secure email from one of his researchers.

Results remain inconclusive. Prism deformities absorb significant energy. Apparatus becomes unstable and prone to failure.

He sighed. "Failure" was an innocuous way to say the damn device melted down and threatened to explode. Project Faustus was in jeopardy, and it'd be on his head. When they were forced to pull out of their university research partnership the prior year due to the scandal and the resulting Congressional investigations, he'd felt certain they were close enough to a functional prototype to keep the project alive at SCCD. He'd assured the brass they could build it. If he had to admit that instead, they'd built an expensive, unpredictable bomb that tended to erupt like a volcano, his commission would be on the line.

Quantum electronics and optical amplification were outside Finke's field of expertise, but he delved deeper into the results anyway. He didn't hold multiple PhDs in engineering and physics, hadn't risen to his current role and rank, because he couldn't figure things out, dammit. He enlarged a chart depicting megawatts versus pulse frequency so his eyes wouldn't strain to see the tiny numbers.

Finke lost himself in the dense research findings until he heard the quiet thud of a door latch. His head snapped up. This floor was empty but for him.

Should have been empty.

The basement labs below ground were occupied by researchers at all hours, but not the fourth-floor meeting rooms and leadership offices. Across from Finke's little cubicle was the much larger and much grander office of the CO, but she'd left for the day hours earlier, as had her second-in-command. Visitors came and went via the security entrances on the ground level.

He should be alone. There should be no doors opening. Certainly not the one that led to the roof. Finke knew telltale click of that latch like he knew the timbre of his own voice.

Someone had just crept in from the roof.

Sidearms were not permitted in the SCCD, but Finke kept a knife in his top desk drawer. He yanked it open, fingers closing around the leather-bound hilt. But he didn't pull it out yet. He could be overreacting. A researcher had probably gone up for air while Finke went down to the mess for coffee. Or while he'd been lost in the research materials. He tensed, waiting for the rational explanation to reveal itself. Footsteps would come down that hall any minute, as some authorized person made their way from the rooftop stairs to the internal staircase.

Nothing.

Finke slid out the knife and pushed back his chair, giving himself the space to spring.

The hallway remained silent.

He swallowed and shook his head. It was late and he was under stress. Between his investments and the pressure to get Project Faustus operational before year end, he wasn't resting well. Sleep deprivation could make you hear things, right? As the silence stretched on, he began to feel silly, tensed like a man in a combat zone instead of a researcher in an office. Rolling his shoulders to shake off the crawling sensation that plagued him, Finke dropped the knife into his drawer, sank into his chair, and let his head fall to the desk. He needed a break if he was jumping like a scared rabbit while sitting in the most secure building on base. He was due leave; he'd put in for a week off tomorrow. As a bonus, that timing would give him a chance to poke around on the internet, do some crypto investing, make up the losses he was undoubtedly suffering right now. His holdings were in bad shape after the last year's market volatility. A less devoted believer would walk away from the losses. But not him. Finke knew that's when you had to be ready to buy, right? When the market was low. That was when opportunity was at its greatest. And if he turned a few bucks quickly, he'd be able to transfer coin to dollars before his wife tried to pay the mortgage this month and bounced the check. Maybe he could even double his profit. He'd managed that once before. He'd tell his wife he had a paid speaking engagement. She didn't ask too many questions when he told her that.

Hey, it wasn't like the promotion at the SCCD came with a big jump in pay grade. Should have. Longest hours on base. Highest degree of secrecy. Most important contribution to the mission. He could quote the soundbites from the onboarding speech as well as the next officer. Hell, he stepped in and gave that speech when the CO was off-base. Best of the best of the best— except when it came to pay. Sue him for making up the difference between his military salary and what he could have raked in by going into the private sector with some extracurricular, not-exactly-authorized crypto deals. It was a neat solution that let him keep serving humanity and himself and no one really got hurt. A soldier did what they had to do, right? So it was a risk. Was it any worse than the soldiers who—

Whoosh.

The sound caught him off guard, startling him. He picked his head up, fumbling for the knife he'd already discarded.

Too late.

A figure slipped inside his office, too fast for him to see. Defying the physics of ordinary movement. As always. It was just there suddenly, in a rush of sound, a swirling of a cloak.

"Good evening, Colonel," the low voice said.

He swayed on his feet. It had never found him on base before.

"You don't seem happy to see me."

That glow. The faint yellow luminosity that emanated from the depths of the hood made him sick. His scientist mind rebuffed explanations of how a being could do that. He'd stopped trying to analyze what caused the phosphorescence. Not because he doubted his ability to figure anything out, he told himself. But because he didn't want to know the answer. Asking prying questions of this—this *thing* was a road to doom. He'd learned that the hard way, early on, when he demanded a name and the creature responded by cleaning out his crypto wallet.

"Why are you here?" Finke gulped.

"Here is where you are, Colonel."

He loved being addressed by his rank, loved the acknowledgement of the sweat and heartache that had gone into earning those eagles. But not like this. It wasn't a sign of respect from this creature.

"Would you like a debrief on how the Swarm performed in real-world conditions?" The figure edged closer, hemming him in behind his desk. "Perhaps I should file an after-action report."

Why had he faced his desk toward the door? He should have made sure his escape route was clear. Finke forced himself to focus on the creature's words. "'After action'? You built them? *Used* them?"

There'd been chatter earlier on secure channels about an odd occurrence in the suburbs outside New York City. An email from an Air Force colleague, Alexander, asking if he could ID some kind of UAV. He'd been distracted. Hadn't really listened. Hadn't clicked on the picture Alexander forwarded. Had never imagined it could be the Swarm. The AI drones had been a design— blueprints, some incomplete code. A concept, for God's sake. Far from reality. The tech wizards downstairs imagined all sorts of nonsense no one would ever seriously build. He'd told himself it had been harmless to give those designs to this creature, when it first came asking for weapons in exchange for a haul of crypto coin. You'd need a massive budget to create a composite metal with glass-like properties, fill it with sensors without compromising aerodynamics, not to mention developing code for an artificial intelligence capable of processing information in nanoseconds to adapt to combat conditions. This department dealt as much in fantasy as in reality, and he'd thought the Swarm was firmly in the not-remotely-possible camp.

"Do you invent weapons of war to display them in a museum exhibit, Colonel?"

"You—you said you were going to experiment with a prototype. For research."

The figure laughed, a higher pitched, more tinkling sound than seemed justified given the deep voice. "Surely you didn't really believe that."

"We were cutting red tape. Avoiding unnecessary delays. It was only theoretical. You assured me."

"Once you heard the amount of coin on offer, you stopped asking questions. Much like your wife doesn't ask where the money for those five-star vacations comes from. You think she's weak for that. You despise her a little, for not being suspicious." The figure leaned a hip against the chair it stood beside. So casual, for a creature that was trying to ruin him. His pulse picked up. "That's interesting, don't you think? Despising in her your own faults."

"I don't know what you're talking about."

"Don't you?" That laugh again. It pierced his last remaining bubble of self-confidence, spewing liquid fear into his insides. "You've found yourself in a little trouble this week, haven't you? Your digital wallet is empty."

"It's a temporary setback. The market'll bounce back. I'm not worried."

"Your increasingly reckless trading history suggests otherwise."

He gulped. How did it know? How did it always know what he was doing online? The transactions were supposed to be anonymous.

"Tens of thousands of dollars in supposed value evaporated overnight. Your retirement savings more fiction than fact. Bills coming due, bank account bare. And yet, you persevere," the creature went on. "You never can resist the temptation to risk more than you have. Is it the thrill, Colonel? Is that why you're a gambler?"

Finke backed up, bumped into the credenza behind his desk, a fighter shoved against the ropes. The heavy wooden piece with its brass hardware and polished surface had been chosen by his predecessor, but he kept it because it looked rich, like it belonged in a colonel's office. Nice things were evidence of status. It didn't matter whether they were his personal taste, whether he actually liked them.

"I don't gamble." This thing didn't know him. He'd never been to a race track, didn't bet on sports. He didn't even participate in the base March Madness pool. "I *invest*."

"Stocks are a rich man's horse race. But you don't have the money for real trading, do you? Your investments—they're what a man who *wants* to be rich can access."

His mouth curled. This was absurd. He was a full colonel in the SSCD. He didn't need to be threatened by some mystical glowing creature. Why was he listening to this, frozen against a desk like a cowering fool? The creature had never gotten physical with him. He could put an end to the taunting right now.

But. He didn't. Because he knew what would come at the end of this barrage of insults. Because his digital wallet was empty. Because there was a new NFT he had his eye on and this one would mint him money. He was sure of it. If he held out, this creature who somehow knew all his secrets would offer him a trade.

"Did you come here to torment me?"

The hooded head tilted, as if, in the shadow of the dark fabric, the creature was studying him more closely. "I need Project Faustus."

Finke blanched. Few people were aware of the project's existence, let alone its parameters. It was as if this thing lived inside his brain, knew everything he knew. He had never mentioned Faustus around the creature. He was sure of that. Someone else in SSCD had to be leaking. *He* couldn't be the only source. Could he?

"The Swarm was insufficient."

Insufficient for what? Finke ground his back teeth, thinking fast. There'd been an attack on American soil, if he'd understood the gist of the earlier reports. On civilians. And the figure wasn't professing research motivations now. No pretense of legitimacy, no guise of scientific discovery, remained. He had spared little consideration for what would happen if he was revealed to be the source of a leak of top secret information. Thinking through it now sent his pulse into overdrive. There'd be an investigation; they would not have trouble tracing the tech back to SSCD. To him. Finke hadn't bothered to obfuscate, to layer diversions around himself, to construct a safety net. The possibility of getting caught had seemed so remote.

It was clear how narrow-minded he'd been. How naïve. God, what a gut-punch to think of himself that way. This creature had outsmarted him. Finke bristled, recalling that dismissive, pitying laughter. Its assumption that it already owned him.

No! He wasn't done for. He just needed a payout. If he netted enough coin, he could still build himself a fallout shelter—metaphorically speaking. The results of an investigation wouldn't matter if he could run. But he needed a high dollar offer. He had to be careful to give no hint that the Project Faustus tech was… unstable, at best. The creature wouldn't pay for a half-finished liability. He had to play this coy.

Finke squared his shoulders, calculating coin values and property values and fees for the untraceable kind of banks. "Project Faustus is classified."

"It'll be worth it to you."

"The designs—"

"I want the device. Nothing I have to manufacture. No code I have to write."

He thought of the halfcocked prototype six floors below them. "The device would be hard to remove from its current location." And doing so right now would implicate him immediately.

The incandescence beneath that cowl mesmerized him. He didn't want to see the face hidden in the folds of fabric, even as that was precisely what he desperately wanted. He clenched and unclenched his fists, willing himself not to bend. Not yet. He needed a way to get the device to the creature without outright handing it over. Perhaps, if he made it vulnerable to being stolen... Finke gnawed on the inside of his cheek as his mind cycled through possibilities. Yes, engineering a theft, that might work. If the attack happened elsewhere, he might have time to get his affairs in order. Put an escape plan in place. Find his way out of the ten-foot hole he'd dug himself into. He'd be court-martialed once the prototype was stolen. But that would only matter if they caught him.

"It's too well guarded here."

The creature's cloak rippled as it loomed. "Move the device. I'll handle it from there."

He licked his lips, holding back a nervous but triumphant smile. "I might be able to make that happen."

"See that you do."

9

"IT'S BEEN more than twenty-four hours since anyone has heard from her," Carol said, barreling through her apartment and into her bedroom. She set the phone to speaker and tossed it on the dresser so she could change. "She would never leave Gerry unless something was wrong."

They had just talked about this scenario, but Carol hadn't needed to hear her friend say the words. No matter how dicey any situation had ever become, Jess did not disappear. She always made sure Gerry was safe. *Always*.

On the other end of the line, Tony sounded pinched. "Does someone have the rug rat?"

"Lindsay is with him, but she's worried, too."

"Jess's phone's off. I can't track her."

The tension buzzing through her ratcheted up a level. Carol had been in the process of pulling on a long-sleeved thermal T-shirt, but Tony's words froze her in place. Jess was missing. Those drones had come out of nowhere. This side-project to help Tony figure out what was going on with DigiTech and watch out for Mara had quickly turned into a Mission with a capital

M. And that meant operational readiness, at all times. She let go of the civilian attire and called upon her powers to weave matter into fibers, fibers into fabric, fabric into the Captain Marvel suit. Energy crackled and sparkled around her for the space of a breath, and when it dissipated, the familiar red-and-blue suit hugged her form again. Manifesting her suit through matter manipulation used up energy she typically preferred to preserve for a fight, but Carol was now certain they *were* in a fight, even if their opponent remained shrouded in mystery. She gripped the Hala star securing her sash at the waist, holding on for a moment. The physical reminder of her power settled her nerves. Whatever was going on, Carol would, could punch her way through it.

"Carol!"

Tony's voice was muffled, her phone lying under a pile of cast-off civilian clothing. She dumped that onto the floor and launched into her plan. "I'm going to find out where Faber lives and—"

"Look at the alert I just sent you. Quickly!"

"You know this burner phone doesn't have internet—"

"Open your damn computer, Carol, fast! Find a news site."

Carol flipped open her laptop. A red-and-white banner headline assaulted her eyes as soon as a browser loaded.

BREAKING NEWS: SPIDER-WOMAN WANTED FOR MURDER

Laurence Faber, 67, was found dead in his penthouse on Central Park this afternoon. According to the deceased's assistant, Faber had a meeting with private investigator Jessica Drew scheduled for this morning, and he grew worried when messages to Faber went unanswered. Police investigators state they have messages between Faber and Drew in which they argued over Faber's failure to cooperate with an investigation Drew had been hired to conduct. Police briefly took Drew into custody, only for her to break out and disappear within hours. Drew is currently on the run and wanted by the Metro Police. A law enforcement spokesperson advises anyone who spots her to call the tip line. Consider her dangerous and do not approach her on your own.

Okay. What the hell happened at that meeting?

"Tony—"

"I know, I know. I'm digging into the MPD systems to find out what they have."

Carol hung up. He didn't need her in his ear while he did his computer genius thing. She paced the length of her apartment, firecrackers exploding in her legs. She wasn't built to sit and wait while others acted. She needed to find Jess. She needed to figure out who was behind that drone attack. No way were they unrelated. Could Faber be responsible? They hadn't looked into him very deeply before Jess went off to meet him. Had he timed the attack to keep Carol busy while he—what? Battled Jess? Attempted to kidnap a well-known super hero? That was a wild theory, full of leaps of logic, and Carol knew it.

She sat on the edge of her bed and stilled her mind. She needed to comb through her thoughts, ordering them into an action plan. A pilot couldn't have a jumbled mind. The past was a compass, and it would guide her. Somewhere in the steps leading to this moment was an arrow pointing to Carol's next move. She began by focusing on Faber, revisiting what little they'd learned about him and shifted her focus a few degrees to see what had come before the meeting.

A tip. Jess had been told to reach out to Faber. Where had that information originated? Carol pictured Jess, standing in the tiny kitchen of her apartment, cooking macaroni and cheese for her son. She'd reported putting out feelers among her network of P.I. friends and someone had turned up specific, if obscure, intelligence about a disgruntled former shareholder within hours. At the time, it was just a possible lead. Carol knew dozens of random tips came in whenever Jess issued a call for information to her fellow investigators, and though each was probably more likely to be a dead end than a key to the mystery, her best friend was thorough, looking into them all. But it was beginning to feel like they should have looked harder at that particular tip. Why would someone have been able to point them to Faber so quickly? What had seemed earlier like any other potential lead, now seemed too timely, too coincidental.

Perhaps Mara's pattern-spotting penchant was rubbing off on her, but Carol decided she needed to know more about that tipster, pronto. Starting with their identity. She raised her burner to call Tony. Maybe he could hack into Jess's phone records and see who she'd been talking to. Before she could hit a single button, a shrill ring from her computer caught Carol off guard. She'd forgotten Tony had synched her computer with her original phone. Carol thumbed a button to answer without quite meaning to.

"Carol, it's me."

Jess! A fraction of the tension that strung Carol tight as a livewire loosened. "Thank—"

"Call me from one of your burners at this number."

She rattled off numerals almost too fast to catch and disconnected. Dammit! Carol fumbled the flip phone, singing the string of numbers Jess had given her to a tune she'd used in her military days to memorize senseless sequences of digits. Jess wasn't prone to playing spy games for no reason, so if she didn't trust regular comms channels, Carol wasn't going to take that lightly. She managed to punch in the digits, praying to the Supreme Intelligence that her old memory trick worked.

Jess answered on the first ring, her voice strained, her cadence on high speed. "I'm on what is possibly the last remaining payphone in the city. But I didn't kill Faber. I swear it."

"I believe you," Carol said fiercely. Their missions didn't always have fairy-tale endings. Sometimes people ended up dead, but Jess was no murderer. Evidence or not, she'd hear her friend out. "Care to explain why we're calling each other like it's 1986?"

"Don't trust my phone. You probably shouldn't trust yours either."

Carol frowned at the computer sitting on her desk, wondering if that counted, too, if she should disable it. "You dodged the cops?"

A breath blown directly into the phone speaker crackled the line. "That is a long story."

"That you don't have time to tell me?"

"This payphone is at the back of a laundromat. Someone's going to ID me sooner rather than later. I need a place to go."

To hide, she meant. "None of this makes sense, Jess. Two days ago, you'd never heard of Faber."

"Tell me something I don't know. I'm being framed, Carol. And it's really pissing me off."

Carol clenched her fist around the phone, the flimsy plastic strained nearly to cracking. *Her too.*

"I can't turn myself in. There's enough evidence to hang me. I need time. Carol, please. You've got to help me stay free while I figure this out."

Jessica Drew was officially a fugitive—one with a dicey recent history of dark behavior. Yeah, she'd moved past that and most people would put her back on the hero roster, but turmoil was a major running theme in her life. She and Carol had that in common. No matter what they did, they were always dead center in the Venn diagram of *being a savior of humankind* and *being a menace to peace and order.*

It took Carol less than an instant to decide. Not only was Jess her best friend, but she was also in this predicament because she'd been helping Carol. "The lair. I'll program it to—"

"Really? Lair? That's what you're naming it? I was partial to the Carol Cloister, myself."

She snorted. Even in the middle of a scrape involving a murder accusation, Jess had jokes. Another tiny tension knot in Carol's back untied itself. This was an official mess, but if Jess's humor was intact, they weren't beaten yet. "Hey, I know it's been a minute since I've been on a date, but that doesn't make my HQ a nunnery. Do you need a hideout the PD can't find or not?"

"I need, I need."

"Want me to get Gerry?"

"He's safer at home until we know more about what's going on. Besides, if they're watching my apartment and you show up, they're going to follow you straight to me."

Carol was confident in her ability to get in and out of a New York apartment with one small child in tow without a patrol car latching onto her. But Jess got the final say when it came to her son. "Need me to call Lindsay, let her know it might be a while till you can get home?"

"Already did."

<hr>

CAROL SWEPT up the coast, hands balled into fists, flying as fast as she could without causing a fiery meteor trail to appear in her wake. A mysterious shooting star being spotted off the northeast coastline wouldn't be very incognito. She cringed. Since her identities had become public, she hadn't invested much time in keeping her activities discreet and she'd forgotten how much effort it took. Trying to make the extraordinary seem normal was like trying to lower the brightness of a light without a dimmer switch. Ineffective and frustrating.

She dropped altitude as she approached Harpswell Sound, admiring the view despite her haste. While she preferred the greenery of summer, Maine was pretty gorgeous snow-covered too. She skimmed over barren trees, fields of icy drifts, until she reached the sound, which, thankfully, wouldn't freeze over even in deep winter. Sinking rapidly, she landed one foot at a time on her dock. The wood was beginning to warp from weather damage. Again. When she had free time—ha!—she'd have to tear this whole thing out and rebuild it. Good grief, was Carol tired of rebuilding broken things.

She pushed off again, not hard enough to propel her skyward, but with the perfect amount of force to clear the end of the dock. She hovered a moment, waiting for the entrance to her lair to open, admiring the rush of water as the vacuum tech sucked the lake downward into the most beautiful man-made circular waterfall Carol had ever seen. Technically, it was the only man-made circular waterfall in existence, but she was still sure it was darn beautiful. Well designed, too. The water wicked away from the aircraft canopy she'd repurposed as an entryway. One of her better ideas, to be honest. Climbing into her lair felt like climbing into the cockpit, the one place in any universe where Carol felt certain of herself and in control.

Miraculously dry, she dropped to the metal floor of her lair and rolled to her feet. She glanced around the cavernous room, eyes skipping over her professional-quality gym equipment, the jet parked at the far end, the display cases housing her Marvel suits, the wall of screens Tony had insisted she needed and... there! She found what—or rather who—she was searching for in the comfy corner her friends fashioned after their first visit involved sitting on the chilly floor. Monica picked out a couch and chairs, Jenn gifted her an area rug, and the very woman now sitting there slumped, elbows on her knees, head in her hands, had provided a minifridge and microwave.

Jess's long dark hair shielded her face, but Carol didn't need to see an expression to know how her friend was feeling. The anxiety radiated from her in powerful waves.

"He was dead when I got there, Carol," Jess said. She'd lost the sparkle and wit of their earlier conversation, which was a bad sign. Reality crashing on her, no doubt. Carol had been a fugitive before. It weighed you down. "Door unlocked, penthouse empty, body collapsed over his desk."

"Could you tell how he died?"

"No obvious signs of violence." Jess shivered—stress, probably—and Carol tossed her an old Air Force sweatshirt that had been hanging on the back of the chair. "Could have been a heart attack, for all I know. I called the cops immediately."

A heart attack? A vague recollection tugged at Carol's mind, like a fish brushing past a hook without grabbing on. She couldn't quite call forth the connection her memory was trying to make. "Online news says his assistant did that."

Jess's head popped through the neck of the sweatshirt, her mouth pursed. "Maybe the assistant did, too, before me. Cruisers arrived way too fast to be responding to *my* call. PD doesn't get anywhere in Midtown traffic in three and a half minutes. But that begs the question—how'd Faber's assistant know he was dead? I'm telling you, there was nobody but me in that penthouse when I arrived!"

"So someone—the assistant—found him before you got there, then ran and called the cops?" Carol joined Jess in the comfy corner. She perched on the arm of a lounger, too keyed up to sink into it. "Possible but…"

"Odd. I know." Jess flopped back on the cushions of the couch and directed the rest of her monologue to the ceiling. Like she couldn't spout off wild and unsubstantiated theories while looking Carol in the eye. "Maybe whoever got there first is innocent and scared. Or maybe it was the killer who called the police on himself to divert attention. All I know is, the minute they showed up, the cops came at me hot. Even a couple guys I know from past cases. It was door breach, hands up, *boom!* Instant interrogation. One guy grabbed Faber's phone from the desk and started reading messages from me to Faber—messages which I did not send."

"How'd he know the guy's phone passcode?"

"Excellent question." Jess, still prone on the sofa, pointed a finger in Carol's direction. "Possible the phone didn't have a passcode, though that seems like a rookie mistake for a guy like Faber. He was a sophisticated investor. Surely he understood basic internet security. But more than that. Why would the cops go straight to his phone messages? Without even examining the body or looking around the room for a murder weapon? Protocol is to send electronic devices to be analyzed by the crime tech lab. They skipped right over that step, which makes me wonder if whoever called the police before I did gave a really, really specific tip related to that phone."

"What were the messages? The ones you didn't recognize."

"Something about stock market fraud. They made it sound like I was pressuring him to let me in on a deal related to his most recent stock sale. And believe me, I wish I had spare cash lying around to be engaging in suspicious securities transactions. But unless buying a Christmas gift for the guard at Gerry's mommy's morning out program counts, I got nothing."

A jolt ran through Carol, bringing her back to the moments before Jess called, when she'd been sitting on her bed, sifting through the information they knew. A feeling that Faber wasn't the real story had begun to crystallize and it grew more solid now. "Didn't he just sell off a bunch of DigiTech stock?"

Jess paused, her rant receding as she considered this fact, wheels turning, her brain pulling forth all the data they'd turned up in their research. She sat up, finally. "Yes, he did. We keep circling back to where we started, Carol. DigiTech."

10

A SUDDEN sucking sound sent Carol and Jess to their feet. Water rushed overhead. The entry was opening. Without a command from her?

She strode toward her control panel. "Were you messing around with the settings?"

"Who am I, Stark?" Jess said, close on her heels. "I can resist pushing buttons on gadgets I don't know how to use!"

Carol kept her trusted inner circle small, and the list of people who knew of the lair's existence was even smaller. Lauri-Ell. Jess. Jenn. Monica. Tony. And every single one of those people knew better than to drop by unannounced.

If there was an intruder breaching her lair, they'd have to make entry from the canopy. She'd be waiting. Her hands formed into fists and she rose, floating a few inches off the ground. Below, Jess, still in her street clothes, dropped into a crouch, positioning herself just to the side of the canopy, ready to leap. Even without her trademark red suit, her movements were fluid, elastic. Spidery.

From above, they heard a muffled squeal, a thump, and a groan.

Carol snorted. "Amateur." The fall from surface level was

deceptively long—an optical illusion of proximity created by the water and the reflective paint job on the capsule that contained the lair.

"Not a flyer," Jess said.

Good point. Someone with flight ability would have caught themselves before the thump. "If the Fixer's found me here, I will turn that tech-pack of his into *dust*."

Jess eased off her crouch, just a hair, to twist and look up at Carol. "And why exactly would Norbert Ebersol be the first one to come to mind?"

"I might have ruffled his feathers a little after the drone attack."

"*Drone attack?!* Sounds like you've got a long story of your own."

Had that whole drone battle taken place just hours ago? Earlier this evening felt like a distant memory. She really did hate the time warp phenomenon she experienced while on a mission. "Can I help it if you miss things when you're on the run from the law?"

"All I know, ma'am, is that once we're done kicking this trespasser's butt, you've got explaining to do."

Whoever was clomping around Carol's roof wasn't likely to be much trouble, if their stealth skills were any indication. Possibly they weren't even trying for a sneak attack. Which meant they were super strong or super arrogant. She'd knock either or both right out of the person. Only Carol got to wield those two character traits around here.

The descriptions could certainly apply to Ebersol, though she couldn't imagine how he'd found this place. Hack? Was her security up to par? Maybe her director of IT, i.e. Tony Stark, was the one with explaining to do.

Quicker than Carol liked, the rooftop visitor figured out the aircraft canopy hatch system. Which suggested either a former pilot or a smart cookie. Still, they'd be no match for her. Having Spider-Woman by her side for a fight with one little old non-flyer seemed overpowered. With a yell worthy of a winning tennis player striking a ball, the prowler wrenched open the hatch and tumbled inside gracelessly. Carol powered up her hands, then caught sight of a cloud of frizzy hair and a streak of bright yellow.

"Oh hell!" She swooped forward, catching the mass of flailing limbs inches before they smacked into the floor, pulverizing a bone or two, at least.

Carol gently lowered Mara Melamed to the ground. The young woman's legs weren't yet steady enough to hold her, so she ended up in something of a heap on her backside, hunched and panting, trying to calm her pulse, which was probably close to heart attack range.

Jess had gone back into her crouch. "Did you rescue an intruder from a fatal fall so you could see the whites of her eyes when we trounce her? And you said *I* went through a dark period."

"No!" Mara gasped. She flung one hand out, as if she could hold off two super-powered heroes with her palm. "Please don't hurt me. I—I didn't mean to break in. Exactly."

"Jess, meet Mara Melamed," Carol said.

"Wait, Melamed? As in—"

"As in the family that's at the center of our investigation into DigiTech." Carol knelt beside Mara, setting a steadying hand on her shoulder. "What *exactly* were you trying to do here, Mara?"

"I have information. It was urgent, and I didn't know how else to get in touch with you. You aren't answering your phone."

The phone she'd lost in the drone fight or the burner she'd ditched back at her apartment? Both had been discarded, which meant Mara was telling the truth. Carol been incommunicado for hours. "But how did you find me?"

"With help from Professor Stark."

Jess choked. "Professor?"

Tony would never have given up the location of the lair. Or at least, he wouldn't have done it without warning her. Carol narrowed her eyes.

"Okay, with a little help from Stark's systems." Mara straightened her glasses and ducked her head. "A little unauthorized help."

Carol couldn't help but laugh. The kid would never last through an interrogation, if she cracked that fast under a stern look. She gestured for Jess to stand down.

Jess rose from her crouch, but remained at the ready, limbs loose, hands curled nearly into fists. "You trust her?"

"I don't have any reason not to," Carol said.

"Except for the whole stalking you and breaking into your secret bolt-hole thing."

Touché. "What've you got for us, Mara?"

"A pattern."

"What, like floral?" Jess said, layering on the sarcasm. "Polka dots are in this year."

Carol understood Jessica's tension, but snark wouldn't help her—or any of them at the moment. She shook her head, warning her friend to ease up.

"Mathematical patterns." Mara's anxiety set her talking too fast, bordering on incoherent. "They're my thing. Remember I said there was a pattern of weird stuff going on related to DigiTech? Ms. Drew is part of it now. I think someone set her up for that murder she's accused of."

"Well, that makes three of us." Jess's posture relaxed, and she brushed grit from her hands and righted the sweatshirt that had drooped off her shoulder while she was in her crouch. Apparently Mara's declaration of her innocence was all the vouching Jess needed. "So. You're Tony's hacker, huh? The one who started all this?"

"I'm not a hacker. Exactly," she said, with a sheepish glance at Carol, no doubt remembering that she was only standing in Captain Marvel's secret lair because she'd hacked into Iron Man's computer systems. "Just when I need to quickly find someone who's pretty off the grid."

Mara pushed herself to her feet, a bit gingerly. She wore the same blue ombre glasses and yellow puffer coat Carol had first seen her in. Another chin-high turtleneck poked out from beneath the zipped collar, though the beanie was gone. She had a black pack strapped over her shoulders. With legs finally steady enough to hold her, Mara pulled her backpack around, undid a series of complex zips and ties, and removed a slim computer, examining it carefully. Her face remained tight until she'd verified it was intact. The tenderness of her gestures, the tension and quick relief, reminded Carol of the way Tony fussed over his gear. Endearing, almost.

Carol took a seat at her tech panel. The newcomer lingered on her feet, one hand gripping her computer tightly, the other clutching her bag to her chest like a shield.

Jess returned to the couch, kicking her feet onto the already-battered coffee table, eyes fixed on Mara. "Tell me what makes you so certain of my innocence. I mean, I am totally innocent, but the news makes it sounds pretty grim for me."

"It all comes back to DigiTech. Right after Carol—uh, Ms. Danvers—I mean, Captain—"

"Carol," she said firmly. She jerked a thumb toward the other super hero in the room. "And Jess."

A relieved smiled pulled up the corners of Mara's mouth. "Right after you visit DigiTech's HQ, you're attacked."

Carol, catching the confused look on Jess's face, gave her a quick rundown of her run-in with the drones.

"And you," Mara said, looking to Jess, "go in search of a former DigiTech shareholder and get accused of murder. Not to mention they stole my grandfather's technology and made my mom disappear."

"These are all strange occurrences, troubling on their own, for sure," Jess said. "But the problem is any connection is circumstantial. It's a series of coincidences."

"It's a pattern," Mara insisted.

"Maybe so." Carol stood, her arms crossed just below the Hala star on her chest. "But you're looking at these facts through an emotional lens and drawing an unsupported conclusion. Your mom is missing, but there's no proof DigiTech had anything to do with that. And the technology wasn't stolen. DigiTech acquired it legally in a public records release."

"If my grandfather had been in his right mind, that never would have happened."

"His right mind?" Carol said, her tone sharp. "The picture you painted of your grandfather was of a man in such perfect health his death from a heart attack was shocking, despite his age."

Mara hung her head, tucking her chin between her jacket collar and her turtleneck. She rubbed it back and forth, in what Carol was beginning to recognize as her anxiety tell. "I wasn't lying. He was in good health. Physically. But he was also in treatment with a psychiatrist for the last year or two of his life. My—my mom knew about it, but she didn't tell me until later."

From the way she stumbled over that last bit, Carol could tell it rankled. A flicker of memory lit up her brain. The lines of a news article describing Mara's mother as having been raised by strangers. "You weren't close to her, were you? Your grandfather raised you."

"Yes," she said, tears forming along the rims of her eyes. "When Mom was little, when he was at the height of all his most important research, running the lab jointly with the DoD, he wasn't around much. She went to boarding school, but it was for the best. She knew that. And then, by the time she had me and my dad died, my grandfather was mostly retired. He had more time for—you know. Family stuff. I know it sounds like a strange family arrangement, but it made sense to us."

Carol was the last person to judge anyone's family situation, and by the silence from Jess, she knew her friend shared the reluctance to criticize.

"I was closer to him than I was to her," Mara admitted.

"It must have hurt that she kept information from you about his health," Jess said, casting a side-eye at Carol.

Carol looked to the ceiling, trying to control the spike of emotion that seared her. She forced her shoulders to relax, pulling them down from around her ears, aware that she towered over Mara by a good six inches and that she looked intimidating as hell when she stood, fully suited-up, arms crossed. "I know what it's like when your family keeps secrets. It's hard when they don't live up to our expectations."

Mara pulled her head out of its turtle pose and sniffled. "That's not it. My mother claimed my grandfather started raving about how he was the cause of civilization's demise. According to her, all the stress, all the revelations of his involvement in that government weapons testing scheme sent him over the edge. Caused a break from reality. But he started talking about the danger *before* that information leaked. I spoke with him right after BOS-MA was declassified and DigiTech bought it to use as a platform for civilian use. He was already saying it was a threat to humanity."

Carol met Jess's thoughtful gaze. Professor Melamed's concern was yet another intriguing but circumstantial bit of evidence swirling around DigiTech. It raised more questions than it answered.

"Mara, does Tony know where you are?" Carol asked.

The young woman shook her head, miserably. "He was busy looking for Jess when I left. I—I didn't tell him I was coming here."

"There's a secure connection." Carol waved at the bank of screens decorating the wall of her lair. "I'm sure you can figure out how to access it. Go tell him you're okay. And tell him we've got eyes on Jess, too. Supreme Intelligence help us; if Iron Man's out looking for the both of you, he'll stir up a whole hornets' nest of unwanted trouble and attention."

Still clutching her bag like a security blanket, Mara wiped her nose and approached the computer system. Carol plopped onto the couch beside Jess, who leaned in close. Their shoulders pressed against one another, offering the comfort of wordless support. For a few minutes, they listened as Mara video-called Tony and confessed to hacking his systems and dropping in on Captain Marvel, unannounced. Tony, predictably, paired a relieved rant with an admiring cross-examination into how she'd done it.

"You believe her?" Jess asked, a hint of amusement putting a lilt into her words. Mara was handling the grilling well, all things considered.

Carol sighed. "I don't *not* believe her."

"Me too. Me either? Ugh. She is right about one thing. You and me, we're targets—"

"Jessica!"

The sharp edge to Tony's voice brought them to their feet. He held up his phone, the screen blurred beyond recognition.

"Tony, none of us can read that," Carol said. "You'll have to—"

"It's from Lindsay." He lowered the phone and looked straight into the camera, his mouth flat and tense. "It says, *Child Protective Services paid us a visit.*"

Carol's heart sank. She should have thought of this earlier. Of course the police, searching for Jess, would visit her apartment, find her son with only his nanny.

"Gerry!" Jess screeched. She leapt for the ladder to the canopy, using the desk to launch herself into the air. "They're going to take him!"

"Wait, Jess." Carol pushed off and zoomed upward to grab Jess, who'd been spidering up the ladder in record time.

"We don't know why CPS went to your place," Tony said. "Maybe the cops send a social worker as a matter of protocol, whenever—"

"The kid's mother is wanted for murder?" Jess flailed a leg, trying to kick Carol loose. "And on the lam?"

Yeah, okay. When she put it that way, it didn't sound great.

"It could be a pressure tactic." Carol fought to maintain her hold on Jess's ankle, preventing her from fleeing. "Trying to draw you out. It doesn't sound like they attempted to remove him from Lindsay."

"*Yet.*"

"Or maybe CPS got an anonymous tip," Mara said suddenly. Carol started. She'd almost forgotten about her unexpected guest. Three pairs of eyes bore down on the young woman, who sat before the wall of screens that made up Carol's command center. "The police got a call that sent them to Faber and implicated Jessica. How do we know this isn't related?"

Carol frowned. Mara and her patterns. Tenuous hints of association, links that never quite joined. But, as with her other ideas, they couldn't rule out a connection. "We need to know more about what prompted the visit."

"I need to get my son out of there!" Jess shouted, kicking Carol again. Her parental furor swelled, imbuing her with a bonus boost of strength on top of her powers. Anyone other than Captain Marvel would have been no match for the double whammy.

"I could see what I could dig up," Mara said, raising her voice just enough to be heard over the sounds of Jess's struggle to get free.

Hack into a government database, she meant. Mara looked from Carol to Tony, like she was waiting for permission. Her fingers hovered over a keyboard and a flash of intuition told Carol it probably didn't matter what they said. She hadn't listened to the university deans telling her to accept the official explanations given about her grandfather and her mother, even when they threatened her degree. Mara's quiet demeanor hid a rebellious streak. A wave of affection flooded Carol. She knew she'd like the young woman from the first. Defiance bordering on insubordination was a trait she recognized and could love.

Tony, apparently reaching the same conclusion, said, "Carefully, Mara. Government databases are no joke, even local ones."

Mara laughed and shook her head, fingers descending on the keys. Carol watched for a second, wondering if that had been a knowing laugh, if Mara had experience hacking other government databases, and decided she didn't want to know.

Jess had not stopped pulling, trying to free herself from Carol's iron grip. The attempt was futile, of course, but the knowledge didn't stop her. "And meanwhile, I just wait? And what if it is because I'm wanted and we have to figure out who really killed Faber, clear my name? We have no idea how long that'll take! I can't lose him."

"You said yourself, they're probably watching your place," Carol reminded her. "If you show up—"

"I can't leave him and Lindsay unprotected," Jess said, stubbornly.

"I'll go," Carol said.

Tony spoke at the same time. "I'll get them."

Carol looked into the camera and held an entire wordless conversation with Tony. He argued that he was closer. He glanced at the hand she had on Jess's foot. Jess swooping in to grab her son, while understandable, would put her at risk of being caught and jailed. Gerry would be no better off then. They needed to keep Jess out of sight, and Carol was best positioned to do that. She nodded.

The twin offers from her friends finally penetrated Jess's frenzy, bringing her down from the peak. She stopped kicking and lowered her head, staring into the screen, into Tony's earnest eyes. After a long minute, she relented. "Here, Tony, I want him here. Where no one can get to him without going through me."

Tony logged off, swearing he'd get her son safely to her.

"I should never have left him, Carol." The sob in Jess's voice brought Carol close to crying too.

"Child Services has no reason to take him," she said, soothingly, as she pulled Jess off the ladder, flying them to the stability of the ground. "He's safe with Lindsay."

"She's not his guardian," Jess said, rubbing a hand over her face, brushing away tears. "If anything happens to me, if they try to take him, she's not the one designated to take care of him."

"Who then?" Carol asked, thinking they needed to get that person on alert.

The look Jess leveled at Carol nearly flattened her. "You are."

11

WITHIN HOURS, Tony had extracted Lindsay and Gerry and then arranged inconspicuous transportation to Carol's lair. As Jess reassured herself that her son was all right, Lindsay went about industriously transforming the cozy area into a makeshift child-proofed day care, with strict instructions from Carol to keep the kid away from the experimental weapons at one end of the lair and the jet parked at the other. The wicked gleam in the toddler's eyes as he gazed around told her Lindsay was going to be too busy chasing her charge to enjoy the sojourn in a super hero lair.

Carol sat beside Mara. She kicked her feet up, careful to avoid the keyboards and mice and wires littering the surface of the table. Had there been that many this morning or did computer gear multiply in Mara's presence? "What are we missing? There's connective tissue here. We just can't see it."

"DigiTech has been swirling us around and sucking us in like a vortex. We've talked about the company, the CEO, the chief engineer, and the stock." With Gerry on the premises, apparently none the worse for his sudden flight from the apartment, Jess had finally stopped climbing the walls long enough to focus on the mission. She plunked into a desk chair and spun in a circle. And then again. She twirled back around to stare at the gargantuan main screen that comprised the tech brainstem of Carol's lair. "You know the one thing we haven't talked about? BOS-MA."

"The software?" Carol asked.

"Operating system," Jess and Mara corrected in unison.

"Yeah, okay, what about it?"

"We've got a bank hack, leading to diversion of funds. We've got private information going public about shady stock deals by DigiTech investors. Fake messages about me showing up on someone's phone. What's the commonality?" Jess flicked a look at Mara, who shook her head, eyes a little wild. "All devices running the operating system."

"You suspect a compromise? My grandfather's code wasn't prone to defects," Mara said. Jess stared at her, her gaze cool, level, and unrelenting. Mara went red under her scrutiny and shifted in her seat. She reached for the keyboard of her laptop and then thought better of it, lowering her hands to her knees. Carol couldn't help but notice her white-knuckled grip. "But it is true the pattern commences just after the launch of DigiTech's non-military application of BOS-MA."

"Yeah," Jess said. "Are you running BOS-MA on your system, Carol?"

The two women were operating on a wavelength Carol wasn't tuned into. She glanced between them, eyebrows in her hairline. "Why?"

"I don't want to go digging for dirt on a device running the OS," Jess said. "If it's been hacked, we have no way of knowing how widespread the infection is—whether your system has been breached."

Carol shrugged. "We're going to have to call Tech Support."

Tony answered on the first ring and did not take kindly to being asked if he was the IT help desk. Over the sound of Jess's snickers, he confirmed he hadn't yet installed BOS-MA on Carol's setup.

"Good," Jess said, leaning forward to seize a mouse.

"Uh, Professor Stark, if you're on a device running BOS-MA, you might want to cut over to an emergency backup system," Mara said. "One that's sandboxed from your mainframe."

Tony had not been in the frame of the video call, his disgruntled, disembodied voice filtering toward them from off camera, leaving them looking at the main floor of his brownstone, which was half living room and half engineering lab. At Mara's quiet words, his face popped up, huge and Oz-like on the giant screen at the top of the display. He squinted into the camera, presumably studying Mara. And then, without another word, the call disconnected, dimming the room with the loss of the screen light. Before Carol could flick on the lair's fluorescents, an incoming call jangled. Mara answered, and Tony's face filled the screen again. He sat too close to the camera this time, his nose, eyes, and forehead the only parts of him they could see.

"You suspect there's vulnerability in BOS-MA?" he asked.

Jess nodded. Mara put her head in her hands.

"Okay, tech nerds. Time to catch up the fighter squadron," Carol said, feeling grumpy. She hated when she was a step behind the crew she was leading, even if she was grateful she had the smarty-pantses on her side.

"I think someone found a way to hack into BOS-MA. They're able to extract information from devices running the operating system," Jess said.

"More than that," Tony said. "They're able to insert data—"

"Like fake phone messages from me," Jess said.

"—and assume control of devices," Tony finished.

"I get the how," Carol said, slowly. "But *who?*"

"The drones you had the locals send me, Carol?" Tony said. "Military grade weaponry running on the civilian version of BOS-MA. Your pal, Alexander, knew nothing about them. He's checking with a colleague in another division, but he sounded doubtful. Said maybe they'd have funding to build a prototype, but not the number you dealt with out at that soccer field. You know who does have the capability—funds and facilities—to build something like that?"

Carol dropped her feet from the table, bolting upright, the trilled words of the assistant at DigiTech's HQ ringing in her ears. "Before they were software, they were hardware. DigiTech has got manufacturing capabilities—Seales's assistant mentioned something about another location."

Tony nodded. "A few of 'em. A newer one down on Long Island, and one on their compound, used more heavily in the company's early years, before device construction mostly moved overseas."

"On the compound? I thought that HQ was brand new," Carol said.

"Parts of it, yes," he said. "The outbuildings have been around since the '50s—including an old factory that compiled mainframes. That one's defunct. Allegedly."

So, not the Fixer? Unless he had some connection to DigiTech they hadn't yet uncovered, it looked like he'd been right. She'd jumped to conclusions about him. Ah, hell. "Still doesn't explain who sent those drones to attack a suburban soccer game."

"I don't think they were there for the game, Carol. Those drones didn't show up until you did," Mara said.

"I was the target?"

"Right after you start asking questions about DigiTech, you get attacked," Tony said. "Right after Mara questions DigiTech in that blog, she gets ostracized at school. And Jess ends up on the wrong side of the law when she goes to talk to a former shareholder. It always comes back to DigiTech."

Carol glanced from Tony to Jess, eyebrows rising nearly to her hairline. The certainty in their faces was persuasion enough. She swore and kicked at an empty chair, sending it skittering into a box of supplies, which crashed to the floor. All those people who'd been terrified at their soccer game. All because *she* stopped in the wrong place at the wrong time. The mess—all of the mess, she thought, glancing at the spilled supplies—was on her.

And *dammit*. She owed the Fixer an apology.

"But attacking people to cover up a vulnerability?" she said. "Seems extreme. Software gets bugs all the time, doesn't it?"

"Yes. By itself, that's not suspicious. Code gets created with bugs or develops them over time. Sometimes they're innocuous; sometimes, they create a vulnerability a hacker can take advantage of," Mara said. Carol glanced at her. A minute ago, she'd been protective of her grandfather, denying his code would have defects, but the coldly logical conversation seemed to be dulling her defensiveness.

"If your company's wildly successful and popular operating system that's used in everything from phones to banks to military weaponry has a vulnerability that could be exploited, you'd be worried about people finding out about it," Tony said. "You might be especially worried if you knew the bug existed before you released the OS."

Jess picked up from there. "Companies go bankrupt when it comes out they knew about a dangerous vulnerability and ignored it."

"And if you had no fix for the bug?" Tony added. "Well, then you might be worried enough to—"

"Get rid of anyone who's aware of the defect," Mara breathed with something like relief. Her eyes glimmered. "I knew it. I said all along my grandfather's death was suspicious."

If DigiTech was desperate enough to send drones after Captain Marvel, would they be willing to murder the inventor of the operating system? To make their own chief engineer disappear? Perhaps permanently? That didn't bode well for Mara's missing mother. Carol's chest grew tight. She felt as though the pressure in the lair had suddenly dropped, like there wasn't enough oxygen to fill her lungs. She set a hand on Mara's shoulder, squeezing through the protective puffy jacket that Mara had not removed, though she must be baking in the heat of the hideout. She was beginning to suspect the down coat was a form of armor. Mara looked up at Carol blankly, barely responding to the touch. The young woman would have perceived the danger to her mother as quickly as Carol had, the knowledge draining away her momentary satisfaction about being right. Carol found herself wishing for comforting words to offer, but none came to mind. Not believable ones anyway. If they were right, they were dealing with a company dangerously, recklessly determined to keep its secrets.

"We need to know more about DigiTech," she said. "Who's behind the company?"

"Oh!" Mara blinked, shaking herself out of her trance. She swiped away an errant tear and reached for Carol's computer, pulling up several documents on the wall screens. "I've been collecting information about the company's ownership. Very recently, Laurence Faber sold his holdings to a company called Perigee Partners, Ltd., which now owns more than 90% of DigiTech, with the remainder held by executive employees. Perigee has quietly been buying up stock in the company. Since when, you ask? Since right after Seales was hired, originally in a low level position."

"So, Perigee buys all the stock it can grab," Tony said. He'd finally shoved his seat back, enabling them to see more than half his face. He wore a five o'clock shadow alongside his normally neatly trimmed goatee and his eyes were red-rimmed, like he'd been staring at a glowing screen too long. "Seales is promoted to CEO. Melamed dies, his daughter disappears. And all the while, a series of troubling incidents takes place on computers running BOS-MA, but they're so seemingly random no one but a literal genius at recognizing patterns notices they're related."

Mara started and glanced at her former professor, a faint flush brightening her cheeks. Carol hid a smile. From what she knew about Mara's upbringing, she was likely used to hearing her relatives called geniuses, but not herself.

"Who owns Perigee?" Carol asked, skimming the shareholder papers Mara had displayed on screen. Perigee wasn't a public company, so the sale records would be private. She declined to ask where Mara had gotten them, but she was even more certain now that the young woman had been poking her digital nose where it didn't belong. Lucky for them.

"A reasonable question, Captain," Jess said, pointing a finger in Carol's direction. "One without a clear answer. I've done some digging too. Corporate owners upon corporate owners. Overseas registrations. I can't unearth a single individual shareholder of Perigee. They've gone to great lengths to conceal the people behind this company."

Carol crossed her arms. "That's shady, but not necessarily criminal. Corporations create liability shields by forming other corporations all the time."

"You know what else is shady?" Jess said, throwing an image—Seales's severe haircut and picture-perfect digital grin—onto a screen. Jess zoomed in on an overly pixelated spot beside her eyes, vigorously circling it with her mouse. At that magnification, the inhumanity of the avatar stood out starkly. An obvious digital fake. "Her and her avatar shtick. Did you know that even the DigiTech board has not met her in person?"

"For the record, I *said* that was highly suspicious!" Tony piped up, smacking his palms together.

"I don't think the avatar is the whole gimmick," Jess said. "As far as I can find, Seales came into being when she got hired at DigiTech and exists only in digital form. No social media. No college transcripts. No property records. She has zero online footprint other than DigiTech PR pieces. Either she scrubbed her pre-DigiTech personal life more completely than anyone in the history of the internet has been able to or—"

"It's an invented identity." Carol's eyes flickered between the screens, taking in the DigiTech shareholder papers, the untraceable history of the company that owned the company, the fabricated images of one of the most famous CEOs in the world. They formed a hall of mirrors carefully constructed to deflect attention away from whatever—or whoever—was at the center of the labyrinth. Carol had heard enough. The spinning needle of the compass in her mind settled on a single direction.

"You see it now, too," Mara sighed, looking from the set of Carol's jaw to Tony's furrowed brow to Jess's grim smile. She sounded, for the first time since Carol had met her, relieved. "The pattern."

Yes, Carol saw it. Despite a few unconnected dots, the links were beginning to form, and there were too many to ignore. As far as she was concerned, DigiTech, Perigee, and Seales were one and the same and they were at the center of the labyrinth.

"What I don't understand," Mara said, "is why they bothered to discredit my grandfather by releasing embarrassing information about his past if they—if they planned to murder him."

Jess stood, peering across the room toward Gerry. Satisfied that he and Lindsay were reading together from a stack of picture books Lindsay had thought to bring, she turned back to the group. "I can't stop thinking about that video either. His confession of involvement in the weapons testing, that wasn't released as part of the declassification effort. Mara, who might have had that? Did he bequeath his papers to the university?"

"My mother was the executor of his estate. As far as I'm aware, none of his personal papers were ever released. Not the digital ones anyway. I don't know what might have been in analog form. The university locked up his lab after the scandal, and then my mother went missing. I haven't been able to bring myself to clean out the office or sort through his belongings yet."

Much as she might wish Mara had more time to process, or Jess had time to run down every lead, an urgency tugged at Carol. A dubious corporation with a big secret to protect had just deployed weaponized drones in a civilian area. In Carol's world, that counted as immediate peril. It was time to stop researching and start punching.

Or, uh, investigating actively.

Carol pushed back from the desk, the legs of her chair scraping against the floor. "Mara, Tony, I need you on this vulnerability thing. Can you poke around in BOS-MA and identify it?"

Looking slightly distracted, Mara nodded. Tony responded with more certainty.

"We need to pay another visit to Ms. Seales. A little conversation with that digital facsimile of a person is just what the spider ordered," Jess said, standing as well.

"Uh, no," Carol said, as Jess discarded the baggy sweatshirt she'd borrowed from Carol and pushed up the sleeves of her long-sleeve T-shirt. A sure sign she was getting ready for action. "You need to lay low. In case you forgot, you're wanted for murder."

"I'm supposed to hide out here while some mysterious evil corporation ruins my life?" Jess faced off against her friend, a vivid flush rising up her neck and into her cheeks. "Not likely."

Carol squared up, too, arms crossed, stance solid. "You're supposed to hide out here and use my uncontaminated computer system to find out more about the company behind the company." She'd duct-tape Jess to one of these chairs if need be. By the stubborn set of Jess's mouth, she worried for a moment that she might have to do so to prevent her from leaving the lair. But a giggle from Gerry as he paged through his book gave her another idea. She nodded in his direction. "And make sure that if anyone turns up for him, they have to go through you."

"Oh, that's low, Carol." Jess's fists clenched and she glared. "But damn effective. Meanwhile, you're gonna what? Save the day by yourself?"

"I'm just going to do a little digging at DigiTech's fancy HQ. I've taken the official guided tour. I think it's time for a little self-guided look behind the scenes."

"And if you run into Seales, you're going to confront her alone?" Tony asked, leaning close so that one eyeball appeared obscenely large in the screen. "Not a good idea."

"Why the hell not?"

"I doubt your *punch first, think later* approach is going to work on a hologram," he said. "Not to mention she might have another army of artificially intelligent drones."

Carol sighed. "Fine. I'll call in reinforcements. Who do we know who'd be up for a little law-breaking in the name of preventing a friend from catching a case?"

Tony and Jess answered together, wearing matching grins that mirrored from screen to real life. "Spectrum and Hazmat."

12

BY NIGHT, DigiTech's property was less "welcoming tech company campus" and more "intimidating high security compound." A spike-topped fence had sprouted from a metal track embedded in the ground around the circumference of the property. The periodic clicks it emitted told Carol that it was electrified with a high voltage. Over the top, even for a cutting edge company concerned about security. The site had a fortress vibe, the kind of place where you secured people, not digitized information. Shouldn't they be more concerned about computer breaches, especially if their operating system itself contained a vulnerability?

There was another layer to DigiTech they hadn't unearthed yet, she was certain of it.

Meanwhile, she thought, smothering a smug grin, whoever was responsible for physical security here was either ignorant or arrogant. Though the fence looked impressive with its spikes and sparks, it failed to account for the potential of an aerial attack. Captain Marvel didn't need to walk across the perimeter to breach it, nor did her companions that night.

Monica Rambeau and Jenn Takeda had answered Carol's

text instantly and arrived to meet her just outside the DigiTech compound, suited up and ready for action.

"Up and over?" Carol said. In answer, Monica rose a few feet into the air, her Spectrum suit glowing like faint moonlight. In her energy form, she could also fly over that fence. Carol swept Jenn, who did not have flight capabilities, into her arms.

"We aren't worried that electric charge extends upward?" Jenn asked, as Carol powered twenty feet skyward.

As they were talking through comms, Carol heard her as clearly as if they were chatting over a cup of coffee in the quiet of her apartment. She remembered her earliest attempts at flight without a plane, how earsplitting it was to slip through the airstream without a protective metal cocoon. With nothing between the rush of the wind and her eardrums, the intensity of the noise seemed like it could drown out even her own voice in her head. That, to Carol, was what peace sounded like. A state she struggled to find these days.

Jenn spoke at a normal decibel level for comms chatter, experienced enough at fly-along travel not to shout, but her voice shook. "What if it's like those invisible dog fences?"

"You think anyone would be able to get a control collar on me?" Carol chuckled. "If they hit me with a charge, it'll power me up."

"Yeah, but not all of our anatomy works like a damn D cell battery, Captain!" Jenn's voice rose on the final words, spiraling higher, along with their bodies as they neared the fence.

Carol felt her passenger cringe, perhaps bracing for the pain of a shock. It wouldn't hurt Carol, of course, though she'd feel an energy surge. None came. They slipped past the fence and onto the DigiTech grounds without so much as a crackle from the electric fence below.

She frowned, peering through the darkness. Surely that could not be it. Surely some great obstacle to entry awaited them.

Nothing. There was a possibility they'd triggered an alarm or were caught on cameras. But what good would that do after they were already inside? Carol shook her head. The security officer for this place needed a stern talking-to. As they flew undeterred from the fence line toward the center of campus, Carol ruminated on the ease with which they had broken in, plagued by the sense that she was overlooking important details.

She ascended to an altitude of a thousand feet and studied the campus, taking it in from a vantage point she hadn't had on her earlier visit. The new buildings, that glass-and-metal tower and the parking garage and even the manicured lawn, formed a front that concealed a warren of older outbuildings. A few hulked with the size and boxy form of factories and assembly plants, just as Tony had said. Was that where they manufactured the drones?

Monica glided to a stop in the shadow of the main tower, and Carol dropped down beside her, gently lowering Jenn to the ground. Not the world's biggest fan of ride-along flight, Jenn slumped, hands on her knees, started to talk, then heaved and clamped her mouth closed. Her bobbed hair fell like a curtain over her cheek, but she waved one hand at Carol, making an emphatic get-on-with-it gesture.

"What's the plan?" Monica asked.

Momentarily, Carol regretted not bringing Spider-Woman. Would be handy to have someone who could crawl up a building. But this was the last place Jess should be, if they were right about DigiTech's involvement in the accusations against her.

Carol had briefed Monica and Jenn on a few of the urgent details before asking them to meet her, and though they probably had a couple hundred questions, she trusted both to wait until they weren't in the middle of a B&E to ask. "If we find evidence of those drones here or in the factory building behind the tower, we can prove a connection between this place and the soccer field attack."

"That sounds like a job for me," Monica said. She adjusted the wide headband holding back her curls and Carol spied a hint of glittery eyeshadow on her lids. Had she been out, when Carol sent the call? On a date? What had she given up to be here? She'd done to Monica what Tony had done to her—asked her to put a mission first, without thinking about the personal price her team would pay. A surge of guilt twisted Carol's stomach into a knot.

Before she could say anything further, Monica winked and then her face went still, brows lowered, the corners of her mouth turned down. Carol recognized her morphing into Spectrum, that imperturbable game face the first sign she was tapping into her energy powers. There were some commonalities between her powers and Monica's, but they existed so differently for the two women. Whereas Carol called upon her photon energy as a source of power and wielded it, Spectrum seemed to ease the energy into her body, shifting to accommodate the tangible and the intangible. Someday she'd have to ask Monica how she made room for both and whether it felt like suppressing pieces of herself.

Or maybe not. She could imagine what Jess would say, if the conversation ever got back to her: Tell me you're having an identity crisis without telling me you're having an identity crisis.

Carol's sharp eyes detected the briefest shimmer in the darkness, a hint of movement, and then the woman who'd just been standing beside her vanished. If Carol looked hard, she caught an occasional hazy wave, but otherwise, Spectrum was invisible to the naked eye. In this manifestation of her energy form, she could also phase through solid matter, like concrete walls and steel-and-glass towers. Carol grinned. Man, she loved having badass teammates.

"Go cautiously," she warned. "We have no idea how many drones DigiTech might have produced—or where they're housed. Or whether they have human security in that building."

She felt another subtle shift of air, a suggestion of motion, a faint grazing against her arm. An instant later, the mirage effect Carol knew to look for transferred onto a glass pane. It rippled briefly like water beneath a skipped stone, then went flat as Monica phased through the tower, on her way to the building. If you didn't know, you'd think your mind was playing tricks on you.

"Man, will it ever *not* be unnerving to kinda-but-not-exactly see your invisible friend walk through walls?" Jenn asked. She had gotten ahold of her gag reflex, though she still looked a little queasy. She rested one hand on the white stripes running down her bright uniform, blinking at the spot where Monica had been solid then liquid then solid in the span of milliseconds. Jenn rarely needed her containment helmet these days, having gained sufficient control over her radiation powers, and her expression was easy to read. Spectrum's powers awed her and she didn't bother to hide it. The open admiration on her face reminded Carol a little bit of Mara. The two younger women had a frankness that Carol found dear, was jealous of, even, but couldn't emulate.

"Nope," she said, smiling. "It'll be next level spectacular forever."

"At least she's on our side," Jenn sighed. Carol knew the feeling. She thought that about these women at least once a week. "So, what are we doing while she's poking around in there? I know we're not waiting out here like a couple of lookouts."

"How do you feel about taking a walk?" Jenn's eyebrows disappeared under her blunt-cut bangs. "I pulled some satellite imagery of this campus before we left. Other than the tower and the parking garage, what's available online shows no significant structures. But from the air just now, I saw large buildings around the back. And Tony believes there are or were factories here."

"You think they messed with the imagery to hide something?"

Carol considered what she knew of Tony's and Mara's hacking skills. "I doubt it would be all that hard to do something like that."

Jenn nodded. "Let's go for a walk, then."

If anyone was watching, they'd already announced their presence by flying over the fence, so there wasn't much point in keeping covert as they skirted the building toward the grounds in back. The campus wasn't totally dark—lighted paths crisscrossed the courtyard. Probably a safety feature, so employees wouldn't have to walk to their vehicles in the dark if they worked late. Not that they had many employees to worry about here, if that assistant was to be believed. So strange, Carol thought, as they made their way past the south end of the building, avoiding the paths and keeping to the shadows as much out of habit as need. To create all this and leave it mostly empty. Was it just that the company hadn't had time to move into the building? She'd forgotten to ask Tony how newly constructed this building was.

Around the corner, a more profound darkness shrouded the grounds, but Carol could still see the stark differences between the old campus and the new. In contrast to the modern, digitized glass tower behind them, the rest of the buildings were concrete and in various states of disrepair. The manicured lawn gave way to scruffy, overgrown footpaths. And there were no lights at all.

"Which one first?" Jenn asked.

"Or several simultaneously?"

As Carol and Jenn quietly debated the merits of splitting up to cover more ground versus staying together, a crackle sounded over their comms channel.

"Uh, come in, Captain Marvel. Come in. Do you read? Over."

Mara sounded like a kid playing soldier with a walkie-talkie. Carol stifled the laughter that bubbled in her chest. She'd done that plenty, once upon a time, probably sounding exactly the same as Mara. "I read you," she said. "You don't have to use military protocol on this channel, though. You can just talk."

"Oh." Carol could hear the *well-I-feel-ridiculous* in Mara's tone. "Sorry."

"Kinda busy here, kid. Did you need something?"

"Yeah. Sorry. I, uh, tapped into a feed of the security cameras at DigiTech and—"

"You're supposed to be working with Tony to investigate the vulnerability in BOS-MA's code. That's your top priority."

"And you didn't think that was going to entail hacking into DigiTech's systems?" The tentativeness drained from Mara's voice. Now she sounded less like a nervous noob on her first mission and more like a sassy, know-it-all twenty-something. Which, Carol supposed, was exactly what she was—when it came to tech, anyway. "I'm reviewing the code *and* the security feed. I am an excellent multitasker."

"Consider me corrected," Carol said, her laughter insuppressible now. Jenn, who, of course, could hear every word, snickered.

Somewhere on this compound, Monica was probably doubled over from the hilarity. It wasn't every day you heard Captain Marvel get hers handed to her. "What've you got?"

"I'm looking at locations of cameras and guard stands. There are a lot of cameras. Like, *a lot* a lot. Thousands."

"And the guards?" Carol tensed. Her fingers began to tingle with a power surge, as she scanned her surroundings for signs of a patrol.

"Well, that part gets a little odd. There are around ten buildings identified as guard stations, but I ran a script to trace movement around them over the last month using heat signatures and only the front gate seems to be manned. And it only shows heat signatures during ordinary business hours."

"I don't like that," Jenn said. "If they're so hyped up on security, why would they leave this place unmanned?"

This information troubled Carol, too. "You're telling me there are no guards here after hours?"

"Not human ones."

"So, what?" Monica chimed in, from wherever she was. She must not have encountered hostiles yet either. "Either these folks are counting on a show of preventative force or they're incompetent?"

"Maybe they're overconfident in the tech," Mara said. "Maybe it's all digital and AI. With all the camera vantage points, they'd see anyone coming and be able to deploy drones. An ordinary thief isn't going to take on those things. They'd turn back anyone but, well, you guys, basically."

Possible, Carol thought. DigiTech had made its recent reputation on the universality of its OS. It could run any device, any program, any operation. It stood to reason that they'd be seduced by their own logic. Seales didn't strike her as a leader that would entrust important functions, like security, to outsourcing.

"Say that's true," Jenn said. "Why haven't we encountered them yet? If they're watching our every move on those cameras, why haven't they intercepted us? They're letting us get awfully deep into this compound."

"There's only one possibility to explain that," Carol said. She narrowed her eyes, peering around, seeking any hint of movement. She saw none, but the darkness had begun to feel less like cover and more like a threat. Her senses tingled the way they did when a fight was brewing. "They're lying in wait."

Mara hissed. Jenn's head swiveled to inspect their surroundings, just as Carol's had a moment ago.

"New plan," Carol said. "Mara, see if you can find out whether we triggered some kind of alarm and what's about to come out of this darkness."

"On it!"

Carol smiled. The young woman had quickly gone from a reluctant charge Carol was watching over to a valuable team member who was watching their backs. As every good commander knew, if you let people do what they did best, everyone was capable of being an MVP. And scouring the digital world? That was Mara's sweet spot.

"You want me to join up with you, Captain?" Monica asked.

Carol might be a personal daredevil but she was not careless with her team's lives. Still, if they weren't in a tailspin, she wasn't going to pull up. Not until she had a reason to. "Keep a steady course. I want to prove they're producing those drones. If you run into trouble, fall back to our position, and do it loud."

"I'm checking the local emergency bandwidths, Captain," Mara chimed in. "Not hearing any calls to respond to a break-in at the compound. None of the systems I'm hacked into are broadcasting a distress call."

"So DigiTech doesn't think they need law enforcement backup," Jenn said. "Bold of them."

Carol thought so too.

Mara, despite being more confident in her contributions now, sounded anxious for them. "What if you're walking into a trap?"

"We're forewarned, thanks to you," Carol said. She'd halted while they processed Mara's information, assessing their surroundings, but she resumed striding toward the outbuildings ahead of them. "I have a feeling we're right where we're supposed to be. You good to go, Hazmat?"

"You bet, Captain."

"We're going to see what's in these buildings. Mara, you've got eyes on. I want to know what we're walking into."

"Yes, ma'am." Mara's commentary poured over comms as Carol and Jenn made their way across the lawn. They were both at the ready, Jenn scanning the foreground, Carol checking their backs. "According to the external cameras, you're walking toward some of the smallest buildings on campus—the most distant. From the internal cameras, two look like storage. The center one looks like... I don't know. A bunch of small rooms. Offices? Maybe the old executive suite before they put up the tower."

They abandoned all pretense of covertness in favor of speed and operational readiness. Jenn's hands lightly curled into fists and she double-timed her steps, nearly at a jog. Carol called a surge of photon energy, holding it to a simmer beneath the surface of her skin so that it would be there as soon as she needed it.

"See anyone in any of the three?"

"No. I don't—there's a lot of—I'm skimming the feeds and it's hard to—Mom!" Mara's sudden scream launched Carol into the air. Her fingers glowed and she nearly let loose an energy ball, but a quick glance told her she and Jenn were still alone.

"Mara, what—"

"I can see my mother on one of the internal cameras," she sounded frantic, all the calm of the last few minutes gone. "She's in some kind of small room, on a cot. Carol, please, please. My mother. I knew she wasn't dead. *I knew it I knew it I knew it.* Oh my God, you have to get her! Please."

"Which building, Mara?" Carol surged forward, ready to blast through a wall, but which one?

"The—the farthest building. Oh God, I thought it was storage. What if I hadn't looked closer? I could have missed her!"

Carol shot through the sky. She was vaguely aware of Jenn running flat out across the ground below, following in her wake. "Focus, Mara. What are we facing in there?"

"I don't know! Nothing? God. She's not moving. What if she's dead?"

Danger warnings jangled every one of Carol's nerves, but she couldn't heed them. They had a captive to rescue. She smashed through the door to the building and through a wall to a small antechamber. Debris blasted all the way to a bank of screens and computers on the opposite side of the room.

Jenn burst in behind her and called upon her powers to illuminate her body, beaming enough light for them to see their surroundings. A figure sat on a cot in the far corner. Wild curls stood out from her head, sticking up in all directions like she'd put her finger in a socket. The woman fumbled on the floor and snatched up a pair of horn-rimmed glasses, settling them on her face. She blinked into the sudden light, shock and terror crumpling her features.

"What—what—who are you?"

She was easy enough to identify. She was Mara, with twenty-five years' more experience etched into her face.

Mara was screaming over the comms. "Mom, Mom, are you okay? Did they hurt you?"

"She can't hear you, kid," Carol said. She edged closer to the cot, gesturing Jenn over, too. The women took it slow, aware that the sight of two super heroes, one emitting a toxic-looking glow and the other with hands that crackled with energy, might be frightening. "Dr. Melamed, Mara sent us."

"Mara? My daughter?" The woman sounded confused. How long had she been sequestered in this little storage room? The entire time she'd been missing? She was thin, her hair unkempt. When had she last eaten? Showered? "Is she here?"

"She's waiting for you in a safe place," Carol soothed. "If you come with—"

"Captain Marvel," a low, chilly voice hummed through the

room. "I've been expecting your theatrics since you paid me that visit. You're very predictable."

Carol's jaw clenched. She, too, had been expecting this response.

Seales had been lying in wait alright, probably watching this entire time. Nearby, Jenn hunkered in front of the still-muddled computer scientist, protecting their rescue, and looking around frantically for the body to go with the voice. The confused furrow that developed in her brow reminded Carol she hadn't mentioned the CEO's proclivity to hide behind virtual reality. Of course, the hologram was nowhere to be seen, so Seales wasn't even bothering with her digital doppelganger. Carol looked up and saw a speaker system similar to the one she'd seen in the conference room that enabled Seales to project her voice. But from where? She hadn't considered that on her last visit, assuming Seales was in her office on another floor of the tower. Dammit! Rookie mistake. With the sophistication of DigiTech, Seales could have taken that meeting from anywhere. Just as she could monitor after-hours security cameras from anywhere, too.

"Spectrum," Carol whispered into comms.

"Already on my way," came the immediate reply.

"Where are you, Seales?" Carol said louder, speaking to the room at large. There must be mics in here, too. She could only hope they weren't sensitive enough to pick up her instructions to her team. "You've got some explaining to do."

"How disappointing you need it all spelled out for you. You do bring the brawn, rather than the brains, don't you?"

Carol's photon energy surged, setting her hands aglow. Where was this pretentious snot? "Spoken like a true online troll, Seales. Why don't you say that without hiding behind your holographic trickery and see what happens."

Seales laughed. "I need only fear your fists if I doubt my mind. You require someone to pull your strings. I assume you've got Mr. Stark in your ear, issuing commands. Has he come up with a brilliant plan? Or are you just going to fly headlong into trouble, as usual? Has the Fixer recovered from your recent chat yet?"

Jenn frowned at Carol, and she shook her head, unable to explain all of that now, with Seales listening in. Though it seemed perhaps Seales had already listened in. How had she known Carol went after Ebersol? If she had that information, she must be aware Carol had reinforcements with her on the campus. They'd encounter resistance when they tried to leave.

This hologram was forever a step ahead of them.

"Almost there," Monica said. "Coming in quiet."

As Jenn lifted Dr. Melamed out of bed, the frightened computer scientist gripped her strong shoulders tightly, visibly trembling. The sound of her captor's voice must be sending her nerves into overdrive.

A wave of light and movement quivered through the room from the back wall. Monica appeared, letting go of the energy that rendered her invisible. "The good news is, I managed to get a peek into that old factory building. It's been retrofitted with a high-tech automated assembly system. They're definitely manufacturing the drones here."

"Oh! Well look at that," Seales said. "Another member of the squad has reported for duty! Welcome, Spectrum."

Make that two steps ahead. Carol gritted her teeth. If Seales had been unaware of Monica's presence while she was in her energy form, they'd had an advantage they'd just wasted.

"Let's see. We have Spectrum, Hazmat, and Captain Marvel. Quite a lot of firepower to prowl around a software company's headquarters. What are you so afraid of? And where's your puppeteer? Iron Man hiding in his brownstone, with his gadgets and his AI for company?"

"You're one to talk about that," Carol snapped.

Seales spoke in a conversational tone, even, unstressed, unhurried. In fact, she sounded almost delighted to be taunting them from afar. Disturbingly sociopathic, for an ordinary CEO. Warning bells jangled in Carol's mind again, that prickling sense that she was missing something critical overwhelming her. They could not afford to get distracted by Seales's heckling. She turned to Monica. "What's the bad news?"

"They've got thousands of drones," Monica said. "There's about two hundred on the way to this building right now."

Great. Four times the number Carol had fought at the soccer field. At least they wouldn't have to worry about casualties on this uninhabited campus, as long as they extracted Iris Melamed before the photons started flying.

"You encounter Seales?"

"Negative."

This was DigiTech's HQ, but it didn't seem to be Seales's. There was no evidence she was—or had ever been—here. Another oddity Carol didn't have time to parse. "I need you to get the doctor to my place." Monica started to protest but Carol held up a hand. "I've seen these things in action, so I need to stay and fight. Jenn can't fly her out over the security fence. It's got to be you."

"Fine, but I'm getting her to safety and coming right back!"

"We'll be done by then. Besides, I'm counting on you to keep Jess from doing something rash."

"What, like showing up to help her friend take on a couple hundred deadly sentient drones?" Monica said, unable to hold the sarcasm at bay.

"Rash like not trusting Captain Marvel when she says she's got it," Carol said, firmly. Monica's mouth tightened, but she nodded. Carol knew she hadn't heard the last of this argument, but they'd set it aside for now. "Now go."

Jenn approached and tried to shift Dr. Melamed from her arms into Monica's. The woman flailed, clutching at Jenn's bright yellow suit. "No. Wait. I don't—"

She must be disoriented, having been kept here for so long.

"Come on, Dr. Melamed," Monica reached for the woman. "Let me take you to your daughter. She's anxious to see you."

"Mara. She—she is? Where?"

"Somewhere safe. Let us get you out of here."

Dr. Melamed's head rotated from Monica to Carol to Jenn, the doubt clouding her eyes magnified by her thick lenses. Finally, as the buzz of the incoming drones became loud enough to hear through the walls of the building, she nodded and wrapped her arms around Monica's neck.

"Mara," Carol said into the comms channel. "Is there a back exit to this building?"

"My mom?" Mara's voice wavered, though Carol gave her credit for keeping it together this long, without interrupting for an update. She supposed the young woman was monitoring them on the security feeds.

"She's okay. Bringing her to you. Back exit?"

"Um, yeah, let me see—" Mara choked back a sob. "No. There isn't one. It's just the door at the front."

Well, that had to be a fire code violation, Carol thought sourly. Fine. They'd do this the hard way. If there was no emergency exit, she'd create one. Pointing Jenn toward the front door to draw the drones, she signaled that she'd circle around to meet up. Jenn took off running. Monica tightened her hold on Dr. Melamed and then shifted into her energy form, preparing to fly. When all three were in place, Carol released the energy that had been roiling in her hands since they arrived on the DigiTech campus. A blaze of light and heat burst from her fingertips as she raised one fist and shot through the drywall, rebar, insulation, and tiles that formed the roof of the building, smashing them to pieces. Debris rained around her, but she powered forward, out of the hole she'd just made and toward the sound of the drones, twisting in midair to zero in on them. Carol could feel their movement pulsating the air. They overwhelmed the sky, blotting out the clouds, even the moon, reminding Carol of the mega flocks of birds she'd sometimes see on their southerly migration.

The drones, alerted to her presence, redirected their flight path toward her.

This time, I'm not handcuffed by the presence of civilians, she thought, energy crackling around her hands. She wasn't fully powered up, but she had enough juice to blast these suckers to smithereens. And she was going to enjoy doing just that. Carol released a blistering charge from each hand, scoring two direct hits before a stream of projectiles launched in her direction forced her to dodge. She swerved, but took out another drone before veering to avoid taking fire to the chest.

Below, a small glowing figure burst from the building. Hazmat joining the fight. "You got two, Captain."

"Your substance emission won't work on these guys," Carol warned.

"Not quickly," Jenn said. "I could probably cook 'em into goo with something corrosive to metal, if you gave me long enough."

They didn't have that kind of time. Carol could withstand the projectiles and the rain of deadly debris, but Jenn might not be able to. Besides, there were so many of them, becoming overwhelmed or running low on power was a real possibility. They needed a faster strategy than melting the metal and a more effective one than the blast-duck-cover move she'd just executed.

"What about an EMP burst?" Jenn said.

Carol pondered that, flinging energy balls toward a couple of the bolder drones buzzing closer. "Might work. They've got to utilize electricity. Will that knock out our comms devices, though?"

"Not mine. We built in a Faraday cage after the first couple dozen I accidentally deep-fried. But it'll take yours out, if you're within range when I let loose."

"All right. Well, give it a shot. And remind me to tell Tony I'm mad you have a tech contraption I don't and I want one right away."

Jenn snickered. "You drive a few toward me, okay? And don't get too close."

Feeling ridiculously like a border collie, Carol sectioned off several drones from the main flock and zipped behind them. Just as quick as she'd made their six, they spun, tracking her movement, firing as they went. What they lacked in accuracy, they made up for in speed. She dove sharply, retreating from a horde that was now chasing her instead of the other way around. She re-tried the maneuver, but once again, the drones were only a hair slower than she was. She came under fire too swiftly to move them en masse. And while she attempted to air-dance her way around them, more arrived and filled the sky.

"Damn," she muttered, blasting a drone that crept too close, lashing out with one leg to kick another. "Can't herd 'em."

"I *can* EMP them into worthless metal lumps, though," Jenn said. Her voice was labored and Carol zoomed just near enough for a look.

Hazmat's body wasn't lit up anymore—conserving energy for her other abilities—but it wasn't hard to spot the bright yellow suit. A drone plunged into a dive bomb, heading for Jenn, and Carol's throat tightened. Jenn ducked behind the pile formed by the remains of a few drones, using it as cover to avoid detection. Her disappearance seemed to deceive the one rocketing at her, as it pulled out of its dive abruptly, rejoining the larger formation.

Interesting, Carol thought. They were excellent at tracking, but could be tricked by basic deception tactics. Whatever sensors they relied on were perceptive but they didn't possess human-level sentience. More sophisticated than your average autonomous consumer vacuum cleaner, perhaps, but still robot brains. *Well, thank the Supreme Intelligence for that.* Human-level AI was the kind of threat that set even Carol's nerves jangling.

Carol blasted a row of drones and finally managed to separate out a couple of errant flyers. Jenn emerged from hiding, drawing their attention. When they got within range of her, Carol backed off; Jenn clenched her fists, screwed up her face, sucking in her breath and holding it, then emitted a powerful electromagnetic pulse. The approaching drones dropped straight out of the air, smashing to the ground. As had the devices at the soccer field, they shattered upon impact. The boiling metal fallout didn't spread far without a midair explosion, and Jenn managed to evade the worst of it.

"Well done!" Carol called, a note of admiration in her voice. "How many can you take out at once?"

"Maybe half a dozen? That's about as many as come near at one time. I think they know I'm not the main attraction."

She emerged from behind the new heap she'd created, just as a
drove of drones hit firing range and blasted their weapons, surprising

Carol. She'd lost track of how close they were getting. They were mission-oriented, and she was clearly their mission, although they'd focus on Jenn if she made herself a target. Was there a room of remote operators somewhere out there, all with orders to target her, or did they share a networked brain? Had Seales programmed her deadly little minions to seek out Captain Marvel? She cursed her failure to ask Tony for the details of what he'd discovered by dissecting the soccer field drones. Knowing more about how these machines were operated would come in handy right now.

Carol zoomed into a drone and sent it crashing into two others. Debris showered her, slicing into her arms and legs. The Captain Marvel suit protected her skin, but she didn't like to think about how it would feel without that. And she'd been careless with the amount of force she applied, allowing fragments to pour down on Jenn. Who might have the protection of a suit, but not Carol's alien strength and durability. "Jenn, take cover. They shatter like glass."

Jenn dove behind the growing swell of downed drone rubble. "Captain, I've got an idea. You… might not like it."

From among the wreckage, Carol spied not even a stripe of the yellow Hazmat suit. She felt her temperature rising with her stress level. Whatever this was, if she wouldn't like it, it was going to mean Jenn putting herself at risk. "I'm listening."

"Bring them to me. As many as you can."

"And what? You'll EMP them into a mountain that crushes you to death?" Carol demanded. "No way."

"You scoop me out of the way before that happens."

"That is a terrible idea," Carol said, throwing photon bursts. "It would require precision timing and my comms will be dead. Too dangerous."

"Only one way to find out."

The drones swarmed. It was uncanny, the way they acted as a singular entity, though damaging an individual drone had no effect on the collective. As soon as one fell, another took its place. Even at maximum power, Carol could only take out a few at a time and could not disrupt their pursuit of the mission, could not throw them off track, could not slow the onslaught. Their ranks had barely thinned. Who knew how many DigiTech had stored away in its warren of buildings? The drones closed in. At this range, she couldn't blast them without risking Jenn being annihilated by the shatter effect. If she called Tony or Monica, it'd take them time to arrive. "Dammit."

"It's okay, Carol," Jenn said. "We got this."

They were low on options, and before long, she'd be low on energy. And more than that, Jenn sounded calm, but firm. Certain of herself. Ready. Carol knew better, as a commander, than to dismiss out of hand a trusted teammate's good suggestion. Reluctantly, Carol directed her to stand by the building where they'd found Dr. Melamed, which stood in semi-ruin after Carol punched her way through the roof. She ordered Jenn to retreat if it looked like it was going to go badly. The building would at least provide some cover if Carol brought hundreds of drones screaming down on her and then couldn't whisk her away quickly enough.

She swallowed around a lump of trepidation lodged in her throat. She was attempting a cobra maneuver without the 30,000 pounds of thrust or computer corrections you got from a next-gen fighter jet. Carol could match the power easily, but the precision? The timing? She'd need every bit of her Kree-enhanced reflexes to execute properly. If she did, she'd be able to slow her body and let the drones overshoot her and run right into Hazmat's EMP, while she blasted any that survived the pulse, and soared over the falling horde in time to swoop Jenn out of the way. The catch was that last part. The maneuver would drain her energy. She'd be expending speed and generating extreme friction to stop herself midair, not to mention firing photon bursts, simultaneously. If she wasn't careful, she'd have nothing left in the tank to get her to Jenn.

But her friend was right. A combined assault using Hazmat's abilities and hers was the best plan they had. The only other option Carol could think of was abandoning the fight. And Captain Marvel didn't turn her back on a battle until it was won.

Through a clenched jaw, she said, "On my mark."

Carol pressed her legs together, straightened one arm, and flew head-on toward the swarm. Once they'd homed in on her, she flew in Jenn's direction at top speed. The drones rocketed along behind her. She let them close enough to taste success. The first few to get within range fired projectiles and hit their mark. Carol winced and sped up. As she suspected, the swarm grew bolder. They pushed forward. Carol eyed the distance to Jenn and held a steady course, closing the gap between them. Then, she piked in midair. A wave of heat swept over her as she pushed against the laws of physics to maintain altitude while dropping speed. The wind resistance tore at her, but Captain Marvel's body was more supermaneuverable than any jet.

She held firm, battling the force of the air. Daring it to move her. It could not. Would not.

And the drones didn't react quickly enough. They overshot her.

Yes! Exactly as they hoped.

"Now!" Carol cried into the comms. "Jenn, go for EMP. *Now!*"

On the ground, Jenn powered up, and with a grunt Carol could hear all the way in the sky, let loose a tidal wave of electromagnetic energy that crashed over the swarm and spread beyond, darkening lights across the campus, plunging the glass-and-steel tower into darkness.

Carol mopped up the stragglers, rapid-firing photon bursts, as she pushed her tired body beyond its limits, racing to Jenn. Forgetting her comms were gone, she screamed futilely for Jenn to run. The woman's tired body stumbled forward a step, her face turned skyward, searching for Carol, who wasn't going to make it. She wasn't going to reach her. With the last reserves of her energy, she plunged and grabbed her friend's waist, yanking her backward seconds before the first of the burned-out drones hurtled down on the very spot where Jenn had just stood.

She flew out of range of the drone hailstorm and dropped. Her knees nearly buckled, but she stayed upright, Jenn leaning heavily on her shoulder. Drones fell for long minutes, crashing and shattering, littering the ground with smoking rubble. As the noise of the EMP cataclysm dissipated, an eerie silence took its place. They'd taken out a huge number of the drones—more than half. Maybe even most. But not all. Oddly, those that remained did not go back on the hunt. Nor did they retreat or land. They stopped where they were, suspended in the air, hovering.

"Okay," Jenn said, blinking up at them. "That is creepy."

"Coordinated control, rather than individual pilots. Like a central nervous system. Not a bad trick, really, managing so many at once," Carol said, with a wry half-smile. "You okay?"

Jenn tested her legs, which were a little wobbly. "Fine. Mostly. That pulse was a big one. Took a lot out of me."

If anyone understood that, Carol did. She could use a hell of a nap, herself. But they had to hold on. Maybe the drone operator was regrouping. Or maybe the drones would get new orders and fly off. Either way, Captain Marvel and Hazmat needed to remain alert until they knew everyone's status.

"Spectrum, report."

Silence. Oh hell. She'd forgotten her comms were useless. She growled, as Jenn relayed the message through her own device.

"Monica is almost to the lair. Dr. Melamed is okay," she said, after a pause to hear Monica's update. Carol nodded tightly, as Jenn gave a situation report to the crew, who were no doubt waiting anxiously at Carol's HQ. "Something's up here, though. Not sure what, but the drones are behaving strangely." She was silent a moment, listening. Carol eyed the stationary machines. Jenn was right; it was creepy to see them all suspended in midair like that. "Tony wants to know what they're doing."

"They're not doing anything. Like, literally nothing."

Movement from the east. Carol swiveled in time to discern something approaching—on the ground. A flowing motion, a glow. Not like the moonlight glimmer of Spectrum, or even the vaguely toxic yellow light Hazmat emitted. Yet, the shimmer was somehow familiar. What *was* that?

Seales? Must be. She eased Jenn off her shoulder, mustered up her remaining energy, feeling that familiar tingling in her hands, and waited, muscles bunched, body tight. Beside her, on still unstable legs, Jenn took up position, calling on her powers to spread a little ambient light.

The air around them felt pressurized. Like the eye of a hurricane.

The approaching figure finally came close enough to see. They were about Carol's height, wearing a cloak. Too solid to be a hologram. This was the flesh behind the illusion. Slowly, the figure raised their hands and swept off the hood shading their face. Instead of Griselda Seales's short brown hairdo, a sweep of blond locks tumbled free, swishing down over broad shoulders. Carol's eyes drifted over an angular jaw and up to a pair of crystalline blue eyes that made her feel vaguely as if she was looking in a mirror.

Standing before her was Karla Sofen A.K.A. Moonstone.

13

CAROL SUPPRESSED a snarl. She hadn't tangled with Sofen in years, had thought she was safely incarcerated.

"You're Seales?" she demanded, as Sofen strolled to a stop. The shifty psychiatrist was certainly capable of acting as a puppeteer. Perhaps her current marionette was a digital one.

"Oh, Carol." Photon luminosity lit Sofen's face unevenly, carving shadows into her cheeks and shading her undereye in purple. On someone else, it would look gaunt. On Moonstone, it looked ferocious. "I said it right to you. I suppose that sort of hinting goes over your head. Without Iron Man to bring the brains, you're limited to brawn. Griselda Seales is a convenient costume. You know about those, don't you? You've been wearing one your entire life."

"I haven't been Captain Marvel quite *that* long," Carol snapped.

"Oh but you have. The costume I meant was the one you don to seem human. Tell me, what do you think is the difference between me calling myself Seales and you calling yourself Carol Danvers? They're both invented identities that conceal who we really are."

No. That wasn't true. She'd lived her whole life as Carol, before she ever knew anything about Car-El or Mar-Vell or the Kree. *Carol* was who she was—at least in part. That meant something. Didn't it? Her temper flared. "However many identities you adopt, Karla, you'll always be a two-bit criminal hack."

"And yet here I stand, CEO of the most powerful company in the world." Sofen spread her arms wide, palms to the sky, the gesture grandiose and possessive. "Through DigiTech, my reach is limitless."

Energy sizzled through Carol and she clenched her jaw, holding back the surge. The effort compressed the words as they slid out, flattening them. "You're describing a hologram. A person who doesn't exist."

"It's been me all along. Names don't matter, Carol. Form doesn't. Flesh doesn't. All I need is the power to make my own choices and the will to enforce them. I have that now." Sofen dropped her arms, settling her hands on her hips instead. With the cloak pushed back to reveal the gold and pearlescent white of her Moonstone suit, she glimmered. "You wouldn't know about that, would you? With Tony Stark pulling your strings?"

"Me? You think I'm the puppet?" Carol let the energy surging inside her bubble to the surface, coating her hands in gloves of crackling photon power. She rose a few feet into air, wanting the perspective of flight, the reminder of who she was and what she could do. "You take orders from every villain wannabe on Earth. You're a career minion."

Sofen went still, the shadows on her face lengthening as her glow dimmed. She stared at Carol for a long, tense moment. Carol hovered, her patience wearing thin, her muscles vibrating. She didn't mind a little verbal sparring, but she had limits. More than five traded insults, and it was time to punch something.

Carol never had learned to be careful what she wished for.

Sofen stared up at her for one more second and threw up her hands. "Not anymore."

As Moonstone gestured, Carol pushed a palm forward, expecting an energy blast she'd have to deflect. None came. Instead a drone emerged from its frozen state and divebombed another drone. Was she controlling them with her *hands*? From the rapid response, the tech had sophisticated gesture recognition like some kind of hypersensitive, weaponized virtual reality game. Had she been piloting these things like a conductor at a symphony the whole evening? Moonstone was the central nervous system behind this swarm. Thousands of devices available to do her bidding with a literal sweep of her hand. The thought of it sent a chill down Carol's spine.

"I have an army at my disposal now, Carol," Sofen said, her temper and her voice rising together. She sent another drone careening through the air and stilled it above them. And then, she threw an energy burst of her own, blowing up the device overhead.

What in Hala's name? The villain had sacrificed an incredible amount of her own tech tonight. Either she didn't care because she had such a terrifyingly large supply of them, or she hadn't seen how many Jenn could take out at once.

Jenn! Carol's mind caught up to the danger a second too late. Moonstone's blast erupted through the drone, shattering it and spraying them with deadly metal. Carol brushed away the burning shards. Jenn cried out and dove aside, but not fast enough to avoid the brunt of the debris. Carol's pulse thrummed. Jenn's Hazmat suit would fail at some point. Carol could already see rips slashed in the material. The melting metal would tear into Jenn's skin soon.

Carol flung a photon blast toward Moonstone, which she parried easily. The villain tracked her, mirroring her moves. If Carol sped up, Moonstone gave chase, twisting in midair, firing photon blasts. Carol dodged through the sea of drones, but Moonstone spun them, keeping the barrels trained on Carol. The pair wove an uneven path as they darted through the Swarm, remaining tantalizingly within range of one another but out of reach.

"Whatever you're after," Carol shouted, "you might as well give it up."

Moonstone tsked. "Who says I don't already have it? Your

imagination is limited, Carol. Once, I thought that of all my obstacles you'd be the most formidable. How disappointing to find I was wrong."

Moonstone blew up two more drones. Carol yelled a warning to Jenn. She had to get her out of here and grab Moonstone. And she needed to do the two things simultaneously. As long as Moonstone had control over those drones, Jenn would be a target.

"Jenn, I don't suppose you'd get out of here, if I told you to?" she said, flying as close to her friend as she dared, throwing energy balls to keep the drones at bay.

Jenn snorted. "You really suggested that."

"Had to try."

"Well, quit wasting your time on silly ideas. It's beneath you, Captain," Jenn said. But there was no venom in her tone. She sounded almost teasing. "Can you get her close to me? Unlike her tech minions, she'd be vulnerable to a radiation blast."

"Small problem with that. She's going to be tough for me to get a hold of."

"What's she packing?"

Moonstone had been off Carol's radar for a while, but she could hardly forget Karla Sofen's powers. They were derived from a Kree source—a gravity stone she had stolen from the original Moonstone and absorbed into her body. "Speed, strength, stamina, agility. Flight, under certain circumstances. And photon energy."

There was a pause as Jenn processed that. "So… your abilities?"

Moonstone's powers were, in essence, Kree, and yes, disturbingly similar to Captain Marvel's. Carol flinched. She hated thinking of it that way. "Yeah."

"She wishes!" Jenn snapped. "Hear me, Carol? Whatever she's got, it's not what you have!"

Karla Sofen had what Carol *thought* she had all those years—a human body altered by Kree technology. The reality was Carol was an alien, whereas Moonstone was just augmented by an alien stone.

She's a pale imitation of you, Carol reminded herself. *Right down to the washed-out blue of her eyes.* She wouldn't be daunted by this off-brand Captain Marvel. And she wouldn't be goaded into risking her friend's life. No more dodging and feinting. Karla wanted a big obstacle? Fine. Carol could manage that.

She put on a burst of speed and flew toward the villain, head on. It took only seconds for Moonstone to realize what Carol was up to. Carol braced for a photon blast, but instead Moonstone used her minions to counterattack. She twirled her hands— looking more like Strange and his sorcerers casting spells than a warrior like Carol. Moonstone *would* be the sneak attack type.

The drones enveloped Carol. Surrounded like chum thrown into shark-infested waters, she whirled and fought, lashing out with arms and legs and photon energy just to clear herself a path. The drones dived, fired projectiles, made an aerial battle with Moonstone an impossibility. And Carol's energy was sapped. She needed to take out more of them at once. And it needed to be fast. She hated to involve Jenn, who had to be as drained as she was. But it couldn't be helped.

"Jenn," she yelled, her voice booming over the noise of the machines. "I need to down these drones, pronto."

Her friend didn't hesitate. "Bring 'em, Captain. I'm ready."

Carol twisted and extracted herself from the melee, diving toward Jenn, whose glow amplified, her chest puffing as she powered up. Carol flew in fast, and dropped low, but she didn't have enough energy left to pull off the maneuver she'd used before. Her feet touched the ground, skidding along the grass and tearing up a size 9 trench as she slid to a halt within inches of Jenn and threw up both hands, firing blast after blast to give them a little room.

"Waaaaait for it…" Jenn intoned, as the drones accumulated around them. She clenched her fists, then expelled another electromagnetic pulse. This one wasn't quite as large as the last, but it still rocked Carol. She dropped to her knees, her head foggy, her energy completely depleted.

"Carol!" Jenn cried.

She pushed aside past the pain and disorientation. Her thoughts were clear enough to realize drone fragments were falling on them.

She leaped sideways, knocking Jenn to the ground, covering her with her own body, waiting for the burning metal rain to cease.

When the storm finally slowed, Carol pushed herself off Jenn and to her feet. Sofen hovered in the sky, too far away to discern an expression. Carol surged into the air, but the instant she did, a blinding flash of light exploded from Moonstone. Carol flung an arm over her eyes a second too late. She veered off course, spiraled toward the ground and crashed, her momentum digging yet another crater into the dirt.

By the time she blinked the glowing circles from her vision, Moonstone was gone.

14

THE CROWD in the lair outnumbered available seating.

After Carol flew herself and Jenn back, the crew—absent only Tony—regrouped. Using an improvised stretcher comprised of empty gear crates, Monica tended to Jenn's wounds. Jess and Lindsay sat inside the makeshift play area, where Gerry napped peacefully in a portable crib. Also inside the play area, Dr. Iris Melamed had been tucked into an armchair, a gray military-issue blanket pulled up to her chin. Only her head and a hand, clutching one of Carol's energy drinks, stuck out from beneath the blanket. Her hair was wet and pulled into a tight bun. Her eyes sagged behind her glasses, but she sat upright. Mara perched on the coffee table before her mother, as if unwilling to let her out of arm's reach.

Carol cleaned up and swapped into a fresh suit. At the pace trouble was finding them, there was no time for civvies. She headed to the bank of monitors, which she considered command central of her hideout. Hideaway? Ugh, neither felt quite right. She hadn't yet settled on what to call this place, something that didn't feel comically pompous. She absolutely wasn't going to take Jess's suggestion that they refer to it as the *cloister*, though.

For a moment, she observed the muted chaos around her. Admittedly, Carol had never planned to host this large a party at the retreat—nope, still not right—and the space was nearly bursting at the seams. But her pulse slowed as she laid eyes on each member of her crew—even Tony's face filled one of the monitors on the wall, once Mara connected a video call. A funny thing that, she thought, shaking her head at herself. Having them here both crowded and calmed her.

Jess patted Gerry gently on the back, smoothing his pajamas and whispering an instruction to Lindsay, who then lay down on the sofa beside the crib and closed her own eyes. No doubt it had been a stressful and exhausting few hours back here too, listening to the fight at DigiTech transpire. Jess joined them at the computers, sagging into a chair. Carol tossed her an energy drink and a silent question. Jess turned the can over in her hands without opening it. Carol frowned. Like her, Jess's ability to fight fatigue was super-powered. But she looked ready to collapse.

While the rest of the team caught Tony up on the revelation regarding Moonstone, Carol leaned close to her friend. "Jess. What is it?"

Worry dragged the corners of her mouth into a deep frown. "My picture is still all over the news," she said, softly. "There's video now too." She handed a tablet device to Carol and called up a clip: Faber standing before French doors to a balcony, back to the room, Spider-Woman creeping in. The footage cut off abruptly as she leapt on him.

Carol strained to pick out details in the images, which had the grainy quality of surveillance footage. "Could this have been faked? Edited or something?"

"It has to be." Jess scrubbed a hand over her face. "I'm in the suit in that footage, but I went to see Faber wearing slacks and a blazer—my P.I. clothes. I haven't had a chance to scrub the video for signs of manipulation. But meanwhile, *Spider-Woman Attacks!* is the narrative the media is running with. I've gotten word that three of my clients terminated contracts. They don't want an alleged felon investigating their cases. Even if I prove I'm innocent, my livelihood might be ruined." Jess sighed and cast a furtive glance at her son and her nanny. "How am I going to take care of them if I have no income?"

"Jess, we're going to make this right." Carol grabbed her friend's hand and squeezed. "We're going to expose that video as a fake and Moonstone as the villain behind all of this. I'm not giving up until your name is cleared."

Jess met Carol's determined gaze and smiled, faintly. "Yeah. Thanks." She answered Carol's squeeze with one of her own and then let go, pulling a laptop closer. She raised her voice, drawing the rest of the team back into the conversation. "Meanwhile, I've been channeling my anxiety into research. Moonstone is Perigee Ltd. I mean, *of course*. Even the company name was a clue. Once I knew what to look for, I picked up connections between Karla Sofen's prior known aliases and the stock sales. She's spent the last couple years buying enough stock undetected to own DigiTech."

"But how did she get involved in DigiTech in the first place?"

Monica put the final touches on Jenn's bandages and helped her to sit up. "Yeah, how would she identify BOS-MA as a target for her schemes?"

"The way she always identifies her victims," Jess said.

Carol leaned back in her chair, far enough to tip the front legs into the air, and used her strength to balance. The ceiling, though comforting in its resemblance to the fighter jets she loved, provided no answers. Carol closed her eyes, blocking out the present, and searched her memories. Reaching into the past and the story of how Karla Sofen came by the gravity stone. "Patients! She has a history of manipulating her patients to take things from them."

"Bingo!"

"Mara," Carol said, letting her chair legs bang back onto the ground. She crooked a finger, summoning the young woman to join the group. "Your grandfather was in therapy for a while, right?"

Mara glanced at her mother, whose face was blank, though her eyes were trained on Carol and the rest of the group. She hadn't spoken a word since her rescue. "Yes, but I don't know the name of his therapist."

Jess pulled up a website on one of the screens. "I found something about a program at Ravencroft."

"A—what?" Mara asked.

"A prison for superhumans," Carol explained. "Sofen was incarcerated there for a while—but isn't it defunct? And you know—destroyed?"

"Our friend, Karla, did call a cell at Ravencroft home," Jess said. "She was also on staff."

"Well, that's messy." Jenn propped herself on one elbow and looked incredulously at Jess. "Talk about the inmates running the asylum!"

"I think the powers that be meant it to be on the up and up, but what do you expect when you let a guy like Wilson Fisk finance the rebuilding of a psychiatric institute? Shenanigans ensued. Including giving Karla Sofen another shot at treating patients. There was a lot of wild stuff going on at Ravencroft at the time, but here's the really interesting part. The institute apparently also operated a short-lived program offering therapy for veterans. Some experimental thing to determine whether the therapies practiced on super villains at the institute might be helpful for service-associated trauma."

"Wasn't Reed Richards involved with the facility at that point?" Monica asked. "I can't believe Mister Fantastic would have let super villains meddle with experimenting on veterans."

"The vet initiative was short-lived—and pretty hush-hush— but from what I can tell, it was run by outside researchers and the participants were supposed to be kept separate from the villains," Jess said. "With Ravencroft gone now, along with most of their records, I can't be sure if Sofen got involved with the program. But the timeline works—Moonstone was hanging around that facility with more freedom than she should have had around then."

"My grandfather wasn't a veteran, though," Mara said. "Why would he be in that program?"

"A lot of his early research was funded by the DoD," Tony said. "He could have had connections who would refer him."

"Moonstone was my grandfather's psychiatrist? No wonder he was struggling so much!"

"So, we think she manipulated him into telling her about the bug during treatment?" Monica asked.

Mara gnawed on her lower lip, processing this. "And then, what? Developed a virus to exploit a vulnerability?"

Tony scoffed. "She wouldn't have the skills to pull off something like that."

"Even if she did, why buy enough stock to own the company? If she was after an opportunity to get rich quick, why not just make a virus to hack a bunch of banks?" Jenn asked. Carol's eyes slid over the bandages on her legs, where she'd suffered the worst of the drone damage. Blood was seeping through the layers, but less, she thought, than before. Thank Hala.

"It doesn't make sense," Mara said. Her hand went to the collar of her shirt and gripped hard, skin stretching over her knuckles.

Moonstone had been at Ravencroft during the time when the facility offered an experimental veterans' therapy program, where Sofen may or may not have come into contact the inventor of BOS-MA, who may or may not have participated in the program. After the facility was destroyed, Sofen created a false identity in order to go to work at a computer hardware company that had recently acquired the flawed operating system, while simultaneously buying up massive shares in the company. As Jenn pointed out, money likely wasn't her only goal. But then, what was she after?

There was too much missing connective tissue to form a solid theory.

"Actually—" Tony began. Before he managed another word, the screen showing his face went dark.

"Did he just hang up on us?" Carol jiggled the mouse, trying to bring the image back to life.

"Maybe a screen died?" Monica suggested.

"I just had these installed," Carol said. "Well, technically,

Tony just had them installed. I doubt he'd let faulty tech get through his rigorous testing."

An incoming call lit up the monitor, a picture of Tony in Iron Man garb flashing on the Caller ID. His face filled the screen as soon as she accepted. "What the hell, Danvers? Are you sick of me already? At least tell me you're hanging up before you do it."

"I didn't do that. You did."

"I certainly did not."

As they began to bicker, Tony's face disappeared and the screen went black again.

"Oh for God's sake," Monica said. "Maybe he's having internet trouble? Or we are?"

Jess tossed a phone to Carol. "Call him back."

Before she could dial, a notification interrupted, blaring a warning from another screen. Carol had alerts set to give her a heads-up about unusual occurrences that might suggest alien activity. They caught a fair amount of earthly disturbances, too. In this case, a major power outage reported in Brooklyn.

"That's right near Tony's place," Jenn said. "So he lost power?"

"Why wouldn't his backup generator kick in?" Carol said, her chest beginning to tighten.

"It's not a coincidence!" Mara's voice was too loud. It echoed off the cavernous chamber. The acoustics didn't normally bother Carol, but then she was usually the only voice reverberating around in here. "She—Seales—I mean, Moonstone is doing this!" In response to the baffled looks Jenn, Monica, Jess, and Carol directed at her, she waved a frantic hand toward the monitor alerting them to the outage. "The OS. It's in the power grid! Some of the earliest to wholesale adopt BOS-MA were the utility companies."

Carol processed the implications of that. If Moonstone had access to the computers that controlled power stations… "She has the ability to bring down an entire city block?"

"The entire East Coast, probably, depending on whether they have decent segmentation in their networks. If there's any functionality connected to the OS in Professor Stark's generator, she could render that inoperable, too." Mara's cadence had sped up, her tone high and squeaky, making her sound a little cartoonish. Adrenaline, Carol thought, coursing through the young woman as she deciphered information. "I think, maybe, she might be able to seize control of any device running on BOS-MA."

"That would be a pretty widespread viral infection," Jess said. "How have none of the security companies identified the virus that exploited the vulnerability yet?"

"And what's Moonstone's objective?" Monica asked. "What motive does she have to mess with a power company?"

Mara's eyes were zoned in to a screen showing a news report. She didn't react to Jess or Monica's questions, too absorbed in the images taken by traffic choppers of the expanding chaos from the blackout. People flooded from darkened buildings; those who'd been on their way to work during the morning commute milled around outside. Traffic lights became inoperable, accidents clogged intersections. Lines of traffic piled up forty or fifty cars deep down the streets. Emergency services would be hemmed out. Crowds would be hemmed in. Panic would ensue. Stampedes. Injuries. "I think it's a warning."

Or an attack. Memories of the drone swarm at that soccer game fired in Carol's brain. If that was where this was headed, if Moonstone planned to send in her drones, the city streets would become a massacre site.

They had to suit up. Now.

A screen lit with another incoming call from Tony. Mara jammed a button to answer. His face came into view, but he managed only one word, "Carol!" before his image dissolved, replaced by Moonstone's angular cheekbones and wintry blue eyes. Her lips were curved into the semblance of a smile, but one devoid of joy.

"Captain Marvel. How good to see you again."

Carol strode forward and put a hand on Mara's shoulder, guiding the young woman to the chair before the monitors. She bent close and covered her mouth so Moonstone couldn't see, before whispering, "Is she in my system?"

"I—I don't think so," Mara hissed, one hand flying across the keyboard, the other manipulating the trackpad. Mara looked up, her eyes wide and wild behind her glasses. "She's in his system—hijacked it."

Tony Stark's systems were compromised. Carol felt like Thor had just hit her with a thunderbolt.

"B.O.S.S. is such an interesting AI," Karla Sofen said. "I'm looking forward to learning everything it has to teach me."

If Tony could hear her, he'd be hitting the fan. Carol didn't want to consider how bad it might be for Moonstone to have access to the systems than ran Tony's suits and the Quinjet and other secret technology. That would have to be a secondary concern. The first was the woman currently on Carol's screen and whatever her real plan was.

"Karla." Carol straightened and faced her camera, mouth pressed into a line, jaw tight. "End this now."

"Or what? You and your merry band of misfits will stop me? You saw my handiwork with the power outage. That's just a hint of what I can do. What I know. What I can *control*. I'm everywhere. The world is mine. Where will you hide from me?"

Carol had never before so seriously considered punching a computer screen. "The better question is where will you hide from me."

"You assume I want to hide," Moonstone smirked. And then she was gone, the feed cut off, the screen dark, the team scrambling in the wake of her chilling proclamation.

15

CAROL, JENN, and Monica leapt into action after Moonstone's disturbing call, but thankfully the downtown chaos didn't turn into a bloodbath. Before they arrived on the scene, power was restored. It happened too quickly and neatly not to have been Moonstone flicking a switch. Despite her taunts, her plan hadn't included attacking those civilians.

As emergency services dispersed the crowds with no more than minimal injuries, Carol glowered at the turmoil engulfing the streets. "What's her scheme?"

Her team's perplexed faces told Carol they had as many questions as she did. Remaining downtown wouldn't bring them answers, however. They needed to regroup.

Tony beat them back to Carol's place by minutes, which they knew because when they arrived, he hadn't yet discarded the suit. In fact, he and Mara were engaged in a standoff in which Mara appeared to be guarding Carol's computer system physically, arms thrown wide, as if she could hold off *Iron Man*. Lucky for her, Tony seemed inclined to explain himself, rather than take a run at her.

"What is going on?" Carol asked, as she descended into the lair.

"He was hacked! He's infected by the virus!" Mara yelled.

Tony threw his arms in the air and let them come to rest on his iron-covered hips, standing in a strangely sassy pose for a human in a military grade metal war suit. "You think I'd install an untested operating system commercialized by a woman I hate in my *suit*?"

That rang true, Carol thought. He'd been vocal from the start that he didn't trust DigiTech or BOS-MA. She groaned, realizing he'd been right all along. His wariness of Seales wasn't just professional jealousy. Tony was never going to stop gloating about that.

"You had it on your systems," Mara said. "I saw it when I hacked into them."

"Yeah—about that," he said, his tone low and menacing.

"Okay, kids, time-out!" Channeling her best stern Auntie Carol voice, she stood between Tony and Mara, holding a palm out toward each of them. The photon energy that had surged during her initial adrenaline rush still crackled under her skin.

"But Moonstone said—"

Carol turned to Mara. "Karla Sofen is a master manipulator. You have to try not to let her into your head. She'll make us mistrust each other, if we're not careful. If Tony says the suit is clear, it's clear."

Tears sparkled in Mara's eyes. She looked from Carol to her former professor. Her hand rose to her collar, knuckles rubbing the skin beneath her chin red. Poor kid was at war with herself. Wanting to trust the people who'd been established as the good guys in her life, who'd been mentors and guides, but also battling with her new-found doubts about her grandfather. She had the air of someone who's worldview was shifting too fast for them to keep up. Carol would know.

Tony doffed his helmet, so Mara could see his eyes. With an earnest smile lifting the corner of his mouth, he said, "I needed to start digging around in the code, but I had BOS-MA pretty well segmented. It had access to some systems—communications, unfortunately—but I have an air gap between all my other systems and the suit. I wouldn't risk any of your lives, Melamed, by bringing dangerous code here with me."

"Tony, just to be clear. You're saying that Sofen was lying when she said she had access to B.O.S.S.? And that none of the tech on you right now is infected?" Carol asked.

"Correct," Tony said firmly. "She's messing with us."

Mara studied him for a moment, then relented, rubbing her eyes with the heels of her hands, scraping away the remains of her tears. Carol expelled a relieved sigh and let the energy that had been collecting in her hands fizzle. The last thing she needed was her two computer experts at odds with one another. She had to admit, though, she was impressed by Mara's nerve.

"You were gonna go toe to toe with Iron Man, huh?" she joked, lowering the tension a notch. Mara drew her collar up over her chin, covering her mouth a second too late to hide her sheepish smile. "You got moxie, kid. I'll give you that."

And loyalty. The young woman had been prepared to take on a threat much bigger than she could handle to protect this crew. She'd shown no fear standing up to a powerful super hero. The spark of affection Carol first felt for Mara roared into a warm, crackling campfire, complete with toasty marshmallows. *Good job sticking to your guns*, she chided herself. She'd been so determined that she wasn't going to collect any more vulnerable strays.

Then again, Mara was not nearly as defenseless as she looked.

After Tony discarded the suit for civvies, he shared what he'd found. "I examined every line of BOS-MA's code. Best I can tell, we're dealing with a sophisticated exploit."

"You mean a defect," Mara said. Although the rest of the crew had taken seats, she stood before the wall of screens, arms crossed, fists balled tightly into her armpits. Her hair had been pulled into a disheveled, frizzy bun that sagged to the side of her head.

"It's not a defect."

"Wait," Jenn said. "There wasn't a bug after all?"

"Oh, there's definitely a vulnerability in BOS-MA. It's just not an error."

"Are you suggesting my grandfather—" Mara's voice rose an

octave, cracked on the last word, "—*intentionally* built a vulnerability into his operating system?"

"Explain that for us non-techies, please," Monica said, and Carol was glad someone else had requested first.

"Look, most security incidents occur when a bad actor finds a way to deliver malicious code to your device either to corrupt your system or to take advantage of a weakness in the existing code," Tony said, pacing before the wall of computer screens, waving his hands as he lectured, his tone spirited. "Those nagging emails you get promising free gifts or asking you to confirm your log-in information or a social post offering an online test to tell you what super hero you're most like? We all know them. You click on the handy link provided and wham! A piece of code is delivered onto your machine to cause trouble—steal personal information, take your system hostage until you pay a ransom, or lie there in wait, spying on everything you do until they find valuable information they can use to extort you."

The team watched with rapt attention. Carol had a brief vision of him standing before a packed lecture hall at Empire State University. If he'd been this animated with the students, he'd likely been a popular professor. She made a mental note to ask Mara later. "You said most incidents. Not this one?"

"Moonstone didn't need to infect BOS-MA with malware to gain control of device. All she needed to do was open the back door." He paused for dramatic effect and was rewarded by intakes of breath from Jess and Jenn, and a pained cry from Mara. Even Monica's jaw dropped. "B.O.S.S. found it. I confirmed it. There's a procedure in the defragmentation subsystem that, when it detects a specific 96 kilobyte sequence of data, grants remote access to the operating system."

"Which means what, exactly?" Carol prompted.

"Shelley Melamed built a back door with a specific key that he could use to unlock and take over any device running BOS-MA—without the device owner giving permission. Without them even knowing it's happening."

"No!" Mara shouted. "He didn't. He wouldn't."

"It's true," a soft voice said from the other side of the cavern.

Heads swiveled to Iris Melamed. She'd been so quiet, sacked-out with Gerry and Lindsay, that Carol had forgotten she was there. She stood now, the blanket that had cocooned her pooling around her feet. Iris Melamed was small and gaunt, with jowls that hung from her face and shoulders that curved inward. They'd found her a pair of Carol's sweats to change into and the clothes swam on her, drowning her in gray fabric.

"You're wrong. My grandfather," Mara said, enunciating each word carefully and distinctly, "would never design code that he knew could be exploited. He talked about integrity in engineering all the time. He said we can't invent amorally. He said we have to imagine the things we can't imagine, predict what the people who follow us will do with the things we invent. He told me we, all of us, have a responsibility to be—well, responsible!"

"Easier said than done, when you're in the throes of inventing." Tony offered his protégé a sympathetic smile. "When you know what you've created is a real innovation. When changing the world is something you can actually do."

Carol realized Stark admired Melamed, who'd invented tech that had changed the world in unanticipated ways, as had Tony and his father. *I guess he'd know all about that*, Carol thought. *I guess a lot of us here do. A family legacy is a lot to bear.*

Though Mara's pain and disappointment was palpable, her defense of the man who'd raised her was colored by her emotion, rather than the unbiased truth. After Carol had learned her mother hid her true Kree nature all Carol's life, she remembered reaching for an explanation other than the bare facts. She'd been willing to believe any rationalization that meant she didn't have to accept her mother's deceit. That anguish still crept over her sometimes, but while she empathized with Mara, her research had turned up plenty of information about the young Professor Melamed's approach that contradicted Mara's view of him. In articles by and about him during his early years, when his DoD-funded research began to garner success and attention, he'd never spoken about responsibility to the future or ethics. He'd spoken with the same heady thrill as Tony did of inventiveness, ingenuity, imagination.

"Inspired, really, hiding code designed to scan for certain data in the defrag subsystem," Tony went on. "If you weren't picking through with the fine-tooth comb, like I did, you'd miss it."

"Maybe DigiTech put it there later," Mara choked. She wrapped her arms more tightly around herself until she resembled a pretzel. "Maybe it wasn't him."

"He built it that way," Iris said. She emerged, finally, from the safety of Gerry's play area and approached the group, stopping a few feet short of joining them. "I'd know. I spent years studying the code."

"I had B.O.S.S. compare the version DigiTech launched to the version released by the government," Tony said, sounding almost apologetic. "It's in the original."

Mara huffed. Her shoulders shook for the briefest of moments and then she righted herself, pushed an empty chair aside so roughly it tipped backward and fell with a resounding clang against the concrete floor. She lunged at her mother, grabbing her arms and shaking her. "You knew! You knew and you released the operating system anyway! You put all your users at risk!"

Jess, closest to Mara, grabbed the young woman around the waist and hauled her backward, Mara's arms flailing at empty air.

"The tech was too good to waste. I couldn't let it languish in obscurity just because your grandfather arrogantly included a back door into the code."

"Why?" Mara demanded. "Why would he have done it?"

"Because he could. Because he liked control. Because he never expected anyone to outsmart him." Iris rubbed the spots on her arms where Mara had held her, her eyes watery, but her tone steady. "He could have revealed the existence of the back door, you know, after we released BOS-MA for commercial use. If it was so dangerous, he could have warned people. But he didn't. Too proud of his legacy to reveal the truth, too cowardly to accept responsibility for his choices."

"Would anyone have believed him, though?" Jenn asked.

Monica nodded. "Right. Hadn't the whole scandal about his participation in the weapons testing broken by then?"

"All part of Moonstone's plan to discredit him, maybe," Carol said. "To make sure no one raised credible doubts about BOS-MA before it could conquer the world."

"I just—I can't believe this," Mara said. "I refuse to accept he intentionally built vulnerable code!"

"Maybe you didn't know him as well as you thought," her mother said, coldly.

Mara clutched her stomach, bending forward as though she'd been punched in the gut. "Maybe you don't! You didn't grow up with him. You barely knew him."

"And whose choice was that, Mara?" Iris asked. Anger drew her brows down and pinched her lips into a wrinkled bud.

Carol shared a look with the rest of the crew. O-kay. Whole lot of family dynamics to unpack. Iris's venom toward her father. Mara's wholly different view of him. But they had to focus on the immediate problem.

"Backstory aside," Monica said, before Mara or her mother could wind up again, "Moonstone currently has access to the device of every single person who installed her damned OS. People's private information, pictures, documents are all available to a villain to exploit."

"Not just individuals. Right?" Carol thought of Mara's certainty that Moonstone had caused the blackout that disconnected their call with Tony. That it was a warning. "Power grids?"

Iris nodded.

"Banks, cellular providers, government systems," Tony groaned. "Remember that slide at the conference? DigiTech's been bragging about how widespread BOS-MA use has become. This system is everywhere."

A murmur went around the lair, as the team processed the incredible amount of access Moonstone had at her disposal.

Jess, who'd been quiet, finally piped up. Her question slid

between gritted teeth and came out rough as sandpaper. "She can extract information. Can she also plant it?"

"Yes," Iris said, tucking her chin to her chest, hiding from the blaze in Jess's eyes.

The gesture was so starkly similar to Mara's own anxious habit that Carol startled. Mara resembled her mother, though she didn't *look* like her. It was more in the eyes and the mannerisms. Carol had looked like her own mother, but she never paid attention to whether they resembled each other in other ways. She presumed not; they seemed so different when Carol was growing up. Would she have changed her mind, given time to know her mother as her true self, as Mari-Ell? Would Carol have recognized her own idiosyncrasies as the product of the alien DNA that her mother worked so hard to hide? Her heart squeezed and she suddenly found it hard to look at the mother–daughter pair in front of her for fear she'd see a reflection of her own lost relationship.

Fortunately, Jess provided a distraction with a shout loud enough to wake Gerry from his slumber. "She planted those messages on Faber's phone. The ones that made it look like I murdered him. And doctored the video. She's probably the one that called the cops, pretending to be Faber's assistant, and reported him dead when she knew I was in his apartment. She set me up. Damn her!"

"BOS-MA is an excellent tool for extortionists," Iris said. "You can even invent secrets, if you know how."

"Jeez," Monica muttered. "Between the blackmail and the misinformation, her influence is almost unlimited. It wasn't just a big dramatic villain speech, her saying the world was hers."

"But what's she after?" Jess asked. She bent her head over the screen of an iPad and pulled up a database of those who'd been incarcerated in Ravencroft. She scrolled through Moonstone's entry. "She's done dirty work for the Dark Avengers, Baron Zemo, those types, in the past. But she was low-level. A minion. A mind-gun for hire. Always taking orders from someone else."

"Karla Sofen wants power," Carol said. "That was her motive. What she lacked was the *means*."

"Means, she definitely didn't have," Jess said. "She grew up practically the ward of some bigtime movie producer, the daughter of his maid."

"Ward?" Tony scoffed. "Was this in the Regency era? I didn't think people still had those."

"Yeah, I don't think she was thrilled about it either."

"So this is a get rich quick scheme, after all?" Monica asked, sourly.

"No," Carol said. "Money runs out. That's not what she's after. Or at least, that's not *all* she's after. Remember, she bought DigiTech, instead of just robbing banks. She wanted control of the vulnerability. She wanted to ensure someone else wouldn't find it and use it for themselves—or fix it. Having an unlimited, perpetual flow of information and access that she can use to manipulate people and institutions gives her enormous reach. It makes her independent for the first time in her life."

Tony threw Carol a troubled look. "Danvers, you read minds now? How do you know all that?"

"As Seales, she said something about you pulling my strings, like a puppeteer," Carol said. "It tweaked me, but I figured she was just the kind of arrogant jerk who can't handle another powerful woman. After we realized Seales was Moonstone, I thought of something my dad used to say: *Remember that when you point a finger at someone else, three fingers are pointing back at you.* That's Moonstone. When she talked about me being a puppet, it's because that's what she's always been. Now, she's pulling the strings. And she's not going to give that power up easily."

Iris edged closer to Carol, her eyes huge dark pools behind her glasses. "You know a lot about her."

The observation pressed on Carol, painful as a thumb on a bruise. No way was Carol going to spiral down the rabbit hole of trying to explain the similarity between them. That way madness and all that. "Let's just say Moonstone and I have a few things in common and leave it at that," she said, ruefully.

"Is this why you got fired? And then kidnapped?" Mara

pulled out of Jess's grasp and rounded on Iris. Carol was grateful someone had deflected the attention from her. And on alert lest Mara lunge at her mother again. "You found out her plan?"

"You're lucky you're not dead," Jenn said.

"It's not—it was never about killing anyone. Seales and I disagreed on many things," Iris said. "In the end, I knew too much."

Carol turned to look at Iris, eyes narrowed. The woman seemed frail. Her voice occasionally trembled, her legs wobbled. But her mind remained sharp. And that answer had been a hair too cryptic for Carol's taste.

"So, now what?" Jenn said. "We have to stop Moonstone. Do we make a public announcement, warn people about the vulnerability?"

"You can't do that!" Iris stumbled forward and skidded into Monica, who caught the agitated computer scientist and set her on her feet. "There's no patch."

"People have a right to know," Jenn argued.

"Know what? That at any moment every dollar might be wiped out of their bank account? That someone can turn off power to the entire East Coast? That their deepest darkest secrets could be revealed at any moment and there's absolutely nothing they can do about it? People put everything in their devices. Contacts, family memories, financial information. Can you imagine telling them it's all exposed and being used against them? That there's no way to fix it, no way for them to protect themselves other than just stop using their devices?"

Hala help them. Stated that way, the threat was overwhelming. Pulling on it felt like tugging a string that could unravel the fabric of society itself.

"Just like Grandpa warned." Mara's eyes filled with tears. "He wasn't mad, at the end. He was afraid. Of his own creation."

"People would panic," Iris said, sounding close to panic herself. "They'd lose their trust in technology itself."

Monica glared at Iris. "They shouldn't trust their technology right now."

"Don't blame BOS-MA for that," Iris said. "It's superior technology."

"That just happens to have a catastrophic design flaw currently being exploited by a ruthless villain!"

"Okay, okay. Everyone back to their corners," Carol said, raising her voice. She cast a stern look around the room, waiting until everyone returned to their seats.

"Doom and Gloom over here might be right," Jess said, waving at Mara and her mother. "It sounds dire. But bugs can be fixed. That's what all the tech companies do—*oops, here's this problem with our code, but look we fixed it!* Hell, sometimes the code is so buggy, they have a designated day of the week you're supposed to install the repairs. Tony, you can whip up a patch for this, right?"

He crinkled his brow and stayed quiet for too long. "It's part of the design of the operating system itself."

Carol didn't have Tony's tech expertise, but she gathered he was saying this was a bigger problem than it seemed. "Iris, you know the code. You could fix it."

An odd expression crossed over Iris's features—two parts frustration, one part pride. "My father was a genius."

Carol rolled her eyes, tapped a hand impatiently on the table. This was why she hated tech sometimes and the people who invented it. Couldn't they give a plain answer for once?

"Not to throw gasoline on this already raging inferno," Tony said. He had several tablets and a laptop set up on the table before him, cobbling together a mini command center that probably rivaled the power of the larger one on the wall. "But I'm not just worried about people's faith in technology. If we announce a vulnerability, it'll be an engraved invitation to the biggest hacking party of all time. Everyone with a keyboard and functional knowledge of C++ would wire in and start trying to exploit it. We'd be exposing people to more risk."

"Or we'd be inviting the community of ethical hackers to help us find a solution," Mara said. Her pitch had modulated back to

its normal range. Talking about the problem, rather than the role her family had played in creating it, seemed to bring her back to herself. This Mara, the one who'd gone public with her suspicions in the face of tremendous pressure not to, the one who'd hacked into Tony Stark's system to find Carol, the one who'd pitted herself against Iron Man to protect her friends, had been in there all along.

Carol was glad to see it. This Mara was an asset to the team, and they were going to need her. Because she was afraid Tony was right. They had a decision to make.

"It would be irresponsible to reveal the truth without a way to fix this vulnerability," she said. As the words emerged, they felt right. "Jenn, Monica, you've got a point. People deserve the truth, and they will get it. Just not today. Not when they're too defenseless for the truth to do them any good. We need to fix the vulnerability. Fast."

16

UNDER THE cover of darkness, four heavy-load semitrucks covered in a honeycomb of olive green hexagons rumbled out of Fort Henry William. They turned on no lights, relying on night-vision headsets worn by their drivers, and drove backroads, avoiding traffic. The transports, known to their drivers as the Chameleons, were invisible, outfitted in a skin that rendered them undetectable even by non-Earth technology. To find them, you'd have to already know where they were. Very few people knew this particular camouflage existed, let alone that it had been deployed. Yet the Chameleons weren't the biggest secret on the road that night.

The soldier-drivers didn't know what their trucks contained. The guards didn't. The brass didn't. Nearly no one who served on the base had clearance to know details about the protype weapon contained in a crate in the back of one of the Chameleons. They knew only that orders to move the payload had been received, authenticated. The orders said *move under highest secrecy*. That meant decoys, though the payload was small enough to fit into one truck. It meant risking one top secret tech to exposure to get another out of harm's way.

Hours earlier, at the comms headquarters charged with monitoring outer space, an alarm had sounded. The NCO assigned to the desk blinked once. Twice. Expected to discover his overactive imagination had invented a false warning.

The alarm sounded again. *Impending attack from outside the solar system.*

He scrubbed his eyes, his reaction time slower than it should have been. It was the interstellar alert siren. The NCO on duty was a newbie, recently out of training. Just the guy who monitors comms on the graveyard shift. He'd been too young to serve last time there was a major threat from another world, barely old enough to remember the terrifying news reports and the floods of people trying futilely to escape the geographically unlimited threat from other universes. Since he'd joined up, space had been relatively quiet. Or at least, the army's role in keeping Earth safe from space had been limited. They had super heroes on duty for this kind of stuff. To ward it off. To keep the other species or planets that turned malevolent eyes—or tentacles or feelers or whatever—towards Earth from harming them.

And yet, that alarm still blared.

Was this a readiness test? He'd only been on the job for a few months, but his commanding officer said the brass did that, sometimes, like a pop quiz. She said they sounded the alarms when there were no incoming green beings, just to make sure you were awake at the desk. You had to react or you'd be punished.

He had to react.

The NCO knew the protocol. Register the alarm, wake up his commander, who was going to be pissed to be roused for another drill. Others who manned comms reported that they'd had two pop quiz drills already this month. Though not this particular drill. *Impending attack from outside the solar system.* A chill ran down the NCO's spine and set his legs shaking. He picked up the phone and started a chain reaction.

o———o

MILES AWAY at Fort Henry William, Colonel Finke, on night duty he'd volunteered for, picked up the incoming call. He knew what to say. He'd planned it. However, as the moment arrived to put his plan into action, his voice shook when he gave the order to put the base on high alert and move Project Faustus. Thousands of soldiers would be mobilized, millions of dollars wasted on a false alarm. And Project Faustus itself would be taken.

Too late. It was done. Finke gulped hard and hung up the phone.

No turning back now. Had there ever been a moment when he could have avoided this? Maybe way back when, before he ever made and lost a digital fortune and got addicted to the idea of recovering that first success. Now? He could see no options other than this one. He picked up the receiver and called the transport department to request a chopper. He said he needed to receive delivery of Faustus and ensure safe arrival at its new secure location.

Finke's chopper would never reach the new base.

Even as he flew under the thumping of rotors, another figure powered itself across the sky toward a prearranged rendezvous point, flanked by a brigade of drones that resembled a powerful, deadly swarm.

17

"CAROL."

The whisper penetrated Carol's slumber and she bolted upright.

Mara jumped back, dodging to avoid a head-butt. "Sorry! I thought you'd be harder to wake up. You were practically hibernating."

"I'm trained to rouse quickly." Carol rubbed the sleep from her eyes and swung her legs over the side of a cot.

Her lair was beginning to resemble one of the small forward bases she'd served on early in her military career, before leaving the atmosphere became a common occurrence. Comms station was her computer area, now with folding chairs so the tech team—Tony, Mara, Iris—didn't have to trade off to sit. They'd set up a few of Carol's stash of cots, so the team could take turns getting rest. Monica and Jenn had foregone the pleasure of camp cots in the cold lair, opting instead for comfortable beds and hot showers in their own homes. Both had promised to return as soon as needed.

Lindsay had strung temporary curtains around the sitting area to give Gerry the illusion of darkness and privacy so he could sleep through the night. Carol peeked around the barrier, checked on them. Lindsay had drifted off, too, finally. She'd spent an exhausting day chasing Gerry away from the jet, remaining awake well into the small hours, trying to settle an excited child to whom an overnight in Aunt Carol's lair was an epic adventure. Jess tossed fitfully on a cot beside her son. She'd probably gotten even less sleep than Carol, between worrying over Gerry and climbing the walls (and ceiling), unable to do more than offer unhelpful suggestions to the computer brigade.

Carol stepped away from the cots, wanting her friend to get at least a few more minutes' rest. She needed it. "What's going on? Breakthrough with the code?"

Mara glanced toward the computer system. It appeared the same as Carol had last seen it, every screen teeming with rows and rows of code. She wondered what a breakthrough would look like. She doubted she'd recognize it, but she trusted Tony and Mara would.

"The drones are back."

The pronouncement jolted Carol. "What?"

"I've been monitoring law enforcement scanner traffic. And I just heard a transmission from a jurisdiction upstate that someone reported a flock of giant mechanical birds sweeping over the countryside." She flipped her tablet screen toward Carol. "I scoured the internet for video and found this."

Carol grabbed the device and squinted at a shaky recording that showed a dark mass moving through the sky. Either the flying objects were too high to capture well or the phone that filmed the video couldn't zoom. Carol couldn't entirely make them out, but the smooth, unified flight certainly resembled Moonstone's mechanical army.

"Could be," Carol said. "Did the locals know what to make of it?"

Mara shook her head. "The swarm was gone before they got units out there. But they gave their neighboring county a heads-up and it turns out someone there was reporting UFOs."

Great. UFOs. She supposed that wasn't a wild reaction, considering she had been stunned by all the unfamiliar capabilities of the swarm. "Okay, so Moonstone is on the move. Or at least her minions are. Do we know where they're headed? Or am I gonna have to chase them across the sky?"

"I don't know their destination, but I can tell you their trajectory. I mapped potential routes across a few counties based on the reports I tracked."

Smart kid. As Carol had noted, the longer Mara spent in front of the code and her devices, the more confident she grew. That was her comfort zone, like Carol's was the sky.

She strode toward the display cases that housed her suits, then paused, catching a glimpse of red and gold. Apparently, while she'd slept, Tony had commandeered one of the cases that held her pre-formed Captain Marvel suits. The Iron Man suit didn't need a mannequin to hold its form, so he'd posed it as if it was dancing with her suit. *You wish, Stark*, she thought with a half-smile.

In minutes, she'd donned a fresh suit and emerged to find Tony part of the way to geared up as well.

"What are you doing?" she demanded in a whisper, so as not to wake Jess, Gerry, or Lindsay. It was a hard balance. She wasn't used to having this many people in her space or to taking this much care before jetting off in response to a call. She brushed away an intense longing for the quiet that accompanied her normal routine. This was the safest place for her friends right now. They needed to stay. She was glad they were here, even if she was feeling like a caged lion.

"Same thing as you." Tony pointed to the sash she was securing around her hips. "Moonstone? Destructodrones? It wasn't all a fever dream, Carol."

She aimed an irritated glare at Mara, who raised one hand, palm up, presenting a picture of innocence. The screen she held showed the map she'd worked up. "I didn't know it was a secret!"

"It's not," Tony said. "Carol, were you planning to single-handedly track a bunch of mysterious drones to who knows where on their way to do who knows what and take them out?"

"Pretty much, yeah. You think I can't do it?"

"Not the point, Danvers."

"I'll have my trusty navigator in my ear, guiding me." Carol pointed at Mara. Which reminded her, she needed to grab a new comms device to replace the one Hazmat had fried. She strode over to a stack of gear boxes and rifled through for more tech.

"And Spectrum and Hazmat." Carol glanced over her shoulder. Mara's eyes were wide behind her glasses. Carol was reminded forcefully of Iris's big-eyed concern earlier in the night. But for the spiderweb of lines around Iris's eyes, these two looks could be interchangeable. "Right?"

"No time to waste." Carol shook her head. "We know where those drones are *now*. I need to move."

"*We* need to move," Tony said.

Carol point at the map on the iPad. "I can handle *that*." She waved a hand in a broad circle in the direction of the computer monitors. "You have to handle *that*."

It was about the only thing she could say that would cause Tony to hesitate. And he did, his mouth pulled into a scowl as he looked from Carol to the bank of screens. There was absolute logic behind this division of labor; he knew it, even if he didn't want to accept it.

"Creating a patch could take weeks," he hedged.

"Which is why we can't afford a delay of even a few hours. You need to stay, Tony. I can manage the drones." She didn't give him time to object, lifting off from the ground and surging toward the exit to the lair. Over comms, she said, "Mara, keep me posted if that trajectory changes. And run some simulations using direction and speed of movement, see if you can identify their target."

"I'm—I'm not qualified for that!" Mara shouted after her. "I'm a programmer. A researcher. A student. I'm not super hero dispatch!"

"You know patterns, Mara. Find me one."

"I MIGHT have something."

She'd only been flying a few minutes when Mara's voice crackled in her ear. "Tell me."

"I'm not sure. I'm not supposed to be listening to this

channel—it's restricted. Maybe classified. They're using a lot of code talk that I can't decipher." Mara's words spilled out in a torrent. If they were in the same room, Carol had a feeling she'd be rubbing her chin—her anxious tell.

"Mara, your instincts haven't failed us yet, have they? Keep trusting yourself and tell me what you think."

"It's a secure military channel."

Tony's voiced piped over the comms. "And no. You don't actually want to know how she got in there."

Carol snickered.

"There's a convoy on the road about one hundred miles to the north of you," Mara said. "It was moving under top secret cover, undetected, but a couple minutes ago, there was a burst of chatter. It sounded like distress signals. I can't be sure but—"

"You think they're under attack?" She'd heard enough. Mara's gut had been right since her mother's disappearance. She'd more than earned the benefit of the doubt.

Carol arced in midair, calling upon her reserves of energy to push forward at top speed. Thank goodness she'd rested. She wasn't at full strength, but she had enough to eat up the miles to the location Mara rattled off.

She found the military convoy right where Mara predicted. The wreckage of it, anyway. There were three trucks, two in various states of destruction, lying askew half in and half out of the road. The third remained centered in a lane on the asphalt, smoke spewing from its engine. Carol's eyes traced debris strewn for nearly a mile—broken rotors, flaming tail pieces, the body of a downed helo bellied up against a tree. There were people, too, the soldiers who'd staffed the convoy. From her altitude, Carol couldn't tell if they were alive. She dropped quickly, eyes peeled for any movement. And yes! There. She saw bodies scrambling to take cover under the carcasses of their vehicles, as a cascade of projectiles erupted from the drones in the air. A responding volley of gunfire sounded, telling Carol the soldiers weren't beaten yet.

But this clearly was not a battle in progress. The trucks had been decimated. Men were hiding, using small arms rather than the heavy mounted weapons on the vehicles. There were fewer drones than Carol had anticipated—fewer than she'd tangled with at either the soccer field or DigiTech HQ.

And Moonstone was nowhere to be seen.

Carol's fists clenched and she loosed an infuriated scream into the air. She was too late. Whatever Moonstone had come for, she probably had it in her possession now, and whether she did or not, she'd escaped. That would have to be a problem for later. There were hostiles in the air and soldiers in need of rescue.

She barked a command for Tony and Mara to alert a military contact.

"DAMMIT!" TONY tossed a power bar into a trash bin. It landed with an unpleasant and unexpectedly heavy clunk.

Mara understood the frustration. "I know," she said. "If I look at one more indecipherable sequence, I might scream."

Tony raised one eyebrow. "Not the code. That!" He indicated the bar he'd chucked into the trash. "Whatever that was supposed to be, it wasn't *food*. Trust Danvers to stock power bars and protein powder. Who can survive on this?"

"Hey, be glad it wasn't MREs," Jess said from the couch. She broke off a bite of cookie-dough-flavored power bar for Gerry, who was the only one of them not ready to launch Carol's collection of survival rations into the sun. He gummed the piece Jess had given him, then grabbed the rest from her hand and shoved it into his mouth whole.

"I wouldn't put it past her," Tony muttered darkly. "If we're stuck down here another couple days, I bet she'll turn up with a pallet load from her pals over at the Air Force."

Tension had escalated since they'd alerted their military contacts of the convoy attack. Tony's exasperation at being stuck behind a screen had him rumbling like a volcano threatening to

174

blow. Mara worried he was minutes away from suiting up and joining Carol in the field, and she was certain she wouldn't be able to stop him. She couldn't really blame him, either. They'd made too little progress on a solution. The code for an operating system as structurally complex as BOS-MA contained tens of millions of lines. Even with AI help, they still hadn't identified the delivery mechanism that granted access to the back door—the key. They knew they were looking for a particular sequence of data, but none of their scans had found quite the right sequence. Nor had they made headway on a repair and or how to implement that. And now Carol was battling another tech swarm and Moonstone had apparently stolen something and gotten away.

Mara wasn't great with sports analogies, but she was pretty sure the phrase "batting zero" applied to their current situation.

She stepped away from the screens, needing a rest not only for her eyes, but also for her brain. There weren't many places to hide in Carol's cavern; it was more a warehouse for Captain Marvel gear than a home. And it was too full of people. The only privacy to be found was the restroom, which was currently occupied by Lindsay, who'd declared she couldn't go another minute without a shower.

With nowhere else to go, Mara joined Jess in the cozy area, where there was, at least, the illusion of comfort. Around them, Gerry crawled through an elaborate fort-slash-maze that Lindsay had constructed out of emptied boxes. Inspired use of the materials at hand, as long as Carol didn't get too mad about the gear now spread across the cavern. Mara sank into the armchair her mother had sat in earlier, curling into the discarded blanket, sighing long and heavy.

Jess reached over and patted her knee. "That super hero life not all it's cracked up to be?"

"It's more like a take-home comp sci exam than I imagined," Mara admitted. "Lots more hiding in a dank basement, eating crappy food and trying to untangle intricate coding problems. Lots less dropping out of the sky to face-punch villains and single-handedly save Earth."

"Unless you're Carol Danvers, who has never met a problem she didn't want to dash off to face-punch by herself," Jess said, rolling her eyes. She glanced at her son, who was currently diving around in his fort, battling some imaginary foe and periodically sending out small electric zaps that would catch the edge of one of the cardboard boxes. Jess had her heavy-soled boots at the ready to stamp out the sparks. It looked like better cardio than an aerobics class. She smiled indulgently at her son's acrobatics. "I guess that is what every kid dreams of, though. The heroics of Captain Marvel."

"Not me."

"No?"

"I know how that sounds. Mara Melamed, too good for everyone else's cliche dreams," she said, adopting a judgmental tone that she'd no doubt heard more than once in her life. "But I don't mean it that way. I didn't want to fly into battle, because I grew up in my grandfather's lab. Making machines do amazing things with code *was* the super hero stuff in my childhood. And all I ever wanted was to do what he did. Not—" she gestured toward Carol's and Tony's impressive warrior suits stored in their display cases "—that. No offense."

"None taken." Jess smiled, jumping up to stomp on another spark. Gerry didn't pack a big enough punch to do serious damage, but Mara could see how quickly it could get out of hand. "Your grandfather is your hero, huh?"

"Yes, though I'm nothing like him," Mara sighed. She looked furtively at her mother, whose head was bent over a screen, eyes fixated on the puzzle of the code. "Or her. I've always struggled to keep up. I was born into a family of geniuses, but I'm not on the same level. It's unavoidably evident, now. The BOS-MA problem, it's too much for me. Lucky we grabbed my mom back. Without her, we'd be sunk."

"You're underestimating yourself, Mara. You're the reason we had any kind of heads-up this was happening. If not for you, and your courage in going public, Moonstone would be stealing secrets and using them to manipulate us and no one would have any idea."

"I wish I could figure out how to put a stop to it, but I'm afraid it could take years. We don't know the code well enough."

"Well," Jess said, pretending to die when Gerry popped out and aimed a zap at her. "Who does?"

"Only the creator, and unless we can time-travel—oh." Mara sat up, fighting to free her limbs from the blanket. Her eyes glazed over. "*Oh*."

Jess grinned. "You figured it out."

"No. I mean, maybe. I mean, I have an idea. But it's kind of harebrained."

Jess yanked the blanket off and tossed it on the floor. "Let's go tell Tony."

"What? No! No way. It's ridiculous."

"Who cares? No such thing as a bad idea when everyone else is all out of them! Share with the group and we'll figure it out together."

Mara looked frantically at Tony, who was munching on another power bar with a grumpy expression on his face, apparently having decided hunger outweighed the horror of the bone-dry bar. "You've clearly never had class with him. He dismisses most ideas as banal and unoriginal and the rest as silly. You've never been on the wrong end of his withering stare when a student pitches a concept he finds boring!"

Mara hadn't been on the receiving end of that stare too often, mostly because she rarely volunteered in class, preferring instead to rely on her written work. But she'd seen it turned on others and the memory of the secondhand embarrassment she'd suffered in those moments was enough to send a fiery flush to her face.

"I promise you can handle a withering stare, Mara Melamed." Jess grabbed her hand and began to drag her toward the command center. Mara resisted, tugging back, trying to stand her ground. Futile, really, trying to withstand Spider-Woman's might. Jess didn't even need to apply much of her super-strength to get Mara stumbling forward. She called, loudly, "Mara has an idea!"

For a dreadful, tension-filled moment, as Tony and Iris lifted their heads, Mara was sure they were both going to roll their eyes. But they didn't. They waited, looking nothing more than expectant. Her pulse throbbed in her throat. She gnawed on her lip, trying to figure out how to make her idea sound less outrageous.

"We were talking about who might know BOS-MA well enough to find the vulnerability," Jess prompted. "You said only the creator would."

"Your grandfather?" Tony said. "I'm afraid he's out of reach."

"Maybe not. What if there was a way we could hear from him directly?"

"Wait, are you telling me you actually did mean time travel?" Jess exclaimed, throwing up her hands.

"Not like you're thinking," Mara said quickly, before Tony's forehead muscles could pull down into his annoyed expression. "What about virtual time travel? As in, looking at his old files."

Tony grabbed a laptop and pulled it toward him. "Yes! Brilliant. What's his preferred cloud storage? I assume you have the login—"

"He never got around to digitizing his old work." She shook her head. "He always said he meant to, but he never wanted to dwell in the past. He wanted to focus on what was next. I guess now we know—"

"Mara," Jess said, pulling her out of the memory vortex into which she'd fallen. "If they're not digitally stored, how were you planning to access his old files?"

"Oh. Right. Well, Empire State barred my grandfather from his lab when he was forced to retire. After he died, I was supposed to go clean it out, but I never did. I don't think they would have thrown away his things without giving me a chance to claim them. Maybe we could find some of his writings or something, his papers. It would be almost as good as talking to him—"

Stark jumped from his chair before she finished the sentence, yanking Mara toward the exit to the lair.

AT THE site of the convoy attack, Carol's mind raced through decision points, as it always did. The soldiers needed help to eliminate the remaining drone threat. At her preferred elevation, she'd been another unidentified flyer in the sky. So she'd dropped low, taking fire from both the drones and the soldiers, until she got close enough to identify herself to the senior commander on the scene. When he recognized her, she hollered out a warning about how the drones operated, letting him know they'd have to ground every single one. The commander agreed to leave the flying objects to her while his crew worked on evacuating the wounded.

Carol knew neutralizing the drones without further harming the convoy survivors would take a lot out of her. She hadn't fully recovered from her two prior skirmishes with the swarm. With a groan, she thought of the system she and Jenn had worked out. It had been an energy saver, luring bots to their doom en masse rather than relying on her strength to plant them in the ground one by one. But bringing Jenn back here would put her friend's life at risk. The memory of the injuries Jenn had suffered, of the damage her Hazmat suit had not be able to prevent, sent a shudder through Carol. One night of healing wouldn't be enough to set her friend right. Of course Jenn couldn't be brought back into combat wounded.

Was it the Kree in her that would even consider such a thing? Kree were born to war. Her mother had sacrificed everything for her mission. Maybe that was the part of Carol that would imagine for one second putting a friend in a battle she wasn't equipped to survive.

And yet, it explained why being a warrior was the anchor stone of her identity. She hadn't developed it. She'd been born to it.

But if her crew knew this was how her mind worked, what would they think? Would they continue to trust her to lead them into battle? The question opened a black hole in her chest that she didn't feel equipped to fight. Not with Moonstone on the loose and drones in the sky and soldiers in danger. Carol breathed out roughly and pushed the thoughts to the back of her mind. She didn't have to give in to whatever instincts pushed her toward endangering her crew. She wouldn't. She'd handle this the hard way.

She zipped through the air, headfirst into the nearest bot, and began the process of tunneling every remaining threat into the ground, absorbing endless projectile fire to get close enough to nab them, one by one by one, dragging them down and smashing them, out of harm's way of the soldiers. Thank Hala there weren't many left. Had Moonstone not needed an overwhelming force or had she taken some of the swarm with her when she departed?

After she'd culled the last one from the sky, Carol sagged, resting on one knee to catch her breath and survey the scene. A flurry of activity surrounded her. Soldiers were attending to their wounded and communicating with their superiors and salvaging gear. This was not the part that suited her best. The aftermath. Her specialty, like her ancestors, was destruction, not rebuilding.

Her eyes skimmed over the chaos and came to rest on the two trucks lying savaged by the side of the road. They were covered in some sort of tech tiles, half of which appeared to have absorbed the color and texture of the shoulder of the road, while the remainder were a mottled gray-black that resembled the asphalt. One of the tiles that had been torn from the truck lay on the ground nearby, and she picked it up, finding it surprisingly pliable. As soon as it touched her knee, the tile grabbed on, stiffening into a tough outer shell. It also flawlessly absorbed the royal blue of her suit. Huh. A neat bit of camouflage. Not to mention insta-armor capabilities that were almost slick enough to be a Tony Stark invention. She touched the newly formed plate on her knee and it softened enough for her to pry it loose. Could this be what Moonstone sought? The trucks had been covered with them, as far as Carol could tell, though most now appeared to be strewn across the ground. Two of the trucks had been torn nearly apart. Moonstone wouldn't have needed to do that to get the tiles. You didn't destroy the box if the wrapping paper was all you were after.

Carole pushed to her feet as the senior officer on scene approached. "I'm sorry about your unit, Commander. Sorry I couldn't get here sooner."

"We'd all have been goners if you hadn't arrived when you did." The man assessed their surroundings, then pulled off his helmet and mopped his brow with a sleeve. "You know the funny thing? For a moment, I thought you were the one attacking us."

Rage set Carol's blood to boiling. She wriggled her fingers and breathed deep, trying to dispel the burst of energy that threatened to explode out of her. Evil doppelgangers were a real inconvenience. "Nah. You'd never catch me flying around in a cloak." He smiled faintly. "Your cargo?"

"Gone." He pointed at the only truck still upright. With the engine facing her, she couldn't get a good look at the rear compartment, but she could see a door at the back hanging nearly off its hinges.

She hissed. She'd suspected from the moment she realized Moonstone had fled that the villain had gotten what she came for, but hearing it confirmed was a blow. And a reminder that she still didn't know what *it* was. "What were you transporting?"

He shook his head. "I don't know, ma'am. Above my pay grade."

Hala help them. Those drones were plenty deadly. If Moonstone had been willing to expose herself to attack a military convoy, she had to have a mighty good reason. The only motive that would justify this kind of gamble was another weapon. A more powerful one. Which was a terrifying thought.

Carol drew near the damaged truck. The rear storage had been torn open, hexagonal tiles littering the ground around the metal carcass like confetti. The space left behind was empty and there was no hint of what might have been contained inside.

Dammit. Moonstone was still two moves ahead of her.

She needed to give a situation report to her crew. She needed an update on the code research. She needed to rest and recharge. But she wouldn't leave until she was certain she could help no further. "Is there anything else I can do here, Commander?"

"No, ma'am."

Carol nodded and rose into the air, calling upon her deepest reserves of strength, and swept the field one last time, to ensure there were no remaining drones. A trail of sparks caught her attention, pulling her in the direction of the wreckage of a helo. Unlike the overturned trucks, no activity teemed there. Likely the pilot and crew were KIA, given the extent of the crash damage. Still. Someone should put eyes on. Carol lifted off the ground, heading toward the ravaged metal shell that held the cockpit. Two sat inside, the pilot too broken and battered to have survived. A full bird colonel sat beside the pilot, unconscious, bleeding from a head wound. Carol reached through the broken plexiglass and set two fingers on his neck, beneath the collar of his uniform. She definitely detected a pulse.

Carol tore the side off the helo, then went after the belt holding him in place. It didn't take much of her strength to rip it from the latch. She gathered the man in her arms, glancing quickly at the name badge on his uniform. "Come on. Let's get you to the hospital, Colonel Finke."

Delirious, he grabbed at her face, turning her chin toward him. "It's too late. It—it has Faustus."

The colonel passed out before he could say more.

18

MARA SHOVED her hands deep into the pockets of her yellow parka and surveyed the familiar downtown campus of Empire State University. Throughout her undergrad, masters and PhD programs, she'd lived in dorms and apartments and sublets around here, though nothing ever felt like home more than this quad.

Was this place still her home? She hadn't technically dropped out, despite the pressure her department put on her to leave when she started making noise about DigiTech. But she also hadn't completed her thesis, hadn't been back here in person in months. If not for Tony putting her in his sportscar and speeding them through the streets of the city, she might never have come back.

Mara had avoided acknowledging the reasons for that, but standing there, staring at the dry fountain and the cafe tables outside the bookstore, a tidal wave of feelings rushed through her. She couldn't dodge them this time. Couldn't turn her face away from the sadness that swamped her after her grandfather died, the anxiety that mounted when her mother disappeared, the intimidation—no, the *fear* that swelled when her department leaders strongarmed and threatened her.

On the morning Tony and Carol met her in the donut shop, she'd been arguing by email with the administration, which was pressing her to TA a small in-person seminar group. Even though remote study was part of the curriculum. And she just—couldn't do it. Couldn't make herself show up to mentor fresh-faced undergrads who still believed this place was a meritocracy. It wasn't for her anymore. It was haunted. She'd been on the verge of telling the admins to go to hell, refusing to teach even though it would disqualify her from the program, making her the first Melamed not to be granted a PhD from Empire State.

She pushed away the dismal thought that that might still become her reality and stared at the blue banners marking each building and the school of study to which it belonged. Maybe not becoming the next Dr. Melamed wasn't the worst thing, considering the legacy of the current Drs Melamed. Her family's now-tarnished reputation cast a shadow over the hope and promise she used to see on this quad. A shadow she was afraid left her in permanent darkness.

But she could definitely not say any of that aloud to Tony Stark. "Looks just like it always did."

He glanced at her from the corner of his eye. "Did you expect something else?"

Mara shrugged. A pair of students wearing heavy jackets and backpacks trudged past, using the courtyard as a shortcut from the north to the south side of the campus. One tromped directly through a gray slush pile, splashing Mara's shins with yesterday's snow. The fountain-side bench where Mara ate lunch in nice weather sported the gloss of wet metal.

"God. All these people are probably carrying around devices running BOS-MA. They're all being *surveilled*. Their information collected by someone who's going to use it against them. And they don't know. If they did, would they be walking to class and buying books and—and throwing a Frisbee like it's a normal day?"

Tony followed her gaze toward the incongruous sight of ten students in rain boots and beanies sloshing through half-melted snow and chasing after a neon pink disk branded with the Empire State mascot. He sniffed pointedly. "Spare me the oblivion of normality."

Mara rolled her eyes. Easy to say when you were Tony Stark, when you had a sandboxed computer system that insulated you from Moonstone's diabolical reach, and a super-powered suit that could fly you out of danger, and a crew of super hero friends you could call on to help you save the world, and... and an all access faculty parking pass. Tony might mistake normalcy for dullness. But not Mara. She hadn't been lying to Jess. Her dream had not been to live Tony's life or Carol's or Jess's. Or Gerry's, for that matter. She never played super-kid when she was growing up. She was happy to leave that to Captain Marvel and co. She'd only ever wanted to sit in a quiet basement office and write marvelous code, like her grandfather.

"You know what I mean."

Tony said nothing, his silence frustratingly noncommittal. They'd verbally sparred most of the night, while they, along with Iris, tried to figured out how to patch the back door access to BOS-MA. Mara held firm that they should go public. Tony still felt exposure created a greater danger. He'd seemed grudgingly impressed when he pointed out that she'd said more in a few hours than she had for the entirety of the semester she was his student, but he hadn't backed down. She argued hard, with Carol's voice resonating in her head, reminding her to trust her gut, but she hadn't persuaded him she was right. And maybe she wasn't. Who was she to think she knew more than Iron Man about this saving humanity stuff?

"Where's the professor's office? CompSci?" he asked, gesturing at a tall, shimmering tower that loomed over the east corner of the quad.

The building, newly built and financed by those alumni donations her advisor and the department head had been so worried about, sat a block off the quad but still dominated the landscape, towering over the old original campus. Mara had spent plenty of time over there, and she knew the building well. The lower levels were kitted out with the finest experimental equipment tech boom money could buy, the middle floors with fully wired lecture halls and seminar rooms, the top floors with professor offices with the best views on campus. That building was the envy of every department in the university, especially those still housed in the century-old brick-and-ivy structures on the quad.

"You'd think," she said. Tony's guess was a reasonable one. The new building housed almost all of Empire State's renowned computer science department. The few holdouts that hadn't moved their offices were the professors emeriti, the ones who should have moved on decades earlier, but were too brilliant and famous to retire or fire, the ones whose names still meant something in the world of research and whose legacy still attracted bright young students to the school.

Professors like her grandfather. Like he'd once been, anyway. When the scandal about his involvement in illegal weapons testing leaked, Empire State distanced itself. Loudly. Publicly. In formal written statements drafted by crisis PR teams and reviewed by the university legal department. And now she knew worse truths about Shelley Melamed, knew that his crimes weren't limited to one event, half a century before. She grabbed the zipper of her coat and pulled it all the way up to her chin. Would they take his name off the website entirely once they learned he'd intentionally built an error into perfectly good code that was then used by an actual super villain to achieve world domination?

"His office is in the old science building," she said, realizing she'd disappeared inside her own mind too long. Her professors had always told her she needed to be more responsive to questions. Not Tony. He actually never minded waiting while she worked out thesis-length answers in her head before saying a word aloud, never penalized her for needing time to think through the work.

"They couldn't give him an upgrade when they built all that?" Tony squinted into the sun bouncing off the glowing windows of new building.

"He didn't want it. He liked his old lab," she said. "Even if he did short out the power now and again with all his gear."

Tony smiled, and she responded in kind. But it faded quickly, as they trudged through the quad, cutting across the spoke-and-wheel sidewalks leading to the dry fountain, and she caught sight of the name etched into the building. It was named after a general. "In the early years, comp sci was a subdiscipline of the sciences, which got a lot of DoD funding. By the time it wasn't, my grandfather was too embedded in all the research to walk away."

"Don't judge him too harshly," Tony said, patting her shoulder. "The things that came out of his lab were extraordinary. He couldn't predict how they were going to be used."

She pressed her lips together, holding back the reply: *He should have.*

The pair turned toward the entrance to the science building, which was one of the oldest on campus, a stereotype of old northern colleges, with red bricks and ivy and ornamental cresting along the roof. The sight of it set an ember aglow in her chest. She'd grown up in these halls, even before she matriculated. Her grandfather would pick her up from the local elementary school, buy her a croissant and a hot chocolate from the cart by the fountain, then hold her hand while they took the stairs down to the basement, where his lab was located. Every office door they passed had opened upon the friendly and familiar faces of the department faculty. In the early days, her grandfather and his colleagues were forging the computer science field from nothing. Those leading minds, those cutting-edge thinkers, had been the Melameds' chosen family. They kept Mara company when her grandfather had meetings, helped her with math homework, and listened to her pontificate about the code she'd someday write.

She was glad, suddenly, that her grandfather never wanted a newer, fancier office in the anonymous tower up the street. Even though the basement offices were all empty now, their inhabitants moved on or passed on, this place felt comfortable and familiar. The warmth of those memories flooded her, imbuing her with a confidence she hadn't felt before they arrived. This place *was* home. She shouldn't have stayed away so long.

Mara stopped outside the door to her grandfather's old lab.

"The lab isn't technically his anymore," she said. "And it's no longer a lab. He kept it for years as a professor emeritus after he retired from teaching and research. And then, after everything happened, the university locked it up. Converted it into storage, along with the rest of the offices down here. It's been kind of abandoned down for a while. Everyone wants an office with a view these days—without rats and mold and faulty heating."

"Am I going to have to shoot out this lock?" Tony asked, glowering at the door handle. "The administration would probably frown on an adjunct professor blowing up things on campus."

"Not if they didn't change the locks." She held up a little silver key, a spare her grandfather had cut for her when she started her PhD. It'd been done without permission from the facilities department, of course. She had an office over in the new building that she shared with another grad student, but her grandfather had winked and given her the contraband key nonetheless. *My best thinking happened down here*, he'd said. *Yours will too.*

A bubble of hope inflated inside her. This whole thing was a puzzle of her grandfather's design. The answers would be here, where he was. Of course they would. Mara caught her breath and wiggled the key into the lock. Possibly she was wrong and they had since repurposed this room. Maybe someone had decided they were willing to put up with a space that was drafty and musty, poorly ventilated and inadequately heated, and didn't have enough power outlets, if only to claim a corner of campus as their own. Or maybe the university had fully and finally given up on the Melameds, thrown away her grandfather's things, barred them from this place forever.

Her throat swelled at the thought, leaving her unable to breathe properly.

When the lock clicked, she wiped sweat from her brow and threw open the creaky old door with a flourish and a relieved grin.

"So," Tony said, ushering himself into the room. "This is where it all happened."

Mara glanced at him as she flicked on the fluorescent lights. Tony Stark wasn't prone to wide-eyed wonder and she wouldn't say that was what she saw on his face right then either. But he certainly looked a little impressed. Guess you couldn't call yourself a true tech fan without being slightly in awe in this lab. Not her, of course. He'd been Grandpa before she ever realized he was *the* Professor Shelley Melamed. But she'd seen this look on others' faces on the rare occasions she brought people to "her" office, the look that made clear they were at a monument to a legend.

"Actually, most of his early work was done at an apartment in Brooklyn, where he and my grandmother lived when they were newly married."

"But BOS-MA happened here." Tony swiped a hand over one of the long tables. A cloud of dust billowed into the air.

Mara sneezed. Had no one been in here since her grandfather died? The layers of undisturbed dust suggested not. It was as if the world had erased him from their memories, to pretend he no longer—perhaps never—existed.

The lab was one large room, much bigger than the new offices at the top of the glass tower, but run down. It had once held an eclectic mix of computing equipment cobbled together by her grandfather and his researchers as the field advanced. All that remained were a few bare tables, a hodgepodge of dinosaur machines on shelves her grandfather referred to as his museum, and his office area in the back corner. Mara's fears were partially realized; it appeared that any modern equipment, anything that might still be useful, had been hauled away by the university, and the room was being used for storage. Large, sealed cardboard boxes which had not been there when Mara last visited dotted the room, stacked against walls and on tables.

"Yes. He started working on operating systems when the university got a grant from the military. They wanted weapons research, and he managed to allocate a few thousand dollars to spend on computing systems that would benefit weapons. I guess that's how the military justified it. Sixty years ago, no one knew how big computers would become. How important they'd be in our lives."

"He knew."

Mara bit down hard on her tongue. If she believed her grandfather was a visionary, she'd have to accept he built a system with a vulnerability, knowing it would one day hurt people. She wrapped her arms around herself and tucked her chin into her collar. If people were trying to forget him, maybe they should. He'd made unforgiveable choices.

"I know code doesn't lie. That the vulnerability was there from the start. But what my mother said about why he did it? That's hard to swallow. He wasn't arrogant. He cared about people. I don't want to believe he'd knowingly put them at risk. My feelings, my memories of him, are hard to reconcile with the video evidence that he condoned war crimes."

"People are puzzles, but the pieces don't always fit together neatly." Tony leaned against the dusty table, watching her with narrowed eyes. Mara supposed he understood her turmoil better than most, given his own family history.

"Anyway," she brushed a hint of a tear from the corner of her eye and gestured at the boxes filling the room. "Here's our time machine."

Tony's mouth turned down in dismay. "We may need reinforcements. Searching all this will take time we don't have."

She frowned. There was quite a lot. Her grandfather always had assorted junk around, but mostly devices and machines and excess wires. Reaching into a box by the door, she discovered a stack of books and pulled out a tattered volume about the history of seventeenth-century Dutch merchants that her grandfather surely would not have owned. She held it up for Tony to see. "I don't think all of this belong to him," she said, checking another box. More books on topics Shelley Melamed had never expressed interest in, all in poor condition. Mara pointed toward her grandfather's old desk. "We should start there."

They made their way to the back of the room, opening boxes along the way to see if anything looked familiar to Mara. Those at the front of the room all contained random storage items, a convenient dumping ground for items the university didn't want to throw away, but that no one seemed to need since they were here, disorganized and neglected.

The corner by the desk was her grandfather's domain and it remained mostly intact. He had come here every day, before the scandal broke, and worked at this desk, holding court with grad students, though their number had grown fewer over the years. In his last year, only a dedicated few with an appreciation for computer science history bothered to seek him out in his little hidey hole.

Tony set a hand on his hip, and with the other gestured toward a dinosaur of a desktop computer, with a heavy rear projection monitor and an internal floppy disk drive. "Do not tell me that Professor Shelley Melamed worked on that fossil."

"Not recently," she smiled. From the bottom of a handmade ceramic pen holder—her childhood handiwork—Mara extracted a miniature key ring with two tiny keys, one silver and one brass, and fitted it into a locked desk drawer, from which she pulled a more modern laptop, albeit one that was already old given how computers age absurdly fast. Only middle-aged at her grandfather's death, but archaic now. "This was the machine he was using when he passed."

The piles of random flotsam and jetsam, the things that clearly were not her grandfather's, made Mara's mouth go dry. It had been foolish to leave his belongings. Mara realized the university could have discarded them at any time, repurposed the space for something other than storage. Especially once she found herself at odds with the administration. But she never imagined she'd need these remnants of his past for anything other than nostalgia. A lack of foresight. Mara pinched the bridge of her nose, displacing her glasses, and tried to ward off yet more tears. She was good at spotting patterns of things that had already happened, but not predicting results. A common critique of her work, she thought, wryly, readjusting her glasses, plugging in the machine and powering it on.

"Is it running BOS-MA?"

Tony's voice sounded too close. Startled, she glanced up to see him perched on the edge of the desk. She'd been so deep in her recollections she hadn't noticed his approach. *Yikes.* She got like this when she was working. Like her grandfather. And her mother, from what she was told. The world ceased when the lines of code started to flow. And memories, she supposed. She shrugged and rolled her neck, trying to physically shake loose of the trance that had threatened to consume her since she stepped on campus.

She couldn't afford to lose focus. This was a mission, not a research project. If this machine was running BOS-MA, it wasn't safe to use. Moonstone would see what they were doing like she had a crystal ball. Mara tapped the keyboard, bringing the screen to life, and realized her grandfather hadn't bothered with password protection. She frowned. He'd never respected security as much as he should. What was that old expression he'd used whenever she caught him taking shortcuts like this? *The cobbler's children go barefoot?* Something like that.

She checked the machine and expelled a relieved sigh. "Not BOS-MA. An old Linux system."

"Good." Tony swiveled the screen so he could see it better. Together, they began to poke through files on the laptop. Tony clicked on directory after directory, fingers flying through commands. "He stored a lot on his desktop. You're sure he didn't use a cloud storage system of any kind?"

"Like I said, only for more recent things. He never bothered to transfer old files. Too much time, too little value, or so he said."

"Maybe it wasn't about inconvenience. Sounds more like old-fashioned reluctance to let his work out of his control," Tony mused.

"Researcher paranoia?" she said, hopefully. "Like, because the fix we need is here and he didn't want anyone to be able to access it?" *Anyone else*, she thought. Because if he had created both the problem and the fix and hid them here, she couldn't deny he meant to be able to use it himself.

But a few hours' worth of exploring files turned up nothing about a vulnerability or a patch. Tony, unable to remain still, ping-ponged around the lab, picking over the detritus on the shelves, opening boxes, shuffling through miscellaneous papers in the professor's desk drawers. In the end, he even turned on the ancient desktop machine and inserted a few of the floppy disks they found in a box under the desk. Lots of code, lots of theory, nothing that resembled BOS-MA. Mara leaned back in the broken chair she'd pulled behind the desk and massaged the small of her back.

"He didn't have a patch ready." He'd made this dangerous thing and he hadn't had a fix. What had he meant to do with it? Was her mother right? Was it all arrogance? Control? To prove he could? All his preaching about ethical development had been *do as I say, not as I do*. The stress headache that had waxed and waned since the night before bloomed in her skull again, making her snappish. "Tony, we have to talk about disclosing vulnerability to the public."

"We've been over that, kid. We have a bigger obligation not to make people more vulnerable."

Carol had said as much, too. They'd been saving the universe a lot longer than she had. Maybe they were right. But it felt wrong. She turned her face toward the screen to hide her irritation, clicking on a folder labeled PERSONAL. They'd searched it already, but found nothing relevant to BOS-MA. Just deeds and estate paperwork. The family lawyer had had copies of those. Idly, she clicked on a file titled Receipts and found an insurance bill. Actually, there were several of them, remnants from some treatments he'd undergone.

"Tony, look." She angled the screen toward him.

"Psychiatric services not covered by the insurance... out of network... participation in experimental program," he read from the image she'd pulled up. "No reference to Ravencroft."

"Look at the date." Mara tapped the insurance bill. "This was *after* BOS-MA came out in the government information release."

"And before Griselda Seales emerged from the ethernet. Who's the primary treating psychiatrist?" His gaze flicked back and forth over the notes. "Not Sofen. B.O.S.S., I'm sending you a name. Find me everything you can about him."

They waited briefly while a series of articles was delivered to Tony's tablet. "Sadly not sorted by relevance. Maybe I should have made this AI a little less narrow—oh, wait. This looks promising. An article in the *Journal of Psychiatric Experimentation* about a research program the author briefly led regarding treatment of stress disorders. I'm sending this to Jess to look at too."

Almost instantly, his phone rang. "Of course these people used an experimental program for veterans as a publication opportunity," Jess sneered down the line. "I guess it was too much to expect Fisk and his cronies to have any medical ethics at all."

Tony scrolled through a long, dense scientific article. "Patients participated voluntarily, methodology designed for treatment of psychopathy combined with injection of mild sedatives blah blah blah—and what do ya know. He credited his additional researchers on the study—magnanimous of him—including one K. Sofen, who observed and performed analysis. Well, Mara, there's our confirmation your grandfather and Moonstone both participated in the Ravencroft program."

"But we can't confirm she actually came into contact with Professor Melamed," Jess said. "This doesn't sound like she was actively treating patients."

Tony flopped into another chair, this one even more badly broken, wheels on two of the legs missing. After nearly falling over, he stood with an affronted huff and paced around to the other side of the desk. "B.O.S.S., find us records for Dr. Karla Sofen. Specifically, convictions involving her patients."

"Here are several records matching that description," the tinny robot voice responded as Tony's tablet screen filled with results.

"Oooh, read the one involving Lloyd Bloch," Jess said.

Mara leaned close to skim over Tony's shoulder while the text-to-voice feature read in a monotone: "Lloyd Bloch, former agent of the Secret Empire. Original codename: Moonstone."

"Wait," she said, looking up. "He's Moonstone?"

"The codename Moonstone is currently associated with Dr. Karla Sofen," the AI said.

"I'm confused. There's more than one?"

"Kid," Tony laughed, "if I had a nickel for every time someone ripped off an identity—"

"You'd have four hundred thirty-seven dollars and fifteen cents, sir?"

"Really?" Mara frowned at Tony's device. "How did he—"

"Don't get him started. We'll never get out of the calculation loop. Back to the article, B.O.S.S."

The computer resumed its recitation. "While in hypnosis treatment with Dr. Karla Sofen, Bloch became convinced the Kree gravity stone he possessed had turned him into a monster. The resulting trauma caused his body to reject the stone, the essence of which was then absorbed by Sofen, along with the Moonstone body armor. The stone's energy permeates Sofen's nervous system, granting her enhanced abilities."

"Like Carol?"

Tony hesitated, then shook his head. But Mara noticed he sounded fractionally less sure of himself than usual. "Not exactly. Carol is Kree."

"And Moonstone was created by them? I don't get the difference."

"I'm not the philosophical type," Tony said. "And Carol's not either. That distinction isn't a problem she can punch, so I doubt she's put much thought into it. Besides, that's not the point."

"What is?"

"Sofen manipulated a patient into revealing information about his powers and then used it to steal them from him." Tony fisted his hands and planted them on the desk. His dark eyes glimmered. "Sound familiar?"

"She's listed as an observer in the article, but if she had access to patients at all, if she had access to my grandfather, she could have manipulated him into telling her his secrets, just like she did with Bloch. And his biggest secret was BOS-MA's back door." Mara's brain whirled as the pattern fell into place. Moonstone had done this before, extracted information from patients and then preyed upon them. A torrent of questions flooded her, but one bubbled to the fore more urgently than the rest. "Oh God. Professor Stark. Tony. Did she kill Bloch after she—"

It was Jess who answered. "Yes."

"My grandfather! That article mentioned sedatives—do you think that's how she murdered him? And my mother! She had my mother captive for months. Who knows how she was manipulating her, what she twisted her into revealing. And probably those two shareholders. And all the soldiers at the convoy. She's hurt so many people. We have to find her. We have to stop her!"

Hearing the panic in her voice, Tony bid goodbye to Jess and rested a hip on the desk beside Mara. He set a hand on her shoulder. He looked her straight in the eye, solid and measured. "We will. Carol is out searching for her now. She's the best one for the job."

Mara knocked his hand away and clutched the arms of her seat, trying to hold back the tension winding her tighter and tighter. "You—you didn't want to leave it to her. You wanted to be out there, too!"

"If you tell her I admitted this, I'll invent a time machine, go back in time, and undo this confession," Tony said, his mouth puckered. "But she was right. We have to focus on *our* job. We're needed here."

"Doing what? What are we even doing?"

"We confirmed our theory about Sofen's connection to your grandfather. We found useful information among your grandfather's things. There'll be more. " He nudged the box of floppy disks beneath the desk with the toe of his boot, rattling the contents. "We'll open every single one of these ancient artifacts, if we have to."

An involuntary giggle burst from her. She covered her mouth and swallowed the vaguely hysterical laugh that threatened to follow, but the pressure building in her chest eased a fraction. All vestiges of the momentary uncertainty when he'd spoken of Carol's heritage were gone. He spoke as if their success were a foregone conclusion, despite all evidence to the contrary. And heaven help her, his confidence was infectious.

Tony smiled gently. "Did your grandfather keep a diary or a journal or anything like that?"

Mara took a breath. As her panic receded, a memory swam to the surface. She glanced at the opposite corner, which was two-thirds hidden behind a haphazard stack of boxes and other junk. Scrubbing her sleeve across her face, she set to shifting the boxes out of the way, carving a body-sized tunnel between them and a broken metal cabinet that listed severely. Mara edged in behind the cabinet and found the remains of an old-school photo studio setup. There was a battered stool, a plain blue photo backdrop, a chalkboard. The tripod and video camera were gone, but they'd sat just there, in a spot that now housed, rather inexplicably, a stack of boxes spilling over with Styrofoam cups. Tony grunted as he attempted and failed to squeeze through the gap Mara had created, then resorted to craning his neck around the cabinet.

At the sight of the dismantled photo studio, he smoothed his goatee, giving her a perplexed look.

"He loved cameras. He bought every new model that came out, and when he wasn't messing around on a computer, he was messing around with the latest home video equipment." She waved at the setup and then at the museum shelves, where indeed there were the remains of outdated home video equipment. "He'd film himself solving complex problems and lend the tapes to his students who were struggling. He was an advocate for video learning before it became popular, I guess."

"Video logs? We did time-travel." Tony clapped sharply. "If I were an archaic media storage device like non-digital film, where would I hide in here?"

They scanned the lab, staring in horror at the heaps of boxes. It could take days to go through all of them. Mara wracked her brain, trying to think where her grandfather might have stored recordings. By the time she'd been old enough to visit him, he was no longer using VHS. Had he given the tapes to the library so many students could check them out? She should ask the university library. Maybe there was an archivist. Mara felt in her pockets, then dug in her backpack, realizing with a pang that she'd left her phone at Carol's lair.

"Tony, can I borrow your cell? Mine is—"

He tossed her an old model flip phone, with no internet access. Of course. He wouldn't want to be on a device running on BOS-MA. She pulled an old university directory book from a drawer of the desk, dialed the number listed for the library, and got an automated message informing her the number was no longer in service. She flinched, checking the year the book was issued. Decades out of date. Ugh. She expended a few minutes trying the numbers of the smaller, subject-matter-specific libraries, before finally achieving a connection with the main campus number, which apparently hadn't changed in a couple generations. Thank God! Once they'd connected her to the library and the front desk had connected her to the research librarian, she posed her inquiry.

"I'm searching for some videos made by a computer science professor. I think maybe he left them with the library, so his students could check them out."

"Lecture recordings? Those can all be found on the EmpireView intranet, if you log into your university account," the woman said. "But your lecturer has to have agreed to have his class recorded. Under what name should I search?"

Mara hesitated. Her grandfather was persona non grata around here. She didn't want to use his name until she had to. For all she knew, she'd be reminding them they had his belongings and that would prompt them to destroy the videos. She definitely didn't want to call attention to the little basement treasure trove they still needed time to search. "Um, these probably would have been made before the university wired lecture halls with recording equipment. In fact, I don't think they would be digital at all. They might be on VHS?"

A peal of laughter erupted across the phone line. "VHS? Oh, my goodness. We wouldn't even have the equipment to watch those anymore. If we ever had such a thing, they'd have been culled years ago. You don't need a library; you need a museum!"

With a sigh, and the librarian's slightly insulting over-the-top hilarity ringing in her ears, Mara snapped the flip phone closed and gave Tony a disappointed shrug.

Together, they turned back to the storage boxes, ransacking them but turning up nothing. Wasting time they didn't have. Mara's limbs began to feel trembly. Sweat pooled under her arms. She knew this sensation, knew that stress was pumping an excess of adrenaline through her. She got this way during exams, when time began to run short, when she couldn't work out a problem. She knew what would happen next. Her hands would develop tremors that would make it hard to manage typing. Her knees would begin to shake. If she was sitting, they'd bounce uncontrollably. If she was standing, she'd stumble, sometimes fall. Mara balled her fingers into tight fists to hide the shuddering from Tony and looked around for a seat. Lying down would be better, but sitting would do. Tony was using one of the broken chairs as a step ladder to reach a shelf near the ceiling. The other was a step too far away. One step mattered, just then. Dizziness would come soon. Mara backed toward her grandfather's desk and plunked onto it.

She inhaled and exhaled, drawing her spine straight and pressing her shoulders back, counting silently. Inhale four, hold two, exhale four. Again. Again. It was hard to concentrate. Something was sticking into the back of her thigh. She swept a hand beneath her leg, brushing aside a tiny little object that clattered softly as it hit the floor.

The key she'd used to unlock her grandfather's desk drawer.

No, wait. Mara's breath caught. The key ring—*with two keys*. One silver and one brass. The silver one opened the drawer. What did the other open?

Mara slipped off the desk, still battling the shakes, and snatched up the ring, examining the keys, comparing the teeth. Definitely not duplicates.

"Tony," she said, praying he couldn't hear the wobble in her voice. He glanced down at her and she held the key ring aloft. "Have you seen another locked drawer or cabinet? Or lockbox?"

"Clever thought. I haven't seen anything that might use a key like that except—"

Tony jumped down from his makeshift ladder and examined the handles of the storage cabinet, which did lock. Silver and too large for that key anyway. He shook his head.

Mara, still crouched behind the desk, double checked the drawers, and then, feeling ridiculous, ran her hands along the undercarriage searching for a possible secret compartment. Nothing. Her muscles quivered too hard to hold her in that position, and her legs went limp, depositing her roughly on the chilly linoleum floor. She leaned back, knocking her head against the desk in frustration, staring at the unremarkable beige ceiling panels which had been here for as long as she could remember. The aluminum grid that held them was battered with age and most of the panels bore brown stains. Mara could vividly picture her grandfather leaning back in his chair, eyes on those panels, wrists crossed and resting on his balding head, as he mentally worked through some complex problem. He'd spent hours that way, thinking.

And plotting? What was behind those tiles? Insulation? Was there space enough to hide something? As Mara's eyes tracked the stains, a pattern jumped out at her. She hadn't ever looked closely, even when her grandfather's grave contemplation of them amused her. But now she saw the water marks didn't match up. Where one should have bled over into its neighbor, the adjacent panel was unblemished. In another spot, in the corner by the narrow, ceiling-height hopper window, a cluster of water stains spread on the far side of the panels—opposite the junction with the window. Away from the place where one imagined a leak might let in water. Of course, there could have been a sprinkler up there or pipes or something else that oozed liquid and stained the tiles. But the spread of the stain seemed—unnatural. It would be easy to miss. Water-stained panels wouldn't seem out of place. And who studied ceiling tiles that closely, other than her grandfather?

Mara rose, fighting off the shakes, and went to stand under the spot that had caught her eye. *X marks the spot?* she wondered, shoving a table into place beneath the stain and climbing atop it. The basement ceiling wasn't high. Stretched onto her toes, she was able to push the tiles aside and thrust a hand into the space beyond. Something scratchy brushed her skin, producing a sharp sting. She gasped and clenched her fist.

"Fiberglass insulation." She started at his voice. Tony had stopped searching the shelves and joined her, holding the table she stood on steady. "Stings to touch without gloves. Try not to breathe the particles in."

"Well, that would have been helpful to know a minute ago," she muttered, thinking wryly of the winter gloves lying useless in her bag. No point stopping now. She ignored the itchy sensation crawling across her skin and rooted around in the insulation, gagging when she encountered a damp spot that was probably mold. A cloud of dust and particles descended, sending her into a sneezing fit, but she kept foraging and finally, finally her hand knocked something more solid than the puffy insulation. Something smooth. She clawed, unable to get a firm grip, scooting it closer and closer until it reached the edge of the grid and tumbled free. A small, heavy metal box fell, nearly braining Tony, before thudding onto the table.

He brushed a hand over his hair, smoothing it back into place rather than checking for injury, and she wheezed from laughter. And probably from the plume of toxic dust she'd just inhaled. Tony helped her down and examined the small, vintage olive metal box lying upside down on the table. Mara bent close and saw, with a satisfied smile, that it had a brass lock. She fitted that tiny key inside and popped it open, revealing a single, rather grimy looking black VHS tape.

Wide eyed, she pulled it from the box.

Tony puffed out his cheeks, his expression torn between triumphant and irritated. "We're going to have to find a way to transfer this onto a medium from this millennium."

"No need," Mara said, thickly, wiping her runny nose. She gestured at the museum.

"Oh God, when I was poking around earlier, I thought I saw—" Tony strode over to the shelves, hands questing over outdated mice, abandoned external hard drives, rear projection monitors, until he saw it. An ancient VHS player. He let out a heavy sigh, hauling it off a shelf and brushing a layer of dust from the top. "I'm going to have to hook this up to something, aren't I? Not an A.V. Club member, kid."

"*Anymore.*"

He glared and she knew she was right. Stark had totally been the president of the A.V. Club back in the day. She snickered, the moment of lightness feeling both out of place and vital to her ability to keep searching for answers. She'd felt hopeless for so long, since her grandfather's death, if she was honest, that finding a genuine reason to laugh felt like a sunrise after gloomy night. While Mara dropped into the desk chair and resumed her deep breathing, Tony jury-rigged a way to connect the VHS to the laptop screen, queuing up a video of young Dr. Shelley Melamed which did, in fact, transport them back in time.

He sat in the corner of the room in which they now stood, the photo background and chalkboard behind him crisper and newer. His hair was as dark and curly as Mara's, but cropped short like a cap. Sideburns rode low on his cheeks. He wore a highly patterned shirt and a pair of high-waisted pants that appeared pastel-ish in the grayscale video. He sat casually on the stool, one leg bent, foot propped on a wooden rung, the other braced against the floor, but the hand clenched on his knee belied his relaxed pose.

Seventies Grandpa, Mara thought. She'd never known this incarnation of him, the handsome young computer geek trying to reinvent the world. This must be thirty years before she'd been born. A few years before her mother was. Had he been married at this point? Yes, she could see on his tight-knuckled fist the plain gold band he'd worn to his grave.

"This is a message in a bottle. Only the bottle is a video," Professor Melamed said onscreen. The quality of the recording wasn't great, a little fuzzy, a little out of focus, the sound wobbly.

Nothing like the glossy footage people captured now with their cell phones. "I don't know if anyone'll ever see it. I hope not. But I can't trust that we won't need it. That *I* won't need it."

Dr. Melamed's voice warbled and the camera's non-directional mic picked up background noise from the lab—the hums and whirs and beeps of old computing equipment. No voices. Had he been alone when he filmed this? Did anyone else know it existed?

Mara leaned closer, soaking in every word. She hadn't known his voice when he was this young. She'd known only the voice that had grown rough and irregular with age.

"My name is Shelley Melamed and a couple years ago, the Department of Defense asked me to help them with some research. The guys upstairs in physics, they were doing the weapons stuff. The bad stuff. Me? I was just making an operating system that would be highly versatile and efficient. That's how we invented the Basic Operating System—Military Application. I built BOS-MA to unify command, control and communications with less than a tenth of the processing power currently needed. The government owns it. And… and they used it to test weapons illegally on civilians."

Melamed hung his head, eyes dipping away from the camera lens. "I was part of it. That wasn't supposed to be the purpose. It was supposed to be for non-operational use only. I objected. Maybe I didn't try hard enough. I admit wanted to know if the operating system worked the way I thought it would. And it did." The words grew strong, clear and powerful and awed. "It's a revolution in computing. It's everything I ever wanted to invent. But when I realized the generals' plans, I tried to stop them, told them I don't want the code used for that. They won't listen. The code belongs to them. They can do what they want. And I can't trust them to use it the way I meant it to be used. I realized I had to take drastic measures."

He shifted uncomfortably on the stool, stared off-screen for a long moment, jaw flexing. "I created a bypass. Just a snippet of code that searches for a particular file. Innocent. Unremarkable because I hid it in a system the whole purpose of which is to search for files. It'll lie dormant, a meaningless little procedure that does nothing unless I use the key. But if I do, it'll give me access to the military systems running BOS-MA. I'll be able to stop them from using my system to commit another atrocity. I can keep *control*.

"And the key? It's just the truth. The one thing they're afraid of. I coded BOS-MA to recognize images of the test they conducted. The massacre. If that 96 kilobyte sequence of data arrives on a machine running BOS-MA, it'll unlock the device. See? A key. And it can't be triggered accidentally. The military will *never* let that image out. Classified. God, how they love to say things are classified. But I have copies. Digital copies. All I have to do is send them to any military device running the OS, the sequence will be recognized, the procedure will execute, and I'll take over the machines. I can stop them from launching weapons. I can stop them from misusing my technology. It's targeted. Discrete. I wouldn't need for the images to get to the public. No, no. That would be a breach of national security. It'd ruin this university and the research program. It'd ruin me. But I'd only need control of devices running on BOS-MA. So it won't come to that."

He rubbed his jaw with his hand, the gesture reminiscent of Mara's own nervous habit. Tears prickled her eyes.

"If it did, though—no. I won't think about that. Anyway, it would be a small price to pay. I think."

Professor Melamed stared into the camera for a long minute with haunted eyes before he stood. His body grew larger in the lens and then the shot cut to black.

"No," Mara said. "That's not it. That can't be all he says!" She edged closer to the screen, waiting anxiously, but there was no more.

"Brilliant." Tony stretched the word, rolling it around in his mouth. "Diabolical, but truly genius. A zero-click exploit triggered by an *image*. Not code that has to execute. Not an action a user needs to take. A sequence of data lands on your machine and a tiny little piece of code embedded in a system you don't think about swings a door wide open."

"Don't sound so admiring!"

"It's elegant," he went on, ignoring her sharp rebuke. "Most sophisticated viral infection scheme I've ever seen."

"Professor Stark. Tony. Stop. Please. My mother was right. He was arrogant," she said, her voice breaking. She tried to control her breathing but her chest was too tight. The dam of emotional control she'd been clutching together stood to break. "And—and not a hero! He was a villain. Tens—no, hundreds of millions of people have no way to protect themselves from Moonstone because of *him*."

He turned to her, eyebrows rising into his scraggly hairline. "He didn't anticipate BOS-MA would be used on civilian devices. You heard him. He developed it for the DoD; he presumed he'd only need to assume control of military computers. Weapons systems. He didn't think—"

"He should have. He preached to me that we have to see past our own limitations, imagine what others can do with our inventions."

"Maybe this incident taught him that lesson," Tony said. "Technology is amoral—"

"But people aren't!" She waved a hand at the now-dark screen. Tony said nothing and she took a moment to breathe, waiting until she could speak without sobbing, though her voice remained heavy and uneven. "Or at least, they shouldn't be. He was so intent on knowing whether his operating system worked that he let the people he worked for test it on human beings. He knew he couldn't trust them. He should have destroyed BOS-MA instead."

"He regretted his choices," Tony said. "He thought he created a way for himself to control it, Mara. He tried."

"It wasn't enough! This is all his fault. And my mother's. And mine."

Tony rocked back on his heels. "You don't really believe you're guilty of your family's sins."

"Don't you?" she snarled.

He flinched. Stark's backstory made that particular shot a direct hit. Mara had read up on him when she learned he'd be teaching her class. A low blow, perhaps, against the only person who'd believed in her for the last year. But the words tumbled from her mouth anyway. She didn't want to assuage the guilt. She didn't want to feel better. And she didn't want someone who knew what *this* felt like to soothe her with platitudes he didn't mean.

"We can fix my grandfather's mistake, Tony. Rather than presume he could maintain control to protect his dirty secret, he should have gone public. We still can."

"We can't, even if I agreed with you that we should." His jaw clenched and he closed his eyes briefly. Mara thought she'd gotten through to him, at least a little, but then he shook his head. "It's an entire operating system, not just a piece of software people can stop using. What would we do, shut down every power plant, cell tower, and TV station? In the world? Shut down banks and government infrastructure? Moonstone has too much control. If we try to wrest it away without a solution, what would stop her from melting it all down?"

She had no answer to that. They had no idea how far Moonstone would go to keep control of the power and information BOS-MA gave her. They knew she was willing to hurt innocent people, like she had when she sent those drones after Carol at a soccer game. Just like the men for whom her grandfather had invented the damn thing in the first place. Angrily, Mara kicked the broken desk chair, sending it lurching across the floor and into a stack of boxes. One tipped and fell off the pile, littering the floor with Styrofoam cups. She kicked those, too, frustration boiling in her blood. It was wrong to continue to keep this a secret. People deserved to know the truth. They were repeating the egotistical mistakes of the past—her grandfather's mistakes—thinking they alone could stop a villain.

Tony leaned against the desk, infuriatingly calm while Mara demolished disposable cups. He let her wear herself out and then said, "We have to get back to the code. Patch the vulnerability. That's the answer that protects people."

She opened her mouth to argue, but the shrill chime of Tony's phone cut her off.

19

"MOONSTONE HAD a mole," Carol announced as soon as Tony answered the phone. "He was military. Weapons research and development. That's how she got the Swarm—at least the plans for them. *Another* defense research project that never should have seen civilian use. And apparently having an army of sophisticated AI drones isn't enough. The convoy she attacked was transporting a top-secret prototype, a directed energy weapon capable of targeting spacecraft."

"What the hell does she need that for?" he demanded.

"Military thinks she's starting an interplanetary war. Meet me back at the lair." Carol hung up abruptly.

"But why?" Mara said. "This doesn't make sense. Moonstone has enormous power to achieve what she wants through stealth and manipulation. She should be laying low."

"Yeah, but now we know about the vulnerability," Tony said. "We could expose it. She must at least suspect we're trying to fix it. And Carol is hunting her. We've disrupted her plans. That'll make a villain nervous."

Mara frowned, her mind shifting through possibilities. "An

207

interplanetary war, though. That's a puzzle piece that doesn't fit, Tony. We're missing something."

"More than one thing," he agreed, disconnecting his makeshift projector, snapping Professor Melamed's laptop shut and holding it out to Mara.

She clutched the device to her chest. All the puzzle pieces were there, floating around in her mind, but mixed up. Disordered. She couldn't yet see which edges aligned. "First, she went after information and money. She barely has anyone working with her at the DigiTech HQ building. She doesn't have an army of human minions because she doesn't trust people. She acquired artificially intelligent drones to protect herself, rather than human security. She's built herself a kingdom of one."

"You're right. The puzzle pieces don't fit." Tony's hands stilled on the backpack he'd been packing up. "Karla Sofen is an excellent psychiatrist—and an exceptional schemer. She managed to manipulate your grandfather into telling her about the vulnerability and handing over the images to open the back door to BOS-MA, despite him guarding that secret most of his life. She's diabolical enough to plot a global data war. But you'd need to be a technologist to control the devices once you have access to them. I don't think Moonstone is acting entirely on her own."

"Maybe not. But that doesn't explain what she's after with a weapon that targets space. She's shown no interest in space so far, and that kind of attack would practically demand that every super hero and alien in the Multiverse come after her. Her plans are most successful when executed in secrecy." Mara gasped as a coherent pattern finally emerged, and the mixed-up puzzle pieces formed into a picture... of their team. "*Oh*. Tony. She went after Carol once she showed up at the DigiTech campus. She targeted Jess, who was exploring DigiTech's stock deals. She took out power to Brooklyn to defang you. *We* disrupted her plans. We're the only ones who know about the vulnerability, because we haven't gone public. If she gets rid of us, she's still the secret ruler of the digital world. But her drone army wasn't strong enough against Captain Marvel. That weapon—it's not for space. It's for us."

Tony instantly dialed his phone. "Carol, evacuate the lair."

Mara's mouth went dry. "But—but the lair is secret."

"Carol's hometown isn't," Tony said. "Moonstone could target it, in an effort to draw us out, and get lucky."

Carol, on speaker, swore. "You think she's coming for us?"

"Mara does."

"Wait." She tugged at Tony's sleeve. "You—you can't just take my word for it! What if I'm wrong?"

He leveled a serious look at her. "Have you been wrong yet?"

"Jess!" Carol barked. "And Gerry!" The phone went dead without another word.

Mara's eyes were wide, wild. "Tony—do you really think—"

"I think we have to evacuate the lair ASAP." He was already on the move. "I've got a suit in the car. B.O.S.S., fire it up."

"And where will we go?" she asked, stumbling after him, grabbing her bag from the floor and trying to shove the laptop in as she went. "Your place?"

He paused, nearly to the exit. "No. Moonstone obviously knows where to find me. We need a location that's unknown to her." He twirled the phone in his hands, thinking. After a minute that stretched into eternity, he tossed it to her. "Stay here."

"What? No, I'm—I'm coming with you."

"This is as good a place as any, in a pinch," he said "I'll bring them back here."

She protested but he held up a hand. "Wasting time we don't have. Let me go help Carol. Meanwhile, Mara, get back to the code!"

20

THE QUIET that followed Tony's departure did not calm Mara's nerves. She glanced around the lab, at its familiar decrepit tables and chairs. Her mind's eye filled the scene in with details from her memories—desktop computers humming on tables, fingers flying over clackety keyboards, servers whirring along the walls of the room, grad students staring at glowing screens or arguing theory in the corners, a perpetually burbling coffee pot on the back counter, the one place where no equipment was stored, alongside a dirty dish bin overflowing with cups for the lowliest grad student to take home and wash. When her grandfather retired from teaching, his lab remained a haven for comp sci students, but each year, it emptied a little more, as other professors became the luminaries and the Melamed name dimmed and lost prominence. Mara had still done her best work at these tables, solved her most complex problems. Spotted the toughest, most obtuse patterns. She'd been so sure the answer was here, among the tattered remnants of her grandfather's legacy.

Maybe she hadn't been looking at it right. Maybe the answer wasn't to be *found* here. It was to be *worked out* here.

She couldn't be with Tony and Carol rescuing her mom and the others. But she could be useful at this desk, behind this screen. And she needed to do something to stymie the adrenaline surge she felt building again.

Mara flipped open her grandfather's laptop and her own.

She kept her head buried in the code until the room dimmed. The lab had always been poorly lit, relying on a strip of hopper windows and the fluorescents embedded in the ceiling grid. With the sunlight fading, the early winter evening cast the room in shadows. A glance at the clock on her computer told her that most of the day had evaporated while she worked.

She rubbed her tired eyes beneath her glasses and checked the phone Tony had left. No calls. She tossed it aside and it skittered across the desk, slipped off the edge with a tiny clatter. On the floors above, students and faculty would be chugging through the grind of an ordinary second semester, late afternoon lectures and lab work would just be ending for the day. The building lobby would fill with noise and people as they began to leave for dinner.

The basement, however, was silent.

Or was it?

A whisper of sound reached her ear. From beyond the open door came a rustle, almost too soft to be heard. Mara squinted, but the hallway, what she could see of it, was dark. There should be nothing there, and yet Mara's skin crawled. Though she'd never before been nervous in her grandfather's lab, she'd never been down here when it felt as empty as a horror movie set. And she was the silly character, alone in the night-dark basement.

She leaned back in the chair, eyes glued to the door. The noise had gone quiet. She'd normally try to talk herself out of being afraid of phantoms, but tonight, her pulse raced and her throat went dry and she could not force her logical brain to prevail over her alarm.

Should she worry that Carol had not called? Or Tony? Or her mother? Perhaps she should try them. Had they run into trouble, abandoned Tony's plan to come here? Did Spectrum or Hazmat have hideouts like Carol? She suspected not or Tony would have proposed regrouping there. Where would they be safe from Moonstone?

Mara stood and a cramp immediately hunched her. One hand to her lower back, she hobbled around the desk, in search of the phone.

Another rustle. She bolted upright, back throbbing, and gasped. A hooded figure stood in the doorway, the swish of the cloak around her ankles the only hint she had just arrived, moving fast.

Moonstone.

Mara recoiled, hip banging painfully into the corner of the desk. She failed to suppress a squeak.

"I suppose I needn't bother with subterfuge," Moonstone said. She lowered her hood. "You know who I am."

Mara dropped her eyes but only managed to keep them trained on her feet for a moment. Her gaze was drawn back to the figure like it was drawn to fire. Mara's stomach writhed, her conscience pushing back against the awe she did not want to feel but could not rid herself of. Under her swirling cloak, Moonstone wore an iridescent pearl suit with an elongated gold diamond centered over her heart. The symbol vaguely reminded Mara of the placement of Captain Marvel's Hala star. She also shared Carol's sweep of long blond hair, Moonstone's curled at the ends like she'd come from a salon. Her eyes were blue as a marble and just as cold. There, at least, this woman was distinguishable from the Carol Mara had come to know. They might stand with sharp jaws clenched and bodies unbowed, but Carol's eyes reflected care, concern. Love. The things that drove Carol were written in her expression.

Moonstone's gaze was blank.

"What do you want?" Mara hissed, trying again to back away. The desk trapped her. The phone! Where was it? She needed help. She had to call Carol. Tony. No, they were rescuing her mother and Jess and her son and nanny. Maybe Hazmat or Spectrum would come. Under the pretense of pushing herself off the desk, Mara did a small sweep with one foot, hoping to make contact with the device she'd dropped.

212   "You look like him," Moonstone said.

Mara had spent much of the last several days consumed by thoughts of whether she was like her grandfather. It was almost as if this villain had seen inside Mara's brain, as if she had mindreading powers. She should have studied Jess's files on Karla Sofen more carefully.

But did she look like him? She grew up wanting desperately to be told she had, indeed, been made in the Melamed image, both inside and out. But no one ever said so. "I don't. I look like my father."

"Ah, the grad student your mother rarely spoke of. Stubborn chin, heavy brows, wide forehead. Yes, you have that—but that's the surface. The wrapper. Your grandfather, I can see him in your eyes. He talked about you, you know. In treatment."

Don't listen, Mara ordered herself, scraping her foot across the floor again. She could not listen to what this monster had to say. "How did you find him?"

"I didn't go looking, if that's what you think. Stumbling upon his well of knowledge was a happy accident."

"You weren't his therapist," she said. "I saw his insurance bills."

"Not officially, no. He volunteered to be a subject in a study. A supporter of research to the end. I was only supposed to observe sessions, offer analysis and comparison to the treatments I provided to other types of patients."

Villains, Mara thought sourly. Ravencroft had been a facility for super villains. *Like her*.

"When I figured out who your grandfather was, his background researching for the DoD, I realized he might be a font of interesting information. I found excuses to visit with him, remain in the room after observing his sessions. No one objected to me keeping a troubled old man company for a few extra minutes. The head researcher on the veterans program was all too eager to mentor me. To believe that working with him had given me a higher purpose." She smiled, coldly. "They're all so committed to their ideals, aren't they?"

"Did he know who you were? My grandfather."

"No one has ever known who I am. Or what I'm capable of. Not from the beginning, when the loathsome man who employed my mother thought he could buy my affection for his daughter. Not Deanna Stockbridge, either. My original frenemy. She imagined herself such a bold and daring girl, but she never made a request of her dear dad that I didn't put in her mind. They underestimated me, Mara."

"So, it really all does come down to daddy issues?"

Moonstone shrieked with laughter. "You tell me, Ms. Melamed."

Mara bent her leg, feeling around the floor again, and this time, her foot brushed against the phone. She edged toward it, keeping her gaze fixed on Moonstone's glowing face. "My father is dead."

"Your grandfather raised you, but not Iris. Isn't that right?"

"Yes, but—"

"He was trying to make up for the mistakes he made with her. Letting her be raised by nannies, sending her away to boarding schools. You were his do over. But he hadn't learned his lesson, had he? Not really. To get his attention, you had to speak code. That was the only language he knew fluently and if you didn't, such a shame, you would never truly be able to communicate with him."

Mara's mother had said as much once. A flash of memory took Mara back to the tiny walk-up her mother lived in before she began working at DigiTech—a one-room number with a bed cordoned off by a shower curtain and a door too warped to close properly. She stayed there occasionally, when her grandfather was away speaking at conferences. She remembered one early visit when she had been excited about a robotics team project. She must have been in fourth or fifth grade. She no longer remembered the details, hadn't thought of it in years, but she knew she'd successfully written code that could execute a function for the first time. She'd been desperate to video call her grandfather, watching the clock until it was a decent hour wherever in the world he was, so she wouldn't wake him in the middle of the night. Her mother, a too-full glass of red wine in hand, had sniffed and said he *might* interrupt his important work since the call was code-related, but Mara should probably text in advance to tell him that or risk him screening the call. Mara remembered how much she'd resented her mother for saying that, how angry she'd been. She also remembered sending the warning text, as suggested.

"Iris understood him," Moonstone said. "Did you catch on, Mara, when you were young, as she did? Perhaps not. You don't quite have the same spark as your mother. The great Professor Melamed tried to teach you the things he'd taught her, before he sent her away. You struggled with it, didn't you?"

The words pounded Mara with the force of a Captain Marvel punch. Her grandfather *had* grown frustrated with her when she took her time and worked things out on paper, instead of blurting answers quickly, working out complex problems in her head. He believed she should be able to do it, since her mother had, his features drooping when she could not. Mara lived her whole life to experience the rare glimmers of praise she earned from her grandfather and told herself they were enough.

But she pushed the hurt from her own mind, never sharing any of that. Not with anyone. How could Moonstone know these things?

"What is it they say about genius? It fades with each passing generation."

"No one says that." Mara's fists clenched, knuckles meeting in a self-fist bump, the gesture protective rather than congratulatory. She pressed her hands to her sternum, covering her heart to shield it from further attacks. "He didn't think that about me. He was proud when I was accepted here."

"Was he?" Moonstone cocked her head. "Perhaps I'm mistaken."

The villain's tone said she didn't believe that could be possible, and Mara's heart echoed the sentiment. She knew her grandfather loved her, but she'd seen how it disheartened him that she could never keep up with his intellect. He'd been quick to farm her out to his professor friends down the hall, rather than work with her on homework himself. She'd persuaded herself that his work was too important to set aside even for a single afternoon. But maybe that had not been the reason. Maybe *she* hadn't been worth his precious time.

"Did you kill him?" Mara steeled herself for the response. She knew, of course. But she needed to hear it. "Overdose him with sedatives?"

"Sedatives? No. Your grandfather died of a heart attack, according to the autopsy." She smiled a chilly smile. Smoothed the shoulder of her cloak. "Now, adrenaline, that's a different story. Too much of that and you might give yourself a heart attack, you know? Plenty of adrenaline to be found in a facility like Ravencroft, too. Lots of emergencies happened there."

Adrenaline? What was the woman talking about? A glow pulsed from Moonstone's body, a slightly dimmer version of the power Carol called upon when she created photon energy balls. If their abilities were similar, could Karla Sofen, too, shoot lasers from her hands? What was she waiting for?

Mara's heart pounded. Surely her time was short. Though her hopes of a rescue had faded, a sliver of determination remained. The least she could do was warn Carol and Tony that Moonstone was here. Keep them from stumbling upon her unprepared. She managed to get the edge of her sneaker onto the phone beside her feet and shifted, drawing it closer, inch by inch.

"Are you going to kill me?" The words slipped out.

"Why would I?" Moonstone shook her head. "Maybe your grandfather and your mother were right and you're the dim bulb. But I think not. You're the only one who had an inkling of what I was up to."

"Yes, and I told Captain Marvel."

"Regrettable. But she won't be able to stop me. Besides, you recognized a pattern you didn't understand. Don't you see I was only hurting those who can stand to be hurt? Billionaire stock holders. Banks. The military. All people who control others, bend them to their whim."

"So you're Robin Hood?" Mara scoffed. "I don't see you out here redistributing the wealth you stole. You used secrets to amass *yourself* a fortune. You became one of the people you're criticizing."

"I'm protecting myself. Ensuring I'll never be subject to the caprice of the powerful again. Don't we all just want to be safe from the true bad guys?"

Moonstone sounded so sure of herself. And bits and pieces of what she said were... true. Compelling. She had targeted people in power. Institutions that wronged others or, at least, acted without conscience.

No! Mara clenched her jaw, fighting to pull her thoughts out of their spiral. That wasn't right. Moonstone was a villain. She hurt innocent people. "What about my grandfather? My mother?"

"You mean the people responsible for creating this vulnerability? They're not innocents. The great Melamed family held themselves up as paragons. Everyone likes to pretend they're out for the greater good. In fact, the crusader types are my favorite. Do you know why? They're the easiest to manipulate. They imagine their intentions matter. Haven't you learned by now, Mara? Technology has no principles. It is neither vice nor virtue. It does not preoccupy itself with notions of human morality."

Tony had said something similar. A flash of righteous anger toward him, her grandfather, all these geniuses that invented without considering the consequences roiled Mara's gut. "That doesn't erase right and wrong! You're stealing information and tormenting people!"

"Did I hurt a soul that couldn't survive it before Stark sent Captain Marvel to my headquarters like some kind of pathetic errand girl?" Moonstone spat, more venom in her tone for Carol than even for Tony. "She caused this, by refusing to leave me alone."

Mara blinked. The foot she'd been inching closer froze as she wrestled with Moonstone's words. Would she have gone on tricking only rich shareholders like some kind of Robin Hood if Carol hadn't tracked her down? Mara had studied the pattern for a year. It wasn't wrong to say Moonstone had originally concentrated her damage on the wealthy and the powerful.

"People are sheep. Those that think themselves heroic are the worst of the lot."

Moonstone flashed forward, too fast for Mara to see, but she was lifted off her feet and thrown backwards, landing on the desk with a crash. Her teeth clacked together and her mouth filled with the taste of iron. She came down hard enough to ache from the impact, to bite her lip, but not hard enough to break anything. When Mara peered up, she saw the phone in Moonstone's gloved hand. No! That was her only means of getting in touch with the team.

"Not me. I trust no one but myself. No one controls me now, and no one will again."

"You didn't get here on your own." Mara spit a glob of bloody saliva onto the desk. "You stood on the shoulders of giants like my grandfather."

"Interesting observation." Slowly, the glowing fingers wrapped around the plastic and metal, crushing them. "I knew you were not as dim as everyone thinks. I don't need help. But I'm not so arrogant as to turn it away when it could benefit me. Us, actually."

"Us?"

"Don't you want to be out of the shadow of your family, Mara?" Moonstone threw the phone corpse to the ground and, for good measure, crushed it to techno bits beneath the heel of her glimmery boot. "The whole of the computer world believes you're a bootleg copy, too full of errors to be worthwhile. You imitated every step of your grandfather's journey, from his alma mater to this office you're cowering in right now. But that needn't be the greatest height you achieve. You can prove to everyone—to the mother who discarded you, to the professors who doubted you, to the university ready to sacrifice you for money, to *yourself*—that you are your own woman."

"H-how?" She hadn't meant to ask that.

"Come work with me."

"*For* you, you mean. Manipulating people."

"Becoming someone beyond disregard."

That wasn't what Mara wanted. Except, it was *exactly* what she wanted. Moonstone was the first person to ever identify the pulse at the heart of her determination. The drive that kept her battling for her PhD long after she should have abandoned the attempt. Her deepest desire was to be deemed worthy of her family name. Why could this villain, and no one else, see it? Everyone who had never believed in her, who had overlooked her, sidelined her. She did want them to realize their mistake. She wanted them to admit that she was as valuable as all the other Melameds, that she was someone. Mara raised a fist to her chin, knuckles rubbing hard against her skin. They came away streak with blood.

"Find me when you're ready. You know how." Moonstone kicked the dust of the smashed phone toward her. "I won't wait forever, though. With me or against me and all those cliches."

With that, Moonstone vanished in a swirl of cloak and a shimmer of light, gone as quickly as she'd arrived.

21

NIGHT HAD fully fallen by the time Carol arrived with Jess, Gerry, Lindsay, and Dr. Melamed in tow, and while the campus had not emptied, the science building Tony led them to was quiet.

"Oh my God! You're okay!" Mara leapt up when they entered the lab and barreled toward them. Until they entered the room, she'd been certain she'd never see them again. Relief made her giddy, and she gathered everyone she could reach into her arms in a crushing hug. She flinched when Carol's arm squeezed her lower back, but ducked her head to avoid Carol's gaze.

Was that a bloody lip? What on Earth?

Before Carol could ask what was going on with the young woman, Jess's head poked over the top of the huddle. "Here?"

"Hey, it's got power, internet, and an absentee landlord," Tony said.

"More than you could say for my first apartment in New York," Carol said, offering an uncertain smile. She extracted herself from the group, watchful eyes on Mara.

"Absentee landlord?" Jess's incredulous tone made it clear she shared Carol's skepticism.

"I had B.O.S.S. check the university records. Professor Melamed was the last holdout with an office down here, and once he stopped coming, they converted it to storage to which very few people have access."

"Okay, on the upside, privacy." Jess moved Gerry from one hip to the other while Lindsay shifted boxes to make room for a playpen. She cocked her head and listened for a second. "On the downside, mice—maybe rats?"

"Now that's definitely something my first apartment had," Carol quipped.

Her eyes carried out a quick visual patrol around the room. As Jess noted, they were unlikely to be stumbled upon by university personnel demanding they relocate their unauthorized rescue-humanity mission. But was the place even habitable? For the humans, not the rats. Carol, too, could hear squeaking along the floorboards at the corners of the room. They'd have to keep Gerry away from the walls.

This office felt as if it had stepped out of time but that also meant it was out of Moonstone's digital reach. They'd have the ability to make sure any computer device they brought in here was BOS-MA-free.

While Tony, Mara, and Iris set up a smaller version of the computer command center they'd had at the lair, and Jess helped Lindsay and Gerry get settled, Carol paced. For all her strength, she was useless now, like she had been as a junior pilot, waiting around squadron HQ for orders that came from someone else. She'd come up as a small cog in a larger machine, most of the time never knowing the full scope of any mission, only able to carry out her small part. Carol had been no good at waiting then. She'd gotten herself in trouble more than once, jumping into action before she should. Her early commanders called it gumption—pluck, when they were being pejorative. Maybe that was why, now that she controlled her own missions, she rarely sat back. Carol never had to reach far to find the part of herself that demanded she push higher, further, faster. *The Kree part.*

Were there some parts of her that were Kree and others that were human? She had a vision of doctors in lab coats parsing DNA the way she'd separated out the marshmallows from the wholesome crunchy oat bits of her cereal when she was a kid. Carol was a hybrid, crosspollinated as if by some medieval monk who wanted to see what would happen when he fused things that weren't meant to be combined. Her hands curled into steel balls and tingled with energy. She hated feeling like a science experiment.

On her tenth—twenty-fifth? She'd lost count—lap around the lab, Jess grabbed her shoulder, halting her. "You're dancing around this room like it's a maypole, Carol, and you're making me dizzy."

She bit back a retort about how Spider-Woman had been literally climbing the walls herself not so long ago. Jess wasn't built for this any more than she was. "I'm bad at waiting."

"Tell me something I don't know." Jess glanced toward the far end of the room, where the computer scientists were back in front of their glowing screens. "I don't think we're the only ones having a hard time."

Carol followed her gaze. Tony had commandeered Shelley Melamed's desk, centering himself with the old man's dinosaur of a laptop. Iris stood just behind him, peering over his shoulder. Off to the right sat Mara. Her eyes weren't on the screens, but rather gazed toward the high windows along the exterior wall, through which little to nothing could be seen.

The pose suggested someone deep in thought. On anyone else, Carol would have dismissed it as no more than that. But one set of Mara's knuckles were planted firmly against her chin. Her anxious tell.

"She was moving a little gingerly earlier," Carol said. "Did you notice?"

Jess nodded. "That lip, too. And there's a busted phone on the floor over there."

Carol's eyes tracked to the spot Jess pointed at and narrowed when they caught on the broken carcass of a flip phone. There'd been some kind of a scuffle. Why hadn't Mara said anything?

What was she hiding?

"Go figure it out, Captain," Jess said, clapping her heartily across the back.

"Mara," Carol called. "There a restroom down here?"

Mara startled, the half-broken swivel chair she sat in wobbling precariously. "Um, yes. Well, it's more like a closet with a toilet. But it's down at the end of the hall."

"Show me."

If anyone thought it was strange that Captain Marvel was worried about getting lost looking for a bathroom twenty feet down a straight shot of a hallway, no one voiced the concern. Mara trailed Carol down the hall to a door with a faded plastic W.C. signed tacked to it that Carol surely could have found herself.

"You okay?" Carol asked.

The young woman blinked. She looked at the closed door. Along the hall toward her grandfather's lab. Down at her feet. "Yeah. I'm fine."

Carol nodded at the red patch along the young woman's jawline. "Then how come you have a split lip and your chin has been rubbed raw?"

Her hand flew to her face, too late to hide the evidence of her anxiety. "It's nothing."

"Look," Carol said. "I may not be the expert at talking feelings. I've been known to avoid Jess's questions like you're trying to avoid mine right now. But you're hiding something. I need to know what it is. Both because I care about you and because it could affect this mission."

Mara put her palms to her eyes, avoiding Carol's probing gaze. Carol waited her out, patience held in check but barely. When Mara pulled her hands away, bloodshot veins and dark circles betrayed her exhaustion. They'd none of them slept properly in days. Carol could handle that, even if she was feeling a little depleted. Jess would bear up too, and Tony. But Mara was only human. She needed rest. Carol promised herself she'd make the young woman take a break, just as soon as she could.

"I can't do it." Her voice was small, a whisper that the echoey hall swallowed whole. "Crack the code. Patch the vulnerability. I can't. You were wrong to put your faith in me. I'm—I'm nothing like my grandfather. Or my mom. Or Tony."

"Mara, what are you talking about?" This wasn't the bold young woman who'd tracked Carol to her lair by hacking into Stark's systems and gone toe to toe with Iron Man to protect the team. The one who'd seen a threat the world could not and spoken up about it despite attempts to silence her.

"I know you don't want to reveal the BOS-MA vulnerability publicly. I still think you're wrong about that." A flash of the confident thinker surfaced, only to be pulled under by doubt just as fast. "But fine. We don't have to tell the world. We just need to tell a few people, so Tony can have a team of real coders in here."

"You're not real?"

A tear slipped from the inside corner of Mara's eye, tracking around her nose and into her mouth. She didn't wipe it away, shaking her head miserably.

"You seem to be forgetting that Tony Stark himself is stymied by this problem. You're asking an awful lot of yourself to do better."

"Isn't that what you expect of yourself? To be the best?"

"Touché," Carol said, cringing internally. "I'd like to tear out my own hair, waiting around like this. I feel useless. But this self-pity talking? It's not you. It's imposter syndrome. It's—"

Carol paused and leaned close, ducking her head to see into Mara's eyes. She tilted Mara's chin up getting a better look at the cut on her mouth. "Did she get to you? Moonstone contacted you somehow? Because all of a sudden, you're doubting yourself and I can't figure out why unless a certain villainous psychiatrist twisted your thoughts."

Mara swallowed hard. "She was here. Just briefly."

Carol swore. "How did she find you? And why didn't you tell me?"

Mara shrugged. "I'm okay. Physically. Mostly," Mara said, her voice cracking. She licked at her sore lip, testing the forming scab. "I'll heal. She confessed to killing my grandfather, though. Something about adrenaline? I didn't follow."

Heart attacks! That was it. The commonality between Melamed's death and Faber's that Carol's brain had been trying to piece together. She knew that if you pumped too much adrenaline into someone, you could kill them without leaving a mark. "I'm sorry," she said. "That must have been difficult to hear."

"The things she said. I—I—"

"Can't get them out of your head?" Despite the dim light of the hallway, Carol's vision picked out the angst in Mara's face. She smiled gently. "I know the feeling. She's a master manipulator. It's kind of her thing."

"But it was true. Or at least, some of it was."

"Yeah, that's her thing too. Diabolically insightful." Carol shook her head. "But she didn't come here just to mess with you. She wanted something. Information?"

"No. She asked me to join her. Go work with her."

Carol leaned back against the wall, digesting that. "Why? I don't mean to increase your imposter syndrome. But it seems like she ought to have everything she needs with her information flow and her drone swarm."

"Maybe she's trying to get to you?" Mara's brow wrinkled as she considered this. "Someone close to you?"

"I don't like it. She's playing chess, setting up a maneuver, and I can't see her next move. I need to think about this." Carol pointed at Mara, her eyes bright. "Actually, I need you to think about it. There's a pattern here and we're missing it. I need your brain power on this problem. The same brain you've had all along—before Moonstone tried to emotionally abuse it into mush. Are you with me?"

Mara held her breath for a beat, blew it out, hard. And then, she nodded. "I got this, Captain."

Carol smiled. "You bet you do."

She started to follow the young woman back toward her grandfather's lab, but hesitated. Despite having led Mara to a clearer head space, Carol couldn't get there herself. Mara's reminder of the debate over whether to keep the vulnerability secret haunted her. She had been sure, earlier, that it was the right thing to do. But every member of her team had a different opinion about what to do.

Carol was out of her depth. They'd been sucked into the vortex of Moonstone's manipulations, which were increasingly hard to fight off. Her lies and half-truths were debilitating to Carol.

Bring a massive formation of artificially intelligent drones out of the sky? All in a day's work.

Knock heads together to get answers? She was your woman.

But this confusion? The discord among her crew? The self-doubt? The ethical issues balanced on the head of pin?

This stuff was tricky.

Maybe she'd been trying too hard to control an uncontrollable. She couldn't do anything about a vulnerability in computer code. She had to trust her crew to handle that. She could deal with the underlying threat. Moonstone. The villain was skilled at deflecting attention. However, without her to steal and exploit information, they'd have the thing they needed most—time.

She'd let Moonstone orchestrate this sick symphony for too long, getting into people's heads, making them do her bidding while she hid, in her cowardly way, behind false identities, behind corporations, behind code and tech. She'd been running Carol ragged, leading her through a labyrinth of smoke and mirrors.

No more.

As Mara disappeared into the lab, Carol pushed off the ground, taking to the air, not even willing to waste the seconds it would take to climb the stairs.

They had to stop waiting for Moonstone to attack. They had to take the fight to her. And hunting down a villain head first, hands blazing? That was Carol's way. The Kree way.

Karla Sofen wanted power and she'd proven she'd stop at nothing to get it.

But Moonstone had underestimated Captain Marvel, who
would let nothing stop her from protecting her friends.

22

LIKE THE last time Carol snuck in for after-hours recon, the DigiTech compound looked deserted. Only Moonstone's drones—and not nearly as many as she and Hazmat had encountered on their last visit—patrolled the skies, but she powered up and blasted them to fragments without hesitation. She had no one other than herself to worry about now. And she didn't need to be careful with herself.

Through the haze of drone detritus that exploded around her, she studied the campus. Where, if she was Moonstone, would she hide out? The glass-and-steel tower rose up before her, the obvious answer. Tony had his offices in the most ostentatious, tallest building when he'd headed Stark Industries. Carol had lived in the city long enough to observe the working cycle of bustling companies in the buildings she passed. They bore a certain similarity to the army bases she'd served on: they never went completely dark. Someone always manned the night shift at a base, just like every office had a few workers who kept late hours. She let her body drift higher, seeking a wider view of the building. No corner office with a lighted lamp. No hallway lights. Barely a glint of a red emergency exit sign here and there.

Carol thought back to her first visit to the place, to the fresh paint smell and the pristine hallways. She'd chalked it up to the building's newness. Seales—Moonstone—had said they'd just built it, and Carol figured they were still in the process of moving in. Now she wondered if it would have ever been fully occupied. Maybe this place was never meant to be a thriving company HQ. Maybe it was just more smoke and mirrors. Another kind of costume, like the Seales avatar. Moonstone had said it herself, hadn't she? People focused on the disguise, too distracted by the shiny object to wonder at what lay beneath. Carol looked around the fancy, empty campus and realized it was all for show. A successful tech company would build itself a spectacular campus. It would have been strange if DigiTech hadn't.

But Moonstone didn't need this place for anything other than a distraction, to keep the world from looking too hard at what DigiTech was really doing. She'd bought a controlling interest in the company for the same damn reason—to keep shareholders, the board, at bay, to put them in a position where they had no cause to pull back the curtain and seek the truth.

And, Carol realized, if this place was just one more layer to the disguise, Moonstone wouldn't keep a hideout here.

Carol squirreled away in her home town, on the property she'd inherited from her family. That's where she'd built her bolt-hole. She'd rationalized that it wasn't so far away as to be inconvenient for someone with super hero flight speed. She told herself that it was a practical decision. Mostly. The other rationale? The one she barely admitted to herself? It was sentimental. Home held complicated and painful memories for Carol, but that little plot of land where her childhood home stood was the only place in the universe where all the pieces of her came together. Where the conflicting parts that made up Carol Danvers and Captain Marvel didn't need to be explained or resolved.

There had to be somewhere like that for Moonstone.

Carol flew backward, away from the compound, sifting through everything she knew about Karla Sofen. Exploring that backstory and her motivations was like looking in a funhouse mirror for Carol. Wildly distorted and too familiar for comfort.

Moonstone had grown up in someone else's home, Carol realized.

Little Karla had grown up adjacent to astonishing wealth that wasn't hers, in proximity to extraordinary financial privilege that she was acutely aware she didn't have, a forced playmate to the daughter of her mother's rich employer. An industrial baron of some kind? A magnate? Carol scrolled through her mental database, trying to remember the name. In a pinch, she could call Mara and ask her to search for it, but then she and Tony and Jess would know what Carol was up to. They'd feel compelled to come help, and this was her job. It was up to her to save them, and not the other way around. Her big movie hero moment.

Wait! That was it. Charles Stockbridge, movie producer.

Puzzle pieces rearranged themselves in Carol's mind, shards of information she'd gathered over the last few days fell into place. She wondered briefly if this was how Mara felt when she discovered a pattern. It was damned satisfying.

Stockbridge's eponymously named company owned a defunct studio in New York that had recently been sold, which Carol knew, because the purchaser was none other than Perigee Partners, Ltd. Moonstone's corporate front. She could picture the images Mara and Jess had projected onto the screens back at her lair, a listing of assets, a map that marked Perigee's holdings—their headquarters on the campus of DigiTech, another property near the city.

That's where Moonstone would be.

Karla Sofen had snapped up Stockbridge's property not out of any sentimental connection to her childhood, but because the purchase represented a triumph over the first person to slight her. She owned the Stockbridge legacy now, which had to quench her thirst for emotional vengeance.

Carol took off, racing across the sky, a blur against the backdrop of the rising sun, the heat of her body melting the snow that had begun to fall. She reached the city in minutes and blew past Manhattan and Brooklyn, homing in on an area just north of the airport in Queens.

Among a warren of dilapidated buildings, she sank lower, careful to avoid air traffic. It was always a risk to get this close to planes taking off and landing. She dropped closer to building height, grateful for the darkness that gave her some cover, and circled until she found what she sought. A nondescript warehouse surrounded by a barbed wire fence, marked with only a small card that said: PATROLLED BY PERIGEE SECURITY, INC.

Ha. Perigee Security, her butt. She would bet anything that was a front, too. Moonstone would be as alone here as she was everywhere else.

Carol decided she wasn't going to creep around or probe. Moonstone had the drop on her from the start. Time for a little jump-scare payback. Carol extended one arm, fingers curled into a fist, squared her shoulders, and charged the broadside of the warehouse wall. She blasted it with a photon ball, seconds before she smashed through. The slab gave way and loosed a barrage of mortar and bricks and shattered glass. The rumble of the destruction followed her inside, echoing around the cavernous space. Carol pulled up and surveyed the warehouse interior. It was utilitarian, bare of comforts—no fine furniture or luxury items. No art. Plenty of electronics for Moonstone to conduct her reign of digital terror. Storage for her suits. Warehouse bay doors for a quick exit. With a start, Carol realized it resembled *her* lair, before her friends had gotten hold of it and badgered her into decorating that comfy corner.

A streak of pearly white and gold flashed through Carol's peripheral vision. Moonstone, darting toward the bay doors, which had begun to open. Carol rocketed after, managing to grab a booted foot. Moonstone shrieked, swinging her free leg and clipping Carol's head. Carol grimaced, felt her grasp on Moonstone's boot begin to slip. Before she lost hold entirely, she thrust an arm forward, flinging the villain away. Moonstone soared backward and crashed into the metal catwalk that circled the walls of the warehouse. She tumbled to the floor in a damaged, though not broken, heap, got to her feet, slowly, wobbly but standing.

Carol righted herself in midair, panting, and powered up her hands. Moonstone might not have all of Carol's strength and stamina, but she was no ordinary mortal either. That fall hadn't taken much out of her.

Carol hurled a blast of photons, but Moonstone deflected with a forearm, and the stream of energy diverted sideways, melting the metal catwalk steps. She returned fire, forcing Carol to dodge. She gnashed her teeth, feeling like she was fighting *herself*.

"Nice place you've got here," Carol quipped, building another power surge.

Moonstone flipped a hank of long hair over her shoulder. "It's amazing what you can do with unlimited resources and next day delivery."

"Not your resources."

"I control them. Who's to say they're not mine?"

"*I* say."

"You always were especially self-righteous, Captain. Do you ever get tired of telling people how right you are?"

Carol's pulse spiked. Her arm flew up, a surge of energy at the ready. Moonstone was quicker. She boosted herself into the air and aimed two volleys at Carol. Neither a direct strike, but close enough to send Carol diving to avoid the hit. Before she could find her equilibrium and rattle off another shot, a flash of light obscured her vision, sending a searing pain through her brain. When she pried her throbbing lids open, Moonstone was zipping toward the bay doors again. Her exit strategy. Carol had to cut her off.

Carol raced after Moonstone. With a mighty stretch, she snagged Moonstone's suit, then hooked an arm around her waist and heaved, sending the villain spiraling back. Carol powered forward, seized the doors and hauled them down, calling on her deepest stores of strength to force the heavy hydraulics to move. For good measure, she punched the mechanism, smashing it beyond repair. There, she'd cut off one easy exit. She spun and realized she had lost sight of Sofen. She could hear her though, groaning from the hit she'd taken when Carol hurled her around.

She sped back toward the hole she'd made in the wall, patrolling it so Moonstone wouldn't be able to slip out.

"Tony Stark's errand girl." Moonstone's symphonic tone echoed in the mostly empty space, ringing through Carol's chest. All evidence of the pain Carol had heard earlier was erased. Moonstone's voice was pleasant, melodious. Part of her swindle, as much a tool as Carol's fists. Too bad there were no sea witches around to offer her a bargain for it. "The muscle for hire."

Carol's flight power flagged, and she unexpectedly lost a few feet of height.

"Everyone's colleague; no one's friend. Too different. Too... *alien* to really get close to."

No. Carol pushed herself up, scrambling for some height, for a better vantage point. Ignoring the barbed truth in Moonstone's words: that her Kree heritage set her apart from her teammates. She scanned the dim corners of the warehouse for any smudge of pearlescent white. The longer she listened, the worse it would get. She had to find Moonstone. Stop her from spitting this poison that polluted Carol's thoughts so effectively.

"You wonder how it is that I can speak your thoughts as if I were inside your mind, don't you, Captain? It's because we're the same."

"What?" Carol's voice bounced off the walls and zinged back to her own ears. She sounded wounded, for Pete's sake. Weak. Uncertain. *Get it together, Danvers. Quick.*

"Do you know what they will do when they're done with you? When you outlive your usefulness? They will discard you. Even if you provide years of faithful service, like my mother did for Charles Stockbridge. Even if you are a 'friend,' like I was to his daughter, Deanna. They're never really friends with the servants. We're disposable."

"Stop. Talking." Carol ground the words between her teeth. She wasn't going to fall prey to Moonstone's twisted influence any longer. She wasn't going to listen. She needed ear plugs.

"How close do you imagine you'll still be with Tony Stark when he no longer needs Captain Marvel's magical hands?"

Carol threw a blast toward a corner of the room from which she thought the voice might be emanating. She singed the walls black, but a scuffling sound in the opposite corner told her she'd missed. Or aimed wrong. Moonstone was muddling her focus, disorienting her. Another light flare engulfed the room. Pain shot through her head. Dammit, Carol hated that trick. By the time she could open her eyes, Moonstone was on the move again.

"You're trying to manipulate me. It won't work." *It couldn't*, Carol told herself, forcefully. She needed to keep her head clear of Moonstone's manipulations.

"What do you think your pals in the military were so desperate to protect with that silly convoy?" The voice was quieter now, but no less lyrical. "You and I are not the only source of directed energy in the universe."

The weapon that Colonel Finke mentioned, Project Faustus. He'd been in no condition to give her details at the hospital, and immediately after that Tony warned her that her lair was the likely target. She hadn't had time to think about what the weapon did. Directed energy—in other words, a laser?

"They're trying to replicate you. Your powers, anyway. Make you obsolete. They don't want you, Captain Marvel. They don't need you now they've figured out how to make laser hands of their own."

"You're a liar." And Carol *did not* have laser hands.

Moonstone's laugh trilled, raising goosebumps on Carol's arms. Like nails on an old blackboard. "I may be a bit manipulative, but I'm no liar. These people you fight so hard to protect, they don't care about you. You're not one of them. You're better than them, though you don't know it. There's no one in the world like you—except for me. We're the same, Carol Danvers. The Kree gave us potential. We made ourselves who we are."

None of this was true. But wasn't it? Just a little? Carol was a self-made woman. Everything she'd achieved as a pilot, she'd strived for. Turned every setback into motivation. Prided herself on her grit, her determination, her will to win.

As had Karla.

"No!" A surge of energy filled Carol, radiating up from her hands into her shoulders. "I'm nothing like you, Sofen. You're a villain!"

"And you aren't? You're hiding the truth about BOS-MA. You left people vulnerable to me."

"To protect them," Carol protested. When she said the words aloud, they sounded absurd. Had they been wrong to keep the code's secret? Had she made a mistake?

And where the hell was Moonstone? Carol scanned the space; their battle had created enough debris and rubble that there were several places to hide. There was no trace of the villain, who was smart enough to remain concealed while she taunted. Carol couldn't leave the hole in the outer wall unprotected, unless she had a clear line of sight on Moonstone. She was, effectively, trapped.

Sofen's words reverberated, the terrible warehouse acoustics shielding her precise location. "You could have protected them by enabling them to protect themselves. You didn't trust them to do the right thing."

She hadn't. People had proven over and over that they couldn't be trusted. The very invention of BOS-MA was an exercise in arrogant hubris. How could she leave it in people's hands, just hoping they wouldn't find a way to use the vulnerability to hurt each other further?

Moonstone couldn't seem to help herself, with Captain Marvel as her audience. She went on. "You care too much about what others think of you, even knowing in your heart you're not one of them. And neither am I."

Carol felt the energy she'd been building begin to ebb. Moonstone was speaking her darkest thoughts aloud, bringing to the surface her insecurity about where she belonged. The self-doubt sapped her strength, tore her power from her.

"I'm my own," Moonstone said, her voice loud now, strident. As if the energy draining away from Carol powered her up instead. "The difference is I wear that like a badge, and you wear it like an albatross. You struggle with your true self. I embrace it."

234   A flash of anger seared through Carol. Moonstone called

her Tony's errand girl before—and wasn't there truth in that, too? She'd been on her way to visit Throneworld II when she'd responded to his call. Why hadn't she turned him down? Why hadn't she put her Kree family first? She'd answered the summons like she was his puppet. Carol sank a few feet toward the ground and clutched her head, energy sapped. She closed her eyes, pulled at the very roots of her power, summoning a surge she couldn't sustain, as her anger faded and doubt replaced it.

What of this was real and what was Moonstone's disinformation? There was enough truth in her ramblings to tangle Carol's mind. She'd never been good at this emotional stuff. Carol put up a hand, attempting to throw an energy ball, but it was an anemic swell that faded before it reached its target. She tried again, and again, each attempt less powerful than the last. Her thoughts swirled, something like panic tearing through her. Her powers weren't responding. That wasn't good. That was never good. She needed a minute. She needed to focus, regroup. She needed to block out the venom Moonstone was spewing.

A streak of white and gold emerged on the catwalk overhead. Carol caught sight of it too late, moved too slowly. Moonstone's energy bolt did not peter out, striking Carol directly in the chest, sending her to her knees.

And then another voice—this one familiar and welcome and not at all hypnotic—pierced the silence. "Embrace this, space cadet!"

Jess swung through the hole in the wall behind her, clambering up to tackle Moonstone, who'd been running along the catwalk toward the breach. Monica followed Jess, phasing through the concrete with Jenn in her arms.

Moonstone zoomed backward, screaming. "Oh look. The rest of Tony Stark's misfit girl gang."

"Actually, moon-girl." Jess dropped back to the ground, hooked an arm beneath Carol's and hauled her to her feet, as Monica and Jenn took up stances beside them. "You'll notice Iron Man isn't here. This is Captain Marvel's team."

"Jess," Carol hissed. "You shouldn't be here. Gerry—"

"Uncle Tony's watching him."

Jenn giggled. "How much safer can you get than having Iron Man as your babysitter?"

The image of it brought an absurd bubble of laughter to Carol's throat. She eyed Jess, now outfitted in her black-and-red suit, the second skin moving with her as she crouched in a ready pose. "I see you're finally dressed for the occasion."

"Monica invisibled her way into my place and grabbed me a costume change. You know my worst nightmare is showing up underdressed for a party."

Carol's amusement at the banter faded quickly. "Well, my worst nightmare is putting you all at risk. You shouldn't have come."

"You have got to quit trying to sacrifice yourself to protect everyone else," Jess said, giving Carol a gentle squeeze. Beside her, Monica and Jenn hummed their agreement. "We got into this mess together. That's how we'll get out of it."

"Go on, Carol," Moonstone mocked. She hovered in the air, not bothering to retreat into the shadows. She must know she couldn't overpower all of them physically. She'd be back to her mind tricks. "Let the puppet master pull your strings again, keep dancing like a marionette."

Carol's nostrils flared. Photon energy rushed into her hands. She was done being preyed upon by this devious gaslighter. She was no one's puppet. And she might be an inconceivable bundle of human and alien parts, but she wasn't alone. Her team had shown up, as they had, without question, since she'd arrived at Jess's apartment door asking for help, since the first call she'd put out to Monica and Jenn to join a mission. They had tracked her here. Refused to let her fight this battle by herself. Because they weren't just her team. They were her friends.

Whereas Moonstone had no one. Not even her artificially intelligent drones.

"You know what, Karla? You were right," Captain Marvel said, straightening her spine. Beside her, Jess uttered a delighted oath. "We do have some things in common, which means I understand you. In another Multiverse, we might even be friends. But in this one? There's a crucial difference. You're so busy trying to prove you're independent, you failed to notice you're really just alone."

Jess swung herself onto the catwalk, then crawled high up the wall to make a leap at Moonstone. Spider-Woman was fast enough to keep the villain moving in order to avoid being tackled midair. Sofen managed to throw an energy blast here and there but without any accuracy.

Carol held a hand out to Monica. "You got a boost in you, friend?"

Spectrum grinned. She linked hands with Carol and sent a surge flowing from her fingers. Captain Marvel absorbed the energy lift. Warmth coursed through her, as the photon glow emanated outward, too powerful now to be shielded by skin. She withdrew from Monica as overload approached, careful not to take more than she needed or leave her friend depleted.

A scream drew her eyes up. Moonstone had finally managed a hit, an energy ball slamming into Jess's shoulder and sending her plummeting from the catwalk. She crumpled to the concrete floor.

"Jess!"

"I got her," Monica said, jumping forward. She pointed at Moonstone, who'd made a beeline for the computer equipment. "You get *her*."

With one hand, Moonstone threw energy blasts to keep Captain Marvel at bay, and with the other she typed on one of the keyboards. Carol caught sight of some kind of schematic on the screen. Was that the directed energy weapon Moonstone had mentioned? Project Faustus? On another screen, she'd pulled up coordinates. Carol couldn't decipher any of it before a red OVERRIDE warning flashed on screen. Moonstone clicked.

"What are you doing?" Carol yelled, throwing an energy blast of her own. "Jenn!"

"On it!" Jenn sprinted closer, powering up her body and letting loose a massive EMP. The screen and computer equipment popped and fizzled, glass showering Moonstone. Carol lowered the hand she'd thrown up to protect herself and saw rivulets of blood streaking over Moonstone's mask and dripping onto her no-longer pristine white suit. The villain stumbled over a chair and fell, hard.

Carol charged forward, managed to just reach her nemesis. A leg shot past her, connecting with Moonstone's torso. Carol looked up to see Jess, trailed by a watchful Monica, her suit singed and hanging from one shoulder.

"One more for good measure," Jess said, gesturing at Moonstone, who was wounded but unrelenting, attempting to crawl away.

Carol quirked an eyebrow at her team: Jess, bloodied but unbeaten; Jenn, energy sapped, leaning against a table for support; and Monica, upright, but also worn by the power she'd expended. Each nodded in turn. And then, with a colossal punch, Captain Marvel knocked Moonstone out and discarded her crumpled, unconscious body on the floor.

23

WHILE MONICA and Jenn delivered Moonstone to the Raft for imprisonment, Jess and Carol headed back to the Melamed computer lab to find Lindsay packing up Gerry, and Tony packing up the team's computers. Their youngest, newest crew member, their pattern genius, trailed him, removing every piece of equipment he put in his bag.

"Mara," he exclaimed, throwing his hands up in frustration. "The immediate threat has passed. We can move somewhere more comfortable."

"What's comfort got to do with it?"

"A heck of a lot more than nostalgia, which is the only reason to stay here at this point!"

"Kids, stop bickering," Jess said, reaching for her son. She bounced the toddler into the air and he giggled.

Carol responded in kind. It was impossible not to be delighted by the baby's laughter.

Unless you were the rest of her team, apparently. She glanced from Tony, whose arms were now crossed, to Mara, who was still unpacking computer equipment, to Iris, who stood by the outer wall, wringing her hands. Carol pointed to the two wearing the most stubborn expressions. "What's all this?"

Tony huffed. Mara reached into his bag and removed a mousepad.

"They've been at it since you nabbed Sofen," Lindsay said, dismantling the remains of the portable childcare center she'd schlepped all over the city as they moved Gerry from one unsafe place to another. Not for the first time, Carol wondered at Jess's luck in finding the most preternaturally calm nanny in the universe. She was glad they'd be able to head home, get Gerry back to his familiar—and protected—environment.

The thought brought home an inconvenient reminder. Though they'd captured Moonstone, Jess was still a wanted criminal. Carol's heart squeezed. What good were all the super hero aunties and uncles in the world if they couldn't keep your mom from being falsely accused of murder?

This wasn't over yet.

"Carol, tell her she's being unreasonable," Tony said, his voice dangerously close to a whine. Carol smirked. Iron Man wasn't used to rebellious twenty-somethings who defied his orders. She rather hoped Mara would retroactively accept that job offer Tony made. It'd be good for both of them.

"Mara," Carol said. "What's bothering you? We don't need to hide out here anymore."

"It wasn't really a good hiding spot, was it?" Mara plunked down into her broken chair and swung around, facing away from Tony's grimace and Carol's wrinkled forehead and Jess's narrowed eyes. Even Lindsay and Gerry were giving her exasperated glances. She focused on the shelves, the remnants of her grandfather's museum, the pieces they hadn't looted to set up their makeshift operation. The leftovers. "Moonstone found us—me—so easily. I can't stop thinking about it."

"It's disconcerting to be isolated and manipulated like that," Jess said. She set Gerry down, then hitched a hip onto the desk beside Mara and tugged on her sleeve, pulling her back around to face them. "We've all been through it."

"It's more than that," Mara said. "How did she know to come looking for me here?"

Carol recognized the tone the young woman got when she was quite certain of herself. When she was having a flash of genius and finding an obscure pattern. Tension drew Carol's back straight. Her heart rate picked up. What was Mara seeing that they weren't?

"You mean technically how did she locate you? Did you log into any device using BOS-MA?" Tony asked.

It was a reasonable assumption, Carol thought. If Mara had gotten careless, she could have revealed her location. She was a mission novice, operational security wouldn't come naturally to her.

"Even if I wanted to, I couldn't. All I had was my grandfather's laptop and the flip phone you left with me." Mara's hands gripped the handles of the chair and she propelled herself from her seat. "Professor Stark, you were the first person to believe me when I told you I thought all of DigiTech's shady moves added up to something dangerous. And you, too, Carol. Please don't start doubting me now."

It had been a traumatic few days for Mara Melamed. She'd been thrust into a world of airborne drone battles and world-threatening villain manipulations that was difficult to adjust to even after years of living in it, like the super heroes had. And yet here she was, standing her ground against Tony Stark. Again. And intuition—her pattern spotting ability—had been infallible. They owed her their attention. Carol lifted her chin, fixing Tony with a steady look. "You said it yourself a day ago, Tony, as did I earlier. She hasn't been wrong yet."

A muscle in his jaw flexed once, twice, as he chewed this over, but he quickly reached the same conclusion as Carol. He held his hands up in surrender, took a seat on the desk beside Jess, and gestured for Mara to say her piece.

With the eyes of Spider-Woman, Iron Man, and Captain Marvel on her, Mara's cheeks pinked just a little, but she stopped twisting her fingers into knots and her shoulders squared. When she spoke, her tone was level, her voice determined. "How did she know to come here?"

"What do you mean, she came here?" Iris pushed herself off the wall. Once again, Carol had nearly forgotten about the other Melamed in the room. She'd been quiet since they rescued her, which Carol attributed to the trauma she'd been through. Understandable if she felt out of her depth among the crew, remaining in the background for the most part, resting, recovering her strength and her nerve. But hearing how close her daughter had come to the villain seemed to animate her.

"She turned up here." Mara waved vaguely at the door. "Just appeared one second, standing there. Threatening me. Or trying to recruit me. Both, sort of. Definitely gaslighting me."

"She was in this lab?" Iris's voice shook. "With you?"

"She's in custody now," Jess said. "You don't have worry about her coming back."

The computer scientist whirled on Jess, her eyes bright behind her glasses. Too bright, really. Glassy. "Did she say anything?" She turned to Carol then, putting her under the interrogation. "Before you grabbed her in the warehouse?"

Carol shrugged, her mouth torn between a half-smirk at the memory of Moonstone's capture and a half-frown at Iris's wound-up demeanor. "She did the usual self-aggrandizing monologuing, but she didn't have much of a chance to confess before Jenn knocked her equipment out with an EMP and I knocked her out with this." Carol raised a clenched fist. "Although, she did try some kind of last ditch thing with her computer."

"What?" Iris demanded. "What did she do?"

"You'd think she'd have been too busy battling her way out of there to go back to her little digital terror empire, but she went for her computer command center."

"Sending a message to someone, maybe?" Tony frowned and ruffled his hand through his hair. "I said all along Karla Sofen couldn't be the tech brains behind this. She had to have a computer expert working with her. Maybe she was contacting her accomplice. Could you see what she sent?"

242   "I only caught a brief glimpse before Jenn blew it out. I think

it was a weapon schematic." Carol closed her eyes, trying to picture what she'd seen. The flashing red letters came back to her. "She... confirmed an override."

"A systems security override?" Iris crept closer to Carol with hesitant steps. But she stopped well short, trembling so hard her borrowed sweatshirt twitched around her thighs.

Carol's lids popped open and she zeroed in on the computer scientist. "Yeah. That's what it was."

Iris's entire body jerked. "We have to get out of here."

Iris was sparking like a live wire, and Carol didn't need Mara's intuition to know something was not right. "Dr. Melamed, what do you know?"

"Nothing—nothing. I just have a bad feeling. It's not safe here." She spun in a confused circle, once, twice, finally locating the exit door. "We should go. Out. That way. Quickly. What— what are you all waiting for? Come on. *Come on!*"

Carol cocked her head at Jess, motioning her to take up a position beside the door. Whatever this was, it wasn't good. Moonstone had almost made a break for it earlier. She'd be damned if she didn't cut off another escape attempt before it got that far. Meanwhile, Carol held out an arm to bar Iris's progress, and Tony closed in from the other direction.

Iris's steps faltered. She shuffled sideways, as if she meant to dart around. "We have to get out of here."

"It was you."

Mara spoke so softly, she barely edged above a whisper. She stood behind her grandfather's desk, an iPad clutched to her chest, her blazing eyes on her mother. *Missile lock*, Carol thought. She drew up a small surge of energy and slowly curled her fingers into her fists. She didn't know where this was going exactly, but she trusted Mara. She'd be ready to take action at her word.

Iris froze, her back to her daughter. Without turning, she said, "Mara, don't."

"You were the only one, besides Tony and Jess, who knew I stayed here."

"Mara," Carol said, cautiously. "What are you saying?"

"My mother," Mara said, her voice breaking, "told Moonstone where to find me."

Lindsay gasped. She reached forward and swept Gerry up, the tension in the room driving her to cocoon him in her arms. Iris murmured an unintelligible protest.

Mara flipped the iPad, held it out at arm's length, displaying the screen. Carol squinted at the black-and-white image. A cot, some boxes, a computer bank.

"The DigiTech storage facility?" Jess asked.

"Yes, where we found her." Mara nodded toward Iris, who rocked back and forth, shaking her head. "This is a screenshot from the surveillance video I hacked into. This room, it's full of communications equipment. Was it connected, Mom? If any of this worked, you could have contacted the police—or me—any time."

Iris shrank back a step, but Spider-Woman was right behind her, crowding her away from the door.

"This isn't a holding cell, is it?"

"I—I don't know what you're saying," Iris sputtered. "That's not—no."

"Come to think of it," Jess said. "That rescue attempt did go awfully smoothly. Why didn't Sofen kick up more of a fuss when we kidnapped her hostage?"

"Because she wasn't a hostage," Mara said, oddly calm in spite of the revelations she was speaking. "Tony was right. Moonstone had an accomplice. *You.*"

Carol sucked in a breath. Nearby, she heard Tony mutter a triumphant, "*I knew it!*"

"Please," Iris pleaded. "You have to understand."

"You were her computer expert. And her spy. After we freed you," Mara went on. "You fed her information about what Carol was doing. You told her the team was focused on patching the vulnerability. That's what made her go after the other weapon."

The truth of it hit Carol like a punch. "She didn't lose a

hostage. She gained a mole. We know from Colonel Finke she liked to collect those."

Iris spun in a circle, looking from face to face but finding no sympathetic expression. She twitched toward the door. Carol and Tony both leapt, but Jess was closest. She snared the doctor from behind, locking one arm around her waist, the other looping around her neck.

At the sight of her captive mother, the dam of Mara's control broke. "Mom," she sobbed. "How could you help her? How could you let her twist you into doing her bidding?"

"How could I *let* her?" Iris snarled. The hushed, apprehensive demeanor she'd adopted since they pulled her out of DigiTech's HQ melted away, replaced by a look of rage. She strained against Jess's hold. "You think *she* came up with this? I'm the one who convinced DigiTech to acquire BOS-MA when the government dumped it like so much trash. I'm the one who had the vision to deploy it for commercial use. She didn't show up until later, after she'd conned your grandfather into revealing the vulnerability. Griselda Seales." Iris growled the name through bared teeth. "I didn't know her real identity then. I just knew she listened to me. She believed in my vision. We were partners. I didn't mind letting her be the public face of it. I didn't need to chase fame like my father. I only needed someone to—"

"Respect your work?" Mara asked, through a sniffle. Carol flicked her a look, saw the heartbreak—and recognition—on the young woman's face. Just as Carol knew Moonstone's thinking because it was a warped version of her own, Mara recognized a version of her own dreams in her mother.

"The great Shelley Melamed didn't. My father was too busy being a genius to raise his child. He pawned me off on strangers while he tried to invent software that would change the world. Joke's on him. I made his software into what it should have been all along! Where he failed and quit, I succeeded."

Iris was flailing in Jess's grip. Though Carol had no doubt she could hold her, they'd need a better solution soon. But

Mara, whose shoulders were shaking with sobs, deserved these answers. "You didn't need to exploit the vulnerability to make a commercial version of the software, though, did you?" Carol said. "Moonstone came up with that idea."

"Yes," Iris spat. "She said we should get the credit, the financial reward, not the stiffs at DigiTech. We were the visionaries. If it had been up to them, they'd still have been manufacturing hard drives! Moonstone said she knew a way we could gain ownership of the company. So we could run it how we saw fit."

"And of course, you had access to your father's files," Tony said. "You found the images he'd set as the trigger. All you had to do was leak the scandal to the media and let them publish the photos. Anyone who opened a news feed made their device vulnerable to you."

"Including DigiTech shareholders!"

From whom Iris thought Sofen had wrested control in both their names. For such a genius, she'd been duped awfully easily. Carol almost felt bad for her. Except for the part where she'd willingly been in league with Moonstone.

"Funny thing about working with villains, Dr. Melamed," Jess said, with a chilly laugh. "You can't really trust them. You don't own a single share in DigiTech—only Moonstone does."

"No—no, it's my company too!"

"You leaked horrible information about our family." Mara sniffled. "You smeared your good name—*my* name. And it meant nothing. She outsmarted you."

"As if our name wasn't already mud," Iris said. "Your grandfather could have disclosed the vulnerability. But he'd have had to say why he created it, why he couldn't trust his DoD funders. He'd have had to reveal the part his software played in an atrocity. He wouldn't sully his own reputation. He kept it secret and breathed a sigh of relief when his brilliant creation was buried in the military archives. He lived his whole life denying his best work, hoping the truth never came out, all so he wouldn't have to face the consequences of his decisions. You shouldn't idolize him. He was a selfish man and a terrible parent."

Mara's eyes overflowed again. "Apple didn't fall far."

"At least no one will ever call me 'Professor Melamed's daughter' again, will they? I have my own legacy now."

The word rang in Carol's ears. Moonstone had spun a similar web for Carol, needling her about her Kree heritage, telling her that Tony was her puppet master. She'd said something like that to Mara, too, making her doubt her worth. She'd found three women staggering under the weight of their birthright, wrestling with complex family histories. Three women who hadn't entirely belonged in the family they were born into, who worried they could never live up to their names. The ingredients of self-doubt were in all of them, in her and Iris and Mara. Moonstone had thrown hot peppers into an already boiling dish.

But even as she thought it, she realized they had never been the point. Moonstone had her own agenda. Iris, and Mara, and even Carol. They were tools or pawns or inconveniences. They mattered to Moonstone only to the extent that they could help or harm her.

"She showed up here after Iris told her we suspected she'd go after my lair," Carol said. "Gaslighting Mara was a nice bonus, but it wasn't her real purpose, was it?"

On the cusp of finding the missing piece that had nagged at her all along, Carol began to pace. It was right there—at the edge of her reach. Iris blinked rapidly. Mara's face was a mirror of her mother's, but for one thing. Where Iris's eyes flashed with fear, Mara's welled with sorrow. Though a mist coated her cheeks and tears dripped from her chin, soaking her the collar of her puffy jacket, she regarded Carol steadily, nodding her on.

Mara's relentless pursuit of answers has brought them here. She'd trusted her gut—something which Carol did too, when she wasn't under Moonstone's nefarious influence.

And suddenly, Carol knew.

"The weapon is here," she said, her chest constricting. "Moonstone's real purpose was to plant that weapon nearby, to target us once we evacuated the lair."

"You," Iris hissed. "Just you. You've been the one she wanted all along."

It might almost be flattering, that Moonstone found her a worthy rival, but Carol would not measure her worth by those who sought to hold her down, to harm her. She spent her early life proving herself to people like that. No more. Carol's voice remained deadly calm. "Tell me about the device."

"Project Faustus? Your army pals didn't tell you?"

"Don't get coy, Doctor." Jess tightened her grip on Iris's arms, giving her a brain-rattling shake.

Moonstone had already attempted this gambit, preying upon Carol's insecurities, insinuating she mattered only as a strike force. The villain was better at it, frankly, than Iris, and Carol was prepared. She brushed away the provocation. "How much damage are we talking?"

"Who knows? Powerful enough to reach into outer space," Iris strained against Jess again, yanking frantically. Some reality seemed to come back to her, the distraction of her personal grievances against her father paling in comparison to the reminder of the weapon. "You're dooming us all by keeping us here. Him, too!" She nodded at Gerry.

Her words sucked the air out of the room. Carol's photon energy reacted automatically, bubbling to the surface. Tony snarled. Lindsay tightened her hold on the baby, bending over him like a human shield. And Jessica's face screwed into a terrifying mask. She leaned into her powers, wrenching Iris's arms up behind her back, pulling a scream from the computer scientist. One thing you never, ever did was threaten Jess's son.

"What. Do. You. Mean?" Jess growled.

Iris's response was labored as she spoke through the pain. "Moonstone's military mole lied to her. He never told her the weapon didn't perform well on tests, that it kept overheating, but she found the evidence anyway. There are no secrets in BOS-MA. If you saw her override systems security, she didn't set the weapon to fire. She set it to explode."

The words stunned them into silence for a beat. Carol's mind raced through information, calculating options and responses. An overheating weapon that had been designed to shoot a laser into space? She knew from her own power surges how much destruction that was liable to cause. They were talking about a weapon that could devastate the entire Empire State campus and several blocks beyond.

Jess reacted first. "Gerry!" she shrieked, letting go of Iris and streaking toward him and Lindsay.

Tony surged forward, catching up Iris before she could bolt for the door. Carol shot across the room and punched a human-size hole in the exterior wall.

"Get them out of here," Carol ordered. With rubble still raining around them, Jess swept her son and her nanny into her arms and sped them out into the chilly winter air. "Tony, get Spectrum and Hazmat back here ASAP."

He was already on comms, calling for reinforcements, altering authorities. Carol advanced on Iris. "Where is it, Melamed?"

"I don't know!"

That was, quite likely, the truth. Iris hadn't been as important to Moonstone as she imagined herself to be. Moonstone had placed the weapon nearby, indifferent to the possibility that Iris might end up here, too. Unbothered that Iris's daughter was certainly here, Karla Sofen hadn't warned her chief software engineer of the danger. She hadn't cared whether she sacrificed her so-called partner, as long as she accomplished her goal of taking out Captain Marvel.

They had to find that weapon—fast.

"Mara, what time did you see Moonstone?" Carol asked.

The young woman stepped forward, her hands knitted together again. She twisted them around and around, her anxiety ratcheting up with the mounting danger. She avoided looking at her mother, still caught in Tony's steel grip. "I don't know exactly. I remember it was just getting dark out."

Carol peered out the hole in the wall, making certain Jess's figure had retreated from view and then paced the room. "There would have been people around and a weapon of that power can't be small. She'd need a place to tuck it away without attracting attention to herself."

"Here? The basement?" Tony suggested.

"Maybe." Mara blinked, owlishly, behind her glasses. "I thought I heard noises in the hall before Moonstone came in."

"We need to evacuate this building and search," Carol said. Dammit, they were spread too thin.

A voice crackled over comms. "How about a loading dock?"

Warmth bloomed in Carol's chest. "Monica, you got here fast."

"Jenn and I were already on our way back when Tony signaled and said we're looking for the weapon Moonstone stole from the convoy. I circled the sciences building—there's a loading dock that backs up onto a parking lot cordoned off by a barbed wire fence. Might be a good place to deliver a large object without too many eyes on."

"I'll meet you there," Carol said. "Tony, suit up and check this level. If you don't find the weapon, start evacuations. When Jess returns, you and she coordinate efforts." She turned to Mara and Iris. "You two—"

"I'm coming with you," Mara said. A look of grim determination set her mouth into a firm line. She pulled her hands from their knot and clenched her fists instead. Her chin rose, her shoulders pulled back. The hair was wrong, the heights didn't match, but Carol still glimpsed a faint impression of herself, standing at the ready, prepared to go into battle with her friends. Yeah. *That* she found flattering.

Carol hesitated for no more than an instant before nodding. Mara had earned the right to decide whether she put herself at risk, or not. And Iris should come too. She knew more than any of them about the weapon; she might be useful in defusing it. She gestured to Tony, who shoved Iris her way.

She looped an arm around Iris's waist, hefting the woman into the air as she rose, flying out to the hall, up the steps. Behind her, Tony's voice shouted instructions at breakneck speed—alerting

250

campus security on comms, instructing Jess where to meet him once she'd gotten her family to safety—and feet pounded down the hall as Mara gave chase.

Carol blew through the lobby, ignoring the startled looks of the few people still around, and barreled into the bowels of the building, past a mail room, a boiler room, and finally into a cavernous delivery room. Before the open bay doors stood Monica, dressed in her all-white suit with a white headband holding back her locs, and Jenn, in her bright yellow and black gear, standing a head shorter. Both wore serious, game-face expressions, Monica's eyes alight with her energy powers.

It wasn't hard to spot their target, a metal contraption plunked in the center of the space. Moonstone hadn't bothered to hide it, no doubt believing it would explode before anyone ever noticed and raised an alarm.

How long did they have? It had already been hours. Carol's pulse raced. Years ago, she had lost her Captain Marvel powers, but as a being known as Binary, had gained the ability to channel the energy of a star. When she took her Binary form, it had been an explosion of sorts, violent, unpredictable, unstoppable. Once she hit that moment, when the energy build-up could no longer be contained by her ordinary form, an eruption ensued.

Fabulous. Nothing like an inexorable energy bomb with an unknown timetable and no countdown clock.

Carol's feet touched the ground, as Jenn and Monica raced to join her. She handed Iris over to Jenn's custody, intending to get a closer look at the weapon.

The door behind them burst open and Mara came through, huffing with the exertion of trying to keep up with a super hero. She pulled up short beside the quartet, sparing a brief, pained glance at her mother, before squinting up at the device. "Is that it?

"Unassuming, isn't it?" Carol said.

"I thought a doomsday device would look more like… a giant tank," she admitted. "Or a missile. Or something."

Mara was right. Looking at the thing, you'd never ID it for a laser cannon. The Faustus laser stood on a heavy military-issue gray metal base capped by a long white tube with a domed top. It resembled a miniature portable grain silo. Well, except for the ominous buzz and the blue glow bursting through gaps in the dome.

A grim half-smile lifted one corner of Carol's mouth. "The worst weapons never look like they can do as much damage as they can."

She took to the air for an overhead view. From above, the energy signature was substantial, the light pulsating through the dome grew brighter as Carol watched, the gaps widening. The edges of the metal bore signs of liquefaction.

"Not good," she said to the team. "This thing is melting down fast."

"What if you just blast it?" Monica suggested.

Carol considered that. "We have no idea how it's constructed. If there's anything incendiary in there, it could blow. Maybe I can absorb the energy?"

She swooped down, her feet lightly touching the tube. It teetered under her weight and the dome shifted downward, aiming toward her friends.

"A little warning, Carol!" Monica shouted, diving sideways. Jenn and the Melameds scrambled too, but Carol lost sight of them.

"Sorry! Had no idea it would tilt like that." She crouched and thrust her hands into the laser energy emerging from the dome barrel. A surge of power rushed up through her fingers.

Okay, yes. She could do this. She could siphon off energy, power it down instead of up, give them time to figure out how to shut it off. Trembling with the overwhelming influx of energy, Carol fought to keep her hands in the dome, to absorb all of it, but Hala help her, this thing packed a punch. She couldn't hold it all, couldn't drain the excess quickly enough. The power was still building.

Carol shuddered, brain racing. How much surge could she withstand? Could she render it harmless before the energy triggered a meltdown?

A ray of light erupted from the dome, shooting past Carol's hands, slicing through the concrete wall opposite.

A shout drew her attention, and she saw a flash of yellow. Her head whipped toward the bay doors and she caught sight of Iris making a break for it, Jenn hard on her heels. The computer scientist must have wriggled loose when they dived out of the way of the tilting weapon. Monica joined the chase and flew into position, blocking Iris's lane to the bay doors, forcing the fleeing woman back toward the middle of the room.

"Trying to save yourself, Doctor?" Monica demanded. "What about the rest of us? What about your daughter? Shouldn't you be helping defuse this thing?"

Iris pelted in the other direction. "Why should I help anyone? No one ever helped me."

"Stop," Mara begged, stepping into her mother's path. "Don't run. Help us instead. Make a different choice."

Atop the Faustus device, Carol watched the tableau unfold. Iris skidded to a stop, looking from the super hero-guarded rear exit to her daughter, who was cutting her off from the only other way out. For a horrifying moment, they stood frozen. And then, with an anguished scream, Iris lunged for Mara, grabbing hold of her daughter, shoving her dangerously close to the laser beam shooting across the room.

"No!" Carol yelled, pulling energy desperately, but she couldn't hold any more. Energy leaked from her and flowed back into the cannon, the beam strengthening again. The buzzing grew louder, as did the rumble of the concrete wall being shorn away by the beam.

Mara screamed. "Mom! No!" She flailed and struggled against her mother's grip, but every movement brought her closer to danger, to being incinerated.

"Don't move!" Iris threw a hand out toward Monica, who was advancing on her.

Monica hesitated, glancing at Carol. Carol jerked her chin, directing her back a few paces. Mara was inches from the beam. Monica wouldn't be able to grab her before Iris could toss her into the path of that laser.

"Your own daughter?" Carol bellowed.

Iris flinched, but clutched tighter to Mara. "Just let me go."

Under cover of the conversation, Jenn whispered into comms. "Carol, the weapon. That laser looks unstable."

Jenn was right. Energy bubbled in the device like boiling lava. Carol couldn't absorb it fast enough and she had nowhere to release such a large photon burst that wouldn't bring the entire building down on top of them. "I can't hold much more," she admitted.

"I can absorb some," Monica said. She still stood guard between Iris and the bay doors, blocking her exit route. "But I'd have to abandon Mara."

No. They weren't going to do that. *Think, Carol.* There had to be some way to render this weapon harmless.

"What's your plan, Iris?" she asked, keeping her focus on the sobbing young woman and her red-faced mother. Mara had lessened her struggles, her terrified eyes flicking between Carol and the laser, inches from her shoulder, understanding that every movement put her at greater risk. A flare of energy from the cannon rattled Carol and she gritted her teeth, clenching her muscles tightly to hold her position. "The minute you let her go to run, we'll grab you."

"You won't. You'll let me walk to save her. If I get out of here, I take her with me. We both die or we both live. Your choice, Captain Marvel."

Tempted, Carol paused. She did want Mara out of here, did want her safe. One life was always worth the price. A clang from inside the laser startled her. The device shifted on its base, rocking her; the glow brightened and the heat increased as the metal of the cannon grew soft like putty. Iris was forced to slip sideways to avoid the beam shearing through her. Carol bore down, steadied herself again. If the prisms inside the device were slipping, she had no idea what would happen. It could cease emitting photons and die. Or it could melt the case and burst free. And if anything in there was combustible, it could blow up. She just didn't know.

"Carol!" Mara called, sounding trembly but determined. "Don't risk her going free to save me."

Fury rushed through Carol, raising her already blisteringly hot temperature. *Absolutely not.* Mara's bravery was extraordinary. But this was not a choice Carol was going to make. Not a position she was going to put this young woman in. Captain Marvel didn't sacrifice people to achieve her ends.

"I can see the strain on your face," Iris said. "You're never going to stop that weapon by yourself."

Moonstone's rhetoric resonated in Iris's words, but they were as flawed as her so-called partner's logic. The two of them perceived themselves to be lone wolves, who relied on no one. To their fatal detriment. Carol wasn't alone. Her team—*her friends*—had stood with her every time she needed them. And they'd stand with her now.

Monica edged closer, eyeing the increasingly volatile laser cannon. "We have to cool that thing down before it blows us all the way to Throneworld II."

Throneworld. Cooling…

The idea dropped into Carol's mind like Thor's hammer falling to Earth. What had the engineer called that cooling system they were experimenting with on the *Peregrine*? Thermoacoustic? Radio waves and inert gas. And in this very room, she happened to have her good friends, Spectrum and Hazmat, who could control energy waves and create gas. If anyone could provide the dampening power to stop the Faustus device from going kaboom, it was the three of them.

"I have an idea," Carol whispered into her comms mic. "It's a little wild."

"Hit us," Monica said, and Jenn echoed her agreement.

"Jenn, I need this cannon tube filled with some kind of inert gas," she said. "Can you do that?"

"You're singing my favorite song, Captain. How's a little radon sound?"

"Ladies' choice, Hazmat. Spectrum, you're next. I need to you to block the cannon barrel and power sound waves into it, as much as you can." Thank Hala, Monica could also absorb energy, so that laser ought not to be deadly to her—at least not right away. "I'll stay here and act as a heat exchange."

"I'm on it, but, uh, what the hell is this going to accomplish?"

"Well, if I'm remembering correctly," she said, hoping she'd understood the Peregrine engineer's lecture, "we're going turn this tube into a refrigerator and cool this laser down."

"And what about them?" Monica asked.

Carol followed her gaze to Iris, still holding her daughter a hair's breadth away from the beam. Her eyes locked with Mara's, who seemed to sense they were plotting something. Lacking comms gear, she didn't know what. But she had good instincts. Carol raised her voice and spoke to the room, rather than the comms. "On my mark!" A look of confusion passed over Iris's face. But she didn't process quickly enough to act. "Now!"

In unison, Jenn leaped toward a gap in the metal, grunting as her body began to emit gas that filled the tube. Monica stepped in front of the cannon, pulling her arms back, thrusting her chest forward as she generated sound waves and directed them into the cannon barrel. Carol sent up a prayer to the Supreme Intelligence that this worked quickly or the radon would kill them if the laser didn't get them first.

From the corner of her eye, she saw Mara lift her arms skyward and then go boneless, dropping her weight fast and heavy. She caught her mother off guard. In the moment of surprise, she slipped through her mother's hold and wormed free. Carol tried to keep her focus on the emerging scuffle, but it grew difficult as her body heated, acting as an absorption stack for the gas Monica's sound waves compressed and pushed through the tube of the barrel.

Between the feverish temperature and the energy she had already absorbed, Carol felt like she might explode. She couldn't hold much longer before she burst into Binary form. The last thing this room needed was an explosion of energy from yet another source. The very air around them was supercharged. Doubt and anxiety gripped Carol and she vibrated with tension.

Was this working? Had she now exposed them all to radioactive gas only to fail?

Wait.

Her eyes fixed on one of the gaps in the device's dome. Was the glow growing dimmer? Was she imagining it?

"Carol!" Jenn pressed a hand on the barrel, her face shining with sweat but alight with something else, too. Excitement. "It's cooler!"

Carol groaned and pulled harder at the heat building around her hands. "Keep going!" she shouted to Monica. "Jenn, the good doctor!"

Jenn raced after Iris, who was attempting to escape out the bay doors again, battling Mara, who doggedly held her by one arm, trying to drag her back. As Carol and Monica defused the last of the energy cannon's power, Jenn and Mara halted the fleeing woman's progress, wrestled her still, and held her fast. Iris Melamed must face the consequences of her narcissism.

As the last remaining heat in the Faustus device cooled, Captain Marvel, ablaze and pulsating with energy, blasted off into space to safely release the kind of power burst only she could withstand.

24

LATER, AFTER Carol discharged the excess energy in a location that wouldn't harm anyone, and Jenn and Monica delivered Iris Melamed to the authorities, the team regrouped at Carol's lair, their safe haven again, with the villains locked up.

"We have some decisions to make about BOS-MA." Tony had assumed his customary position at the computer bank, but he faced the circle of teammates, instead of a screen. "We've eliminated the immediate threat, but we're back to our original dilemma. What do we do about this operating system that's corrupt to its core but is also the backbone of most of our technology?"

"We find a patch, right?" Jess said. With Gerry and Lindsay out of harm's way, she was no longer climbing the walls, but her features were drawn and her ordinary sarcastic wit hadn't made an appearance in a while. Her picture still featured on news broadcasts and websites. Jessica Drew remained a wanted woman, an accused murdered. And yet, she said, "That's the right thing to do. Make the OS safe for people again."

Tony grimaced. "That will take time. And in the meanwhile,

it's possible someone else discovers the vulnerability and figures out how to exploit it."

Carol's eyes skimmed the room until she found the person she was looking for, curled tightly into an armchair, covered by that same gray blanket that had once cocooned her mother as she hid in plain sight as Moonstone's mole. "What do you think, Mara?"

Mara shook her head. "I shouldn't be trusted to make this choice."

"Why not?"

"Look at who my family is! Villains. They're the reason we're in this mess in the first place. We've got a bad track record when it comes to decisions that affect humanity. Someone else should decide."

"If we're disqualifying people due to a family history of bad decisions," Jess said, "we can cross me right off the list."

"Me, too," said Tony archly.

"Count me among the not-qualified in that case, as well," Carol said. "Huh. How about that. Looks like none of us passes that particular test. Which brings me back to you."

The young woman fidgeted under the force of Captain Marvel's scrutiny. "What if I'm like them?"

"You *are*, Mara," Carol said, and her breath caught. Those words were a mirror that could be held up to Carol, too, who knew how like her own mother she was. How like the Kree family she'd been avoiding. It was time to stop fighting so hard against her heritage. Her friends had long-since chalked it up as one of the many components that comprised Carol Danvers A.K.A. Captain Marvel. She could do the same, couldn't she?

"You are like your family," she repeated, smiling now. "The good and the capacity for bad. If I've learned anything from tangling with Moonstone, it's that the distance between villain and hero isn't all that far, but it's measured in choices, not genetics."

"People are going to judge me for what my mother did. And my grandfather," Mara said, small and uncertain.

"Some will. Others will judge you by what you're choosing to do. And," she cast a fond glance at the crew gathered in the room, "your teammates will stick by you."

"We're not just your teammates, you mule!" Jess exclaimed.

"We're your friends. Listen, if we can love all of this obstinate, hotheaded half-human, half-Kree, and make her the guardian of our kids—" She tossed one of the cardboard boxes from Gerry's fort at Carol. And they did love her, Carol realized, ducking and grinning "—we can love a genius grad student with a knack for patterns and a complicated family history."

Mara laughed through her sniffles, and Carol joined her. "Come on, Mara. I want to know what you think."

The young woman unwrapped the blanket and stood, squaring her shoulders. "I think it's time to tell the truth. It's hard to admit how wrong my family was. How unethical. How much harm they caused. But my grandfather regretted his choices and I think he wanted to make them right, even if he didn't have the courage to do so. Maybe this is my chance to atone just a little for the Melamed family wrongs."

"I agree." Carol nodded, pride shining in her eyes. "If we tell the truth about everything the vulnerability can be used for, we can also show how Jess was framed. We need to clear her name, get CPS off her case. Make sure Gerry is safe."

"I'm on board for that!" Jess jumped up and threw an arm around Carol and another around Mara, squeezing them into a group hug. Carol wrinkled her nose, but she didn't pull away. "Maybe I can even resuscitate my P.I. business, once I'm no longer a suspected felon."

"It's going to be chaos for a while," Tony said. "People will lose faith in technology."

"We'll get them through it," Carol said. "You won't rest until you've developed a patch."

"I won't," he promised. "And Mara, if you'll agree to work with me, we'll find a resolution faster together."

"You want me on your team?" She peeked at him shyly, her knuckles resting on her chin.

"It wouldn't be a team without you."

"What about you, Captain Marvel?" Monica asked. "What's

next for you?"

Jess raised an eyebrow. "You better say you've got a trip to Throneworld II to resume."

"Yes," Carol said, firmly. "I'm overdue for a visit to my sister."

"Straight there?"

"Well, I have to make one quick pitstop on the way, to talk to an engineer friend about our little unauthorized experiment in thermoacoustic cooling under extreme conditions."

"Carol, this isn't you avoiding again, is it?" Jess asked, in a warning-slash-threatening tone.

Carol paused a moment, interrogating her motives before responding. But when she spoke, she was sure of herself. "It's not one or the other. I have time for both. Now, you all get out of here so I can have my lair to myself again. And Tony," she added, as the crew readied themselves to go, "don't interrupt my next trip to ask for any favors. I am definitely saying no this time!"

"Yes, Captain," Tony said with a salute.

Carol grinned and shook her head, knowing he'd ask and she'd answer the call again. She always did.

ACKNOWLEDGMENTS

WRITING A novel is never as solitary an endeavor as it might seem. In fact, just like Carol, I had a spectacular crew by my side for the wild and amazing journey that was this book.

To the folks at Marvel and Titan Books, I'm honored you entrusted a small piece of Captain Marvel's story to me. Not only was this novel a joy to write, but I got to learn from masterful storytellers along the way, including Jeff Youngquist, Caitlin O'Connell, and Sarah Singer, as well as Sophie Robinson of Titan Books. Thank you so much for all your excellent guidance and support.

To my agents, Tracey and Josh Adams, and the mighty Adams Literary team, thank you for listening to me wax lyrical about Carol and for making my dream of writing her come true. You're the very best agents an author could ask for!

To my subject matter consultants: Scott Gibson, retired U.S. Air Force, who shared with me a bit about how it feels to be a fighter pilot and embrace a warrior mentality; Alex Maghen, who speculated about the really scary parts of technological innovation with me and helped me understand villain-worthy computer exploits; and Daniel and Erin Finke, who fielded more than one barrage of questions about cool weaponry and how to diffuse it. Thank you all for answering the call and jumping into action by gamely responding to a bunch of vague and disturbing hypotheticals—even when all I could say was "I can't tell you why I'm asking but what if…" And thanks for never once wondering (aloud) if you needed to stage an intervention! Any mistakes, inaccuracies or inconsistencies in the amazing stuff you shared with me are, of course, solely mine. You're all real-life super heroes to me.

To my parents, Susan and Mickey, and my sister Stacey, thanks for believing in my dreams and making sure I have the support system to reach for them.

To my children, Noam, Nadav and Shalev, I know I'll never be cooler in your eyes than when I told you I was writing a Captain Marvel novel. Believe me when I say, I've never been cooler in my own eyes than when I became your mom. I have no doubt you'll all live Carol's motto—*higher, further, faster*—in everything you strive to achieve. You're the ones who inspire me.

To my writing friends, I couldn't do any of this without you, nor would it be nearly as fun. Kimberly Jones, Rachael Allen, Maryann Dabkowski, and Mayra Cuevas, in particular, you lighted the way at various points when the path grew dim and I'll be forever grateful for it.

And last but not least, to the 2022–23 TriState Spartans AAA 12U team. As I hunkered down in hockey rinks across the Midwest and raced to meet deadlines for this novel, you guys cheered me on, kept my spirits high and forgave me when I sat in the stands with my laptop on my knees, one eye on the game and the other on the screen. You all rock. Go Spartans!

ABOUT THE AUTHOR

GILLY GREW up in Florida and currently calls Decatur, Georgia home. In addition to being an author, she's the chief legal officer for a group of advertising agencies. Her young adult novel, *I'm Not Dying With You Tonight*, co-written with Kimberly Jones, is a *New York Times* and Indie bestseller and NAACP Image Award Nominee. Her sophomore novel, *Why We Fly*, is a Sydney Taylor Notable Book. Gilly is also a two-time Georgia Author of the Year Nominee.

For more fantastic fiction, author events, exclusive
excerpts, competitions, limited editions and more

VISIT OUR WEBSITE
titanbooks.com

LIKE US ON FACEBOOK
facebook.com/titanbooks

FOLLOW US ON TWITTER
@TitanBooks

EMAIL US
readerfeedback@titanemail.com